I0819566

Ode to the Bones

ALSO BY CAROLYN HAINES

SARAH BOOTH DELANEY MYSTERIES

Doggone Bones
Blue Christmas Bones
Lights, Camera, Bones
Tell-Tale Bones
Bones of Holly
Lady of Bones
Independent Bones
A Garland of Bones
The Devil's Bones
Game of Bones
A Gift of Bones
Charmed Bones
Sticks and Bones
Rock-a-Bye Bones
Bone to Be Wild
Booty Bones
Smarty Bones
Bonefire of the Vanities
Bones of a Feather
Bone Appétit
Greedy Bones
Wishbones
Ham Bones
Bones to Pick
Hallowed Bones
Crossed Bones
Splintered Bones
Buried Bones
Them Bones

NOVELS

A Visitation of Angels
The Specter of Seduction
The House of Memory
The Book of Beloved
Trouble Restored
Bone-a-fied Trouble
Familiar Trouble
Revenant
Fever Moon
Penumbra
Judas Burning
Touched
Summer of the Redeemers
Summer of Fear

NONFICTION

My Mother's Witness: The Peggy Morgan Story

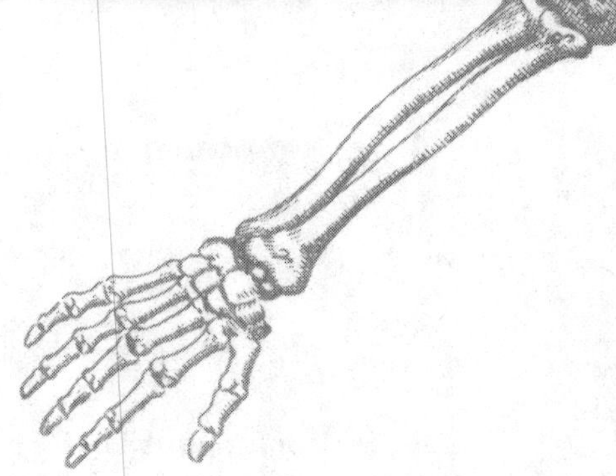

Ode to the Bones

A Sarah Booth Delaney Mystery

CAROLYN HAINES

MINOTAUR BOOKS
NEW YORK

This is a work of fiction. All of the names, characters, organizations, places, and events portrayed in this novel are either products of the author's imagination or used fictitiously.

First published in the United States by Minotaur Books, an imprint of St. Martin's Publishing Group

EU Representative: Macmillan Publishers Ireland Ltd, 1st Floor, The Liffey Trust Centre, 117–126 Sheriff Street Upper, Dublin 1, D01 YC43

www.minotaurbooks.com

The Library of Congress Cataloging-in-Publication Data is available upon request.

ISBN 978-1-250-37767-8 (hardcover)
ISBN 978-1-250-37768-5 (ebook)

First Edition: 2026

10 9 8 7 6 5 4 3 2 1

For Aleta and Thomi—always there when I need a friend.

1

Dust plumed out behind the old Mercedes Roadster as I turned onto the highway that led to the Tallahatchie Bridge in Leflore County. The historic truss bridge, brought so vividly into the collective consciousness by the Bobbie Gentry tune currently playing on my radio, was gone. It had burned in 1972 and a new bridge now crossed one of the iconic rivers of the Mississippi Delta.

Ever since solving the last case of dognapped pups, I'd been blue. I found myself driving over the familiar roadways of my childhood, seeking the solace of a connection that was deeper than blood in the timelessness of the land, the sun, the smell of crops growing. The return of my nemesis, Gertrude Stromm—and her escape from law enforcement yet again—had left me with some big questions about events of the past. I couldn't shake the sense of loss that had crept over me during the past few months. Not even the warm sun and growing cotton could quiet my heart, though they did help. I'd taken to riding the back roads of my beloved home state in my mother's old Roadster, hoping to find comfort in the landscape my parents had traveled. So far, it wasn't working all that well.

Sweetie Pie rode in the front seat and Avalon in the back. With the top down, we flew along the empty road bordered on both sides by cotton fields shimmering emerald-green in the yellow sunlight.

". . . another sleepy, dusty, Delta da-a-a-ay," Gentry sang and I warbled along with her. Luckily, the wind flowing over the convertible was stiff enough to knock my voice away from the dogs' ears. I wouldn't want to harm their hearing apparatus. Sweetie Pie's long floppy ears fluttered in the wind. Avalon was a gray hound/pittie mix, so her ears were more modest. They were both very good girls.

I took the slight incline to the bridge and slammed on the brakes. I put my arm out to protect Sweetie in the front seat, but poor Avalon was bumped into the back of my seat.

"What the heck?" I glanced at the distant figure—a woman in a long white dress stood on the bridge. She stared into the river below her. I glanced back at Avalon to make sure she wasn't hurt, and when I looked back down the road, the woman was gone.

Had she jumped?

Had I just witnessed a suicide?

I froze for five seconds, and then hit the gas. When I got to the place where I'd seen her, I stopped the car, got out, and looked over the bridge in the direction the river flowed. Nothing.

Was she submerged?

I pulled my cell phone from my pocket only to discover I didn't have a good signal. I dialed 911 anyway, but when there was no connection, I gave up. I ran back to the car and drove to the other side of the river, hoping to see the woman crawling up onto the bank and into the brush. She hadn't walked past me, that I could be sure of.

With no sight of her there, the only other possibility was that she swam to the other side of the river in the woods—or that she had jumped and the current, which was hard and fast from heavy rains, had swept her away. I could look for her or drive until I got a good enough signal to call for help.

I considered jumping into the river to help her. I was a strong swimmer. Coleman Peters, Sunflower County sheriff and my main squeeze, had taught junior lifesaving classes sponsored by the Red Cross when I was in ninth grade. He'd given me great confidence in my abilities. I might not be the prettiest swimmer, but I had strength and stamina. But if I jumped in the river and the mysterious woman had run into the woods, I'd be swept far downstream from here with no hope of finding her. And how would I get the dogs or make my way back to the car? No, I'd give a cursory search of the riverbank and then book it to a phone signal and call the authorities. The Leflore County sheriff and the water search and rescue required notification.

I put the car in drive and was about to go when Sweetie Pie jumped into the back seat. Before I could blink, another passenger joined me in the front. I knew her instantly, had seen her a thousand times on the taped Ed Sullivan shows my mother had collected and preserved. "Son of a Preacher Man" was a scandal for the times. Indeed, Dusty Springfield, a British songbird, was sitting beside me.

Even as I stepped on the gas pedal and picked up speed, her perfect bleached-blond bouffant hairdo with bangs cut straight across remained perfectly in place.

The wind did catch the poet sleeves of her satin-and-lace shirt that topped black bell bottoms. She looked exactly as she did when she performed on *The Ed Sullivan Show*.

"Dusty?" I knew it was really Jitty, the resident haint of Dahlia House and my only connection to my family who had passed over. Everyone was dead, but Jitty sometimes fed me scraps of information about them. Mostly, she deviled me. But this was a treat, Jitty appearing as an idol of mine. Jitty never did anything nice!

Her accent was definitely British as she said, "Sarah Booth, your mother has excellent taste in music."

I didn't miss the present tense she used. "Yes, she does." I had an image of my mother and father, playing the records they loved from the big bands, British Invasion, Beach Boys, and branching well over into the country songs that were de rigueur on the local radio stations back in the 1960s and 1970s. Were they up in heaven hobnobbing with their favorite musical stars, laughing and dancing as they had done in real life?

"Your daddy wasn't the son of a preacher man, but he could reach Libby *and* teach her." She cackled at her wit.

At one point in my life, I would have blushed, but no longer. Those tender, naïve days were behind me. "Daddy was a kind of preacher. He was a lawyer and a judge, and he believed in the rule of law."

"Your mother adores him. And he her. They are so happy."

That was all I'd ever wanted Jitty to tell me. Why was she suddenly being so cooperative?

"Jitty, why are you here singing tunes from the 1960s?" It was best to be direct with Jitty. She rarely answered truthfully, but if she thought I was trying to trick her, she'd be even more evasive.

"This bridge, Sarah Booth. This bridge. What a tale it could tell."

The radio in the car suddenly jumped to an AM country station from the distant past. Bobbie Gentry's sultry voice yet again blasted out of the radio, ". . . jumped off the Tallahatchie Bri-i-idge."

"Pay attention to the lyrics, Sarah Booth." Dead silence followed, and with the last flutter of those sleeves, Dusty was gone, too. Sweetie Pie reclaimed the front seat, and I realized that only fifteen seconds had passed since Jitty first appeared.

I was let down. No denying it. I wanted to talk to Dusty about my parents. I wanted details, something to hang on to. Dusty/Jitty knew things and seemed willing to discuss them. But I also had to search for that woman I'd seen on the bridge. Where had she gone? I parked in a sandy spot by the abutment. The area around me was wild with trees, brush, and brambles. No one driving by would notice my car. The dogs and I leaped out, but there were no tire tracks to indicate the woman on the bridge had left a vehicle. There was no sign of anyone. Had I imagined the whole thing? More likely it was Jitty tormenting me again. But I would report it all when I got a signal on my phone.

Sweetie Pie and Avalon coursed along the wooded riverbank, but like me, they found nothing helpful. No broken twigs, prints, or indication anyone had passed that way. It was time to go home. Jitty had hinted there was a clue in the lyrics. But a clue to what? I had no idea. I'd chew on what I'd seen as I drove.

On the way home, I stopped by Hilltop to visit with my partner in the Delaney Detective Agency, Tinkie Bellcase Richmond. Tinkie was a petite keg of dynamite. She was the Queen Bee of Delta society and as different from me as a prom queen to a stall mucker. Somehow, it was a partnership that worked.

"Where's that baby?" I asked when I walked in the door.

Tinkie's daughter—and my godchild—was the best thing that had happened to Sunflower County. Sweetie Pie and Avalon were hard on my heels. They found Chablis, Tinkie's perfectly groomed little Yorkie, and began tearing around the house. Tinkie laughed and waved me back to the kitchen. "Maylin is having a bath. Pauline is in charge. That girl has supernatural talents when it comes to Maylin. She'll let Pauline do anything and when I try, she screams like I'm murdering her."

That wasn't completely true. It was plain to see that Maylin loved both of her parents. But the live-in nanny, Pauline, was exceptional in many ways. Though I was tempted to interrupt the baby's bath, I let it go. I took the cup of coffee Tinkie offered and told her about the woman on the bridge. I'd alerted the Leflore County authorities as soon as I'd gotten a phone signal. They were checking it out, but I knew they wouldn't find anything.

"Do you have any idea who it was?" Tinkie was concerned. She had a big heart and too much compassion.

Truthfully, I'd begun to suspect what I saw was an apparition. A revenant. An echo of geographic resonance. A ghost. "She was tall, slender, and had dark hair. I don't know who she might be."

"Did she jump?"

I shook my head. "I didn't see." I told her I'd reported the incident to the authorities.

"There's nothing else you can do, Sarah Booth."

Nodding, I sighed. "You're right. I just—"

The kitchen door opened, and Oscar walked in, his face pasty and pale.

"What's wrong?" Tinkie jumped up to put her arm around her husband, who also happened to be president of the Zinnia National Bank. "What's happened?"

I stood up. "I'd better head home. Horses to feed, etc."

"No," Oscar said. "Please stay. You're going to be a part of this."

Dread punched me in the gut. Oscar's appearance, his terse voice—something bad had happened. "What's wrong?" I repeated the question Tinkie had asked.

"I need your help. The detective agency. I want to hire you."

"For what?" Tinkie asked. "You don't have to hire us, just tell us what's wrong."

"I need you to find a missing person."

My interest flared. "Who?"

"A man named Danny Anderson."

"Is he part of the Anderson family over near the Basin community?" Tinkie asked.

"That's the one. Danny is an eighth-generation farmer."

"They have some beautiful land." I knew the farm. Though I didn't know Danny personally, I knew the family by reputation.

Oscar sighed. "They do. But farming has had several bad years. Droughts, floods, heat that's killed the crops in the field. You name it, pretty much everything has hit our farmers but locusts or boll weevils, and I expect them any minute. Farmers are hurting."

I'd heard the same from a number of sources. Climate change was killing aspects of the agricultural community around the world.

"Danny is a solid member of the community. Is he missing? Do you suspect foul play?" I asked.

Oscar looked at his feet. He blinked tears away and cleared his throat. "No. I suspect suicide."

"What?" Tinkie and I said in unison.

Oscar held up his hand. "I foreclosed on the Anderson farm

Monday. Danny told me he'd failed his family, that he'd gambled on a new type of corn and soybeans and gambled big. The heavy rains in May killed everything he'd planted. He's upside down on his loans, and the farm was collateral on a big loan."

"You fore—"

I stepped on Tinkie's manicured toes to shut her up. It was clear to me Oscar carried enough guilt.

Farmers often took out loans at the beginning of planting season to get the necessary seeds, equipment, and fertilizer. It was a big gamble, and many farmers had lost too much in the last five years. The entire Delta community was stressed.

"Danny is levelheaded," I said. "He'd never commit suicide."

"I hope not," Oscar said, "but he is definitely missing. His daddy called me, worried sick. He said Danny had been acting erratic, depressed, unfocused. What if he harmed himself because of the foreclosure?"

"Danny isn't a quitter," Tinkie said, then backtracked. "Not that suicide is about quitting. I think there are a lot of reasons people kill themselves, and they shouldn't be judged."

"It's the guilt," Oscar said, stopping to clear his throat again. "He said he'd let his family down and that his parents would lose everything that had been in the Anderson family for eight generations. His ancestors cleared this land by hand with mules. His daddy plowed and planted when he was sick, in the heat, through all kinds of natural hardships. But Danny feels he is the one who will conclude his family's farming legacy. He took it real hard. And it's my fault."

As a person who'd almost lost her ancestral home to back taxes and an unpaid mortgage, I understood how easy it was to get behind the financial eight ball. "How far behind was Danny, if you can tell me?"

"I can't, but just understand I had no other option. I had to do it. As president of the bank, I have a responsibility to the people who do business with us. If this bank were to go under, it would hurt a whole lot of people. But Danny was desperate. Just desperate." He threw up his hands. "I did this, and no one can make it right if Danny has harmed himself."

"Don't worry, Oscar, Tinkie and I will find Danny. I'm sure he's just off at a hunting camp or somewhere licking his wounds. Think about it. That makes perfect sense." I had to get Oscar out of his funk. When Oscar was down, Tinkie suffered, too. She felt everything those she loved felt.

"We'll find him," Tinkie joined in. "Leave it to us."

"Do you know where he was last seen?" I asked.

"I'm not certain. The feedstore, probably. I suspect he was trying to negotiate the bill he has there. It would have been a hard situation, having to beg for time to pay what he owed."

I couldn't agree more, but I didn't want to waste the day sympathizing. Tinkie and I had to get busy. I whistled to the dogs. "Let's get after it, Tinkie."

2

At Tinkie's behest, we ran by the Zinnia National Bank to speak to one of Oscar's coworkers—and one of our best buddies—Harold Erkwell. Harold had helped us with cases more than once, and was an excellent partner in adventures and crime solving. We'd decided to leave the dogs at home with Pauline and Maylin. Oscar and Harold didn't care if they went into the bank, but some customers were finicky. And it was too hot to leave them in the car.

Harold was in his private office and told his secretary to please bring us coffee. Harold was the perfect gentleman—unlike his demon dog, Roscoe. Roscoe's greatest talent was peeing on the shoes of people I didn't like. Of course I adored him. Lately, Harold had also taken in a wire-haired terrorist, Pumpkin, who was living with him for a trial period. Pumpkin's owner, Jody, was traveling in Europe for the summer, and when she returned, they would determine the best place for Pumpkin to reside. Harold wanted her, but he would never jump another's claim for the affection of a pup.

When the coffee was served, Tinkie broached the subject. "You know Oscar won't ever tell me certain things . . ."

Harold shook his head. "So, this isn't a social call. You want something?"

"Yes." I wasn't the type to beat around the bush. "We need financial info on Danny Anderson and his farm. And we need it quickly."

Harold sat back in his chair. "I'm not surprised. Oscar is upset. He feels responsible that Danny is missing."

"Responsible for something specific?" I asked.

"I see." Harold side-eyed Tinkie. "Oscar didn't tell you the whole story."

"Please oblige." I needed to know the facts before I could know where to begin looking for Danny.

"Danny's father came in this morning and lit into Oscar. He said Danny had killed himself over the debt and Oscar was to blame."

"What?" Tinkie went pale. "Danny is dead?"

"That's the problem. No one knows. Danny is missing. Only missing. Mr. Anderson jumped the gun. He's worried sick about Danny, about losing the farm, and the debt Danny incurred in an attempt to save the Anderson land."

"Oscar is distraught. He hired us to find Danny," I said.

Tinkie got right to the point. "Did Oscar foreclose on the farm? For real?"

"Oscar gave Danny several chances. This debt has been hanging over him for more than two years. The weather has been erratic, to say the least. Everyone thought the weather patterns would reverse back to normal. But they didn't. Climate change is impacting farmers hard as they scramble around and try to figure out what to plant."

Billy Watson, the man who leased my land and farmed it,

had talked to me about more drought-resistant plants and trying new schedules of planting and harvesting. The problem was that no matter how hard the farmers worked, if the weather wasn't on their side, they were done. There was no fighting Mother Nature.

"Could Danny pull himself out of the mess?" I asked Harold.

"Oscar tried to help Danny come up with a plan. Maybe take on a partner or sell several hundred acres but keep the best farmland. Danny wanted none of it. He was determined to figure out a way to get the debt paid."

I had a sudden, awful thought. "Did Danny have a life insurance policy?"

Harold nodded. "Yes. He told me about it last year. He said he was worried about the future of farming, and he didn't want to leave his family in a jam."

"Do you know Danny well? Would he do something . . . to himself?" The words to the Gentry song came back to me. . . . *Billie Joe McAllister jumped off the* . . . Had Danny jumped into the river? The Anderson farm was in LeFlore County, not far at all from the Tallahatchie Bridge.

"I've always thought Danny was extremely stable and hardworking. Oscar did, too. Otherwise, he wouldn't have extended the loan again and again." Harold frowned. "There is something else you should know. There's gossip that Danny was having an affair with a preacher's wife. Now, I'm not saying anything happened to him, but if it did, that could also be the reason. It's not the 1950s anymore, but in some communities, adultery is still a sin."

"A preacher's wife?" Tinkie was intrigued.

"It gets even darker."

We leaned in closer. "What?" Tinkie whispered.

"Someone said they saw Pearl Wingard, that's the preacher's wife, up on the Tallahatchie Bridge a few days ago, throwing a bundle into the water."

It was almost as if a strange version of Bobbie Gentry's song was coming to life right in front of me. The truth of the matter was that I'd never fully understood the song. It was an enigma. Everyone had their own interpretation of what it was about and what had happened to Billie Joe McAllister, but many readings involved a baby thrown from the bridge.

"Was it a baby?" Tinkie asked, obviously under the same influence I was.

"No one knows, and the gossip about this is wild and unreliable. Be careful. Pastor Wingard is highly respected in his community. Pearl is also well thought of."

"Do you know them personally?" I asked.

"Only from their visits to the bank. Nice young couple."

But we all understood that "nice" had nothing to do with passion and the predicament people frequently found themselves in. Even nice people.

"Was she pregnant?" Tinkie asked.

Harold shook his head. "I don't know. I didn't pay a lot of attention. They were seated in Oscar's office the last time they were here, and that was eight or so months ago. I only remember because they were talking about a barbecue at their church. They invited everyone who worked at the bank to come for a plate."

That was small-town Southern hospitality. All welcome, believers and non. For decades some of the churches had led the fight for civil and voting rights for all people. In these later years, the mood of the entire country had soured, but good fellowship could still be found.

"Where do they live?" I asked. Grilling Harold was fun,

and I enjoyed his company, but it was probably time to have a chat with Pearl Wingard. She might have an idea where Danny had gone.

I looked at Tinkie and she nodded. She knew exactly what I was thinking. "Thanks, Harold," she said. "If we need more help, we'll be back."

"Proverbial bad penny," he teased. "If I see you coming, I'll escape."

"You know you love us," I said.

"I do. Almost as much as I love Roscoe."

That could either be a great compliment or a slap in the face. Either way, it was time to get busy.

Before we went to the Basin community—which was where the Anderson land was located—we stopped by the local seed and feed. The farmers all knew each other, and Danny's family was a long-standing part of this community. They might shed some light on where he'd gone.

The crusty old gentleman behind the worn counter put a thumb under one strap of his bib overalls and said, "Welcome, ladies." His gaze swept Tinkie in her cute red boots and leggings. "You aren't here for feed, are you?"

"Not today, Mr. Rutherford." I'd known him most of my life. "We're trying to locate Danny Anderson. Can you help us out?"

Mr. Rutherford frowned and looked down at the countertop. He began to straighten a display of fishing hooks. "Haven't seen Danny today."

"No one has," I said. "His family is worried, and we're trying to help them."

He blew out a breath and finally met my gaze. "You promise you aren't starting trouble for that family?"

"No, sir. We're trying to help." I respected how the farmers stuck up for each other. They could be counted on to get in the harvest if one of their friends got sick or couldn't do the work. But many of the older families were dying out. What would become of farming when it was only corporations providing the food and cotton? I didn't want to think about it.

"Danny was in here a couple of days ago. He was really down. He told me he couldn't pay his bill. He said the bank," he cut a glance at Tinkie, "wouldn't extend his loan."

"Oscar—" Tinkie stopped herself. "Oscar is very worried about Danny. He wants to help him. We all do. But first we have to find him."

"Never heard of a banker who really wanted to help anyone but their own bank account." Mr. Rutherford stared at Tinkie.

I knew the older man was hurting. He obviously cared about Danny. "We're really trying to help," I said. "Including Oscar and Tinkie here. She's my partner, and she's sincere in wanting to find Danny. Oscar is sick with worry. Do you know of anywhere Danny might be, someplace he'd go to think?"

"There's a fishing cabin upriver a bit. He might be there." Rutherford had relented.

"Can we get in by vehicle or only by boat?" I asked.

"You can drive in now. When it was raining, access was only by boat. But the sun has baked the land into what could pass for asphalt. This weather," he shook his head. "It's going to break a lot of farmers."

"It already has," I said. "Can you give me the details on how to get to the cabin?"

"Sure." He pulled out a scratch pad and began to write.

We needed to talk to Danny's family, but we decided to check the cabin first. It would be lovely to be able to bring back the news that Danny was safe. To that end, we followed the directions Mr. Rutherford had given us.

"You don't think Mr. Rutherford would send us on a wild-goose chase, do you?" Tinkie asked.

I was thinking the same thing. "Doubtful. But it could happen. Still"—I gestured out the car windows—"look at this beauty. Everything is so green."

"It is getting hotter," Tinkie said. "Why do people keep denying the reality of climate change?" She shook her head. "Willful ignorance. I'm so glad the dogs are home in the air-conditioning. It's only June, but it feels like late August."

She wasn't wrong, but there was no point complaining. I found the dirt road Mr. Rutherford had mentioned, turned down it, and headed into a densely wooded area.

We came up on the cabin suddenly. We rounded a bend and there it was, like something from a Grimm's brothers fairy tale. The old cabin was ramshackle and uninviting. If Danny was in there, there was a good chance he was depressed. Seriously depressed.

"Let me go in first," I said. I wanted to spare Tinkie any tragic scene.

"You're afraid he's dead in there, aren't you?" she asked.

"Just let me check it."

For once, she didn't argue. I got out of the car and walked up to the tilted front porch. The door was ajar—never a good sign. I didn't have a flashlight, only my phone. I pushed the door open, calling out for Danny as I did so. Only silence answered my calls. There was no sign of a living person. Once I confirmed the place was empty, I called Tinkie inside.

Together we searched the small cabin, but found nothing to indicate where Danny was or if he'd even been there. A layer of dust coated everything.

"This is a bust," Tinkie said. "Let's see what his parents have to say."

It was the next logical step. Before we tackled Pearl Wingard.

3

The Anderson farmhouse took me back in time to when I was a child and traveling the Mississippi back roads with my mother as she checked on folks she knew to be in trouble—medical, financial, emotional, and sometimes even spiritual. My father, a do-gooder himself, used to tease Mama, accusing her of running an illegal mental health and medical practice. The religious part, he made no comment on. Looking back on it now, I wondered what my parents' beliefs might have been. I went to a number of different churches with friends, but my parents didn't push me in any direction. "Be a good person and help others." That was the religious instruction they gave me. It was something to ponder another day.

Tinkie and I stepped onto the shady porch that featured two swings, facing each other, and several rocking chairs with lush ferns and spider plants, also called "airplane plants." The scene was lovely, serene, and spoke of a time now gone, when folks would drop by to sit on a porch and visit "of an evening."

Mrs. Anderson answered the door, the smell of lemon and

vanilla following her. "Sarah Booth, Mrs. Richmond, come in," she said. "I'm baking a pound cake, so come back to the kitchen. Maybe you could help me start a pot of coffee. I'll be ready for a cup in two shakes of a lamb's tail."

She was a tall, angular woman with dark hair shot through with silver. The lines in her face were still light, but the evidence of grief was clear.

We followed her back to the kitchen, where she beckoned us to take a seat at a sturdy farm table with eight chairs.

The kitchen—a huge room with fourteen-foot ceilings—was painted barn red with white cabinets. The black cast-iron skillets and pots looked homey. Starched white curtains fluttered at the open kitchen window above a sink and drainboard.

The pound cake she was baking smelled divine.

"Coffee and filters are in the cabinet. I'll be done soon."

Tinkie took on the task of coffee, which was one of the few things she could make that wouldn't kill us. I went to the sink and started the water running hot. It would be a simple matter to wash up the bowls and measuring cups she'd used. I felt at home in this kitchen, and I didn't mind helping out. I only wished Aunt Loulane could see that her lessons about manners and kindness had actually taken root.

"This is the last pound cake I need to make for the church supper. What can I help you girls with?" Mrs. Anderson asked as she turned on the KitchenAid mixer, dropped an egg in the batter, and watched until she was ready for the next egg. Six eggs. It was going to be delicious.

We were no longer girls, but I was warmed by the term when Mrs. Anderson used it. Her motherly nature tapped into something I longed for every day.

"We would like to speak to Danny." Tinkie kept her voice calm and friendly.

Mrs. Anderson blanched. The egg she held in her hand fell to the floor and cracked, spattering everywhere. For a moment we all three froze, and then I got paper towels to clean up the mess.

"I'm sorry," Mrs. Anderson said, recovering quickly. "Danny isn't here."

"We know," I said softly. "You know our families, but you may not know that we're private investigators. We've been hired to find Danny."

"Hired by who?" she asked sharply.

"By my husband," Tinkie said. "He's worried about Danny. Really worried."

I waited for the blast of recrimination, but it never came. Instead, Mrs. Anderson slumped into a seat, put her face in her hands, and sobbed. "I don't know where Danny is. He's never left like this. Never. He's filled with guilt over circumstances he couldn't control or change. I just want him home. We'll sell this place and move. No land is worth my boy."

I dried my hands on a dish towel and went to put a hand on her shoulder. She sobbed harder. The look I exchanged with Tinkie was filled with remorse, but also determination. We had to keep asking questions if Danny was to be found.

I gave Mrs. Anderson some paper towels and she wiped her face and blew her nose and sat up straight. Her dignity was restored. "Why is Mr. Richmond interested in finding Danny?" she asked.

"Because he cares," Tinkie said simply. She poured a steaming cup of coffee and put it in front of Mrs. Anderson, who thanked her for it.

"Oscar feels terrible. He likes Danny. He likes your whole family. No one thought the drought would last all spring. And then the floods," Tinkie said. "Oscar said a lot of farmers had just put out fertilizer and now it's all washed away. Farming is a hard way to make a living."

"He's right," Mrs. Anderson said. "Too right. I'm sorry my husband went down to the bank and jumped on Mr. Richmond," she said. "Peter is distraught. Danny is the only heir to the family land. If he's gone, there's no point keeping it. Peter said we'd let the bank take it and to hell with it all."

"Oscar never mentioned anything about a confrontation," Tinkie said. "He just hired Delaney Detective Agency to find Danny. And we're going to try to do that."

"Peter and I have searched everywhere we knew to look. He's vanished." She brushed more tears away. "Not a note. Not a word. He just didn't come in from the fields. Gone." She stood and walked to the kitchen window to compose herself.

The picture she painted of Danny matched what others had said—a hard worker, reliable, responsible. "Mrs. Anderson, do you know if Danny had a rela . . . was friends with Pearl Wingard?" I asked.

"He never mentioned Pearl or any other girl after Brigette McEachern, who was his high school sweetheart, left the Basin area to go to New York City. She's a successful model, and Danny knows she'll never come back here. She broke his heart, I think. He wouldn't admit it, but he's never been the same."

Brigette McEachern was someone to look into, for sure. But right now, we had our hands full. "When was the last time you talked to Danny?" I asked.

"Yesterday morning."

"Thank you, Mrs. Anderson."

"Call me Opal. If you find or hear from Danny . . ."

"We'll let you know immediately. If you find or hear from him, please do the same."

She nodded, and it could have been my imagination, but

she looked a little relieved to have someone with professional experience looking for Danny. Delaney Detective Agency had solved several successful cases involving missing persons.

"Do you know Pearl Wingard?" I asked her.

She shrugged. "Danny went to high school with Pearl, back in the day. They weren't particularly close, that I knew of. Friendly, but not romantically involved."

"Thank you." It was time to take our leave.

When we were clear of the house, I looked at Tinkie.

"She seemed to be telling the truth," my partner said.

"She isn't mad at Oscar." It was an interesting point for me. Some people would have blamed the banker, even when Oscar was only doing what he had to do to protect the bank. I knew from personal experience that Oscar was no Snidely Whiplash, using his banking clout to try to steal property from his patrons.

"No, she doesn't blame Oscar, thank goodness."

"While we're over here in LeFlore County, let's track down that preacher man and his wife. I want to hear what they have to tell."

"Good plan," Tinkie said. "Remember that terrific Dusty Springfield song?"

"How could I forget?" I so wanted to tell her about the Jitty visitation as Dusty, but I couldn't risk breaking any rule that would keep Jitty from my life. Tinkie and I began to sing together as I drove through the lush beauty of the cotton and soybean fields.

Pearl Wingard opened the door to my knock. She was an ethereal woman, with a startling beauty, and she reeked of vulnerability. The dark circles under her eyes told of sleepless nights. I wondered instantly if she was the woman I'd seen on the bridge. She was tall and slender with dark hair, but I hadn't gotten a really good look at the person—or spirit—on the Tallahatchie.

"Can I help you?" she asked. Ever polite, as all preacher's wives should be, even though it was clear she was in an emotional crisis.

"Are you Pearl Wingard?" I asked.

The question reduced her to tears. I stepped back, undone by her grief. But Tinkie moved in to comfort her, giving her a big hug and patting her back, even though Tinkie was much shorter.

Pearl gathered herself and took in a deep breath. "I'm sorry."

"Come inside out of the heat and let me make you some tea," Tinkie said. She could make tea as well as coffee, but don't expect any scones along with it—her last attempt at the baked goods could have been used for hockey pucks.

Pearl allowed Tinkie to lead her back to the kitchen. Tinkie helped her into a seat at a lovely oak table and motioned for me to put on the water for tea. I filled the kettle and put it on a burner. Tinkie was in charge, and I was glad.

"Pearl, do you need to lie down?" Tinkie asked her.

"No. No." She sat up straighter. "Why are you here?"

Oh, this was going to be hard.

"We're private investigators. We've been hired to find Danny Anderson."

On cue, the waterworks kicked in and Pearl slumped down on her arms on the table. It was clear this wasn't a sham. Even so, I was impatient. I had questions that only she could answer. But my better angels told me to let Tinkie handle this, so I did.

"We don't mean to upset you, Pearl, but time is not on our

side. So, if you can answer some questions, you could help us in our search for Danny."

"The gossip is that he killed himself," she said, looking up with woeful eyes. "Why are you asking me about him?"

"Danny had a lot of stress on his shoulders with the financial situation of the farm, but he doesn't appear to be a man who would self-harm over a debt. What we need to know is if there were other factors involved."

"Factors like what?" Realization dawned on her. "Like me?" She said it bluntly and earned my respect.

"That's right. Were you romantically involved with Danny?"

"What?" She was terrified. "Whoever said that is lying."

"Could I please use your restroom?" I asked, earning a withering look from Tinkie. But there was a method to my madness.

"Down the hall on the left," she said, and the pause gave her a minute to gather herself.

I left the kitchen and headed down the hall, but the bathroom wasn't my destination. I quickly did a scan of the bedrooms and a small home office. Zero baby paraphernalia anywhere in the cottage, from what I could see. If Pearl had ever been pregnant—and she clearly wasn't now, unless it was early stages—they'd gotten rid of any evidence a baby was expected.

I flushed the toilet, washed my hands, and returned to the kitchen. Pearl was more composed and Tinkie was leaning into her, talking softly. The kettle began to whistle, and I made Pearl a cup of tea. When I placed it in front of her, she nodded her thanks.

"We only want to help," Tinkie was saying. "We don't care, and we don't judge. But we need the facts to begin to sort out where Danny might be. Or why he's suddenly disappeared. It could be he owed money to someone bad. That happens, and we'll investigate the financial aspect thoroughly." She hesitated only a split second. "But we have to follow every lead, even when it's only gossip."

"I can't help you." The lie landed quickly, and I knew further pressure wouldn't work. We didn't have any evidence to show Pearl.

"Thank you for your help." Tinkie stood up. She, too, understood it was time to move on. "If you think of anything. Or if you need help in the future, call us." She gave her a business card.

Once we were outside, Tinkie turned to me. "She was lying through her teeth."

"I agree."

"What can we do?"

"Not a thing until we have more evidence." I filled her in on the lack of baby items in the house. "Why don't we go by the library here in Leflore County and see if we can find some high school annuals? I know Danny and Pearl know each other. Perhaps we can find out why she's lying."

4

The resource librarian at the main branch in Greenwood was a helpful young man who had mad research skills. Based on the tattoo on his forearm, he was also a huge fan of Bobbie Gentry's music.

"Nice tat," I said.

"Oh, I love her. She's the best thing that happened to Mississippi in a decade."

"Is she still around these parts?" I asked.

He pulled us into a far corner of the library. "She stepped away from fame without a backward glance."

"Why would she do that?" I asked.

"Lots of rumors and innuendo," he said. "Basically. I think she's just a very private person. I respect that."

"I'd like to talk to her." Yeah, I was a fangirl.

"If I knew where she was, I wouldn't tell you or anyone else. People who want privacy deserve to be left alone."

I couldn't disagree, but my real reason for being at the library was not Ms. Gentry. It was Danny Anderson and Pearl Wingard.

The librarian showed us to a local history section in a snug back corner of the library and I found yearbooks from Leflore County High School. People had no idea what a great resource these "picture" books could be. I calculated the year Danny and Pearl would have graduated and turned the pages of the annual to the class favorites. Sure enough, Pearl and Danny stood wearing their lettered high school jackets, him in football and her in softball. Both voted Most Athletic their senior year.

Tinkie paged through the local Leflore County newspaper articles while I continued flipping through the yearbook. I hit the jackpot on the Senior Day page, where I found a photo of the two of them at a class picnic, him lying on the grass with his head in her lap. They looked at each other with what was clearly romantic love.

I copied the photos and walked over to Tinkie, who was also wrapping it up. I showed her what I had unearthed. "Find anything?" I asked.

"Not much," she said. "Danny was big in the Future Farmers of America. He was well regarded and elected as one of the youngest presidents in the area. Pearl had a scholarship to Delta State University, but she didn't go. A few years back, she became the youth leader at a local church. The church that Micah Wingard now pastors."

"So she became involved in the church before she became a preacher's wife." It was a curious point of interest. "Anything about her and Danny?"

Tinkie shook her head. "The paper wouldn't cover anything like that unless there was a marriage announcement or an engagement party. But we should check with Cece. She has a much wider reach than the small Greenwood paper."

Tinkie was right about that, and once we finished at the

library, we'd visit our journalist friend, Cece Dee Falcon. She knew a little bit about wanting to leave her past behind.

While Tinkie continued perusing the old newspaper records, I turned my attention to finding the names and addresses of any classmates or friends who might have information on Danny. Did he drink? Had he sown his wild oats?

I decided to talk to the county agent while we were still in LeFlore County. I whispered my destination to Tinkie and left her at the library with the car and keys. She could drive over to pick me up when she was done. Maybe we'd have time for some lunch before we drove back.

The county extension office was located on Market Street in a two-story yellow brick building. I found the services offered by this office, and other extension offices in every county across the nation, to be extremely valuable to farmers. I went inside and stood at the counter until a middle-aged man came over to assist me. Yes, he knew Danny Anderson well.

"Danny is one of the farmers we expect will take the Delta into the future," he said. "He's aware that we're facing a climate crisis, and he's willing to try new things. Many of the older farmers don't believe in climate change. They think it's made up. I only wish that were true. People like Danny, who understand science and history, are searching for ways to deal with the big changes coming. He's important to us and the future of farming."

"Have you seen Danny lately?" I asked.

The man was no bumpkin. He instantly knew something was wrong. "Has something happened to Danny?"

"He's out of pocket. That's it."

"'Out of pocket' as in missing breakfast this morning or meaning no one knows where he is?"

I wasn't above lying, but what was the point? "He's missing.

My partner and I are private investigators. We've been hired to find him. His folks are a little worried."

He rubbed his jaw. "I'd say so. Danny is the most reliable man I know. He wouldn't go off and leave his family to worry unless he couldn't help it."

This man didn't know the full story of debt, foreclosure, and potential romance—and I wasn't about to tell him. "We believe he's fine. I just need to locate him and let him know to call his folks. Relieve their minds. You understand."

"You want me to tell you where Danny might be?"

That was the general idea. I smiled my agreement. "We've checked the cabin on the river. No sign he's been there."

"That was my first option. Now, let's see." He went to the coffeepot, poured two cups of black coffee, and pushed one across the counter to me. "Try Sable's Table over on the highway. Folks in there might know where he is. Lots of farmers go there for lunch. I'll check for any meetings of groups he's involved in to see if maybe he's out of town for a conference. Danny is one of the county leaders in confronting issues facing agriculture. He could be out of town on business." His forehead creased. "But it doesn't sound like Danny to disappear without telling anyone."

This man seemed to know Danny fairly well. I had to ask. "Was Danny involved with anyone? I mean romantically. He's a good-looking man and it would be natural . . ." I let the sentence peter out.

"Danny kept his personal life close to the vest. A few months ago, a change did seem to come over him. He became less shy, and seemed truly happy. I assumed he'd found someone. But he never said, and I didn't ask."

I couldn't tell if he was hedging or not. "Do you know Pearl Wingard?" He went pale, and I had my answer.

"Sure, everybody knows Ms. Pearl. She's the backbone of the local church up near the Basin community. Good woman. Loves the community children and makes them feel welcome in the church."

"Did she welcome Danny?" I asked.

He knew what I wanted, and he dodged my question. "Pearl welcomes everyone. Young and old, sick and healthy. She's a jewel, just like her name."

"Thank you." His failure to answer the question honestly had given me the truth. The relationship between Danny and Pearl wasn't the tightly kept secret they might have hoped. Folks knew. And folks were likely talking. The big question was, did Pearl's husband, the Reverend Micah Wingard, know about the . . . friendship? And did he care?

Tinkie called to say she was done at the library and I went outside to stand on the curb while she drove to pick me up. I was taking in the beauty of Greenwood, a town that had once been the central location for much of the cotton grown in the Delta. The bales could either go north via the railroads or south down the Mississippi to New Orleans. From the Louisiana port, the heavy bales were frequently shipped to Europe for the industrial looms that worked nonstop back in the 1800s. Cotton was no longer king, but Greenwood still showed signs of the affluence that once made it one of the wealthiest cities in the state.

Tinkie whipped to the curb with the motor running, but as I was getting into the car, a man hurried down the sidewalk toward me.

"Ms. Delaney," he called out.

I waited.

"I'm a member of the Leflore Savior Church." His stare was so intense I feared it would leave a hole in me.

"Can I help you?" I asked. I'd never seen him in my life.

"You can." He inhaled deeply and stepped too close. I could feel his breath on my face. "Stay out of church affairs. Mind your own business. And leave Reverend Wingard and his wife alone."

"Who are you?" I asked.

"Your worst nightmare if you don't back off."

Before I could reply, he was hurrying away. Tinkie got out of the driver's side and looked over the car. "Who was he?"

"No clue. But he knew me."

"Dammit, I should have snapped his picture," Tinkie said. "He threatened you. We're going straight to the sheriff's office to report this."

Something told me to hold back. "Let's tell Coleman, but not the sheriff here."

"Why not?" Tinkie asked as she got back behind the wheel.

"I think our best option will be to take this up with Reverend Wingard. Not the sheriff. It could be leverage."

Tinkie grinned. "Good thinking. Your brain works more and more like a criminal's every day."

I wasn't certain that was a compliment, but it was true. "Let's go to this local restaurant, Sable's Table. Danny is well-known there. We can ask a few locals about him."

"It won't be as good as going home to Millie's Café, but it's good to try new things," Tinkie said.

I couldn't disagree. I pulled it up on the GPS and we set off.

The restaurant was on the east side of town, and it held all the charm of old-time diners where the food was Southern and the menu was mouthwatering. We took a booth in the back and looked at the four-by-four-inch-square daily printed menu. A meat and two sides for $9.99 or a vegetable plate for $7.99. I went with fried okra, potato salad, and green beans. Tinkie opted for a hamburger steak, fries, and coleslaw. The truth was, not a single item on the menu would taste bad. As we waited for our lunch to be served, we took in the patrons. Most were farmers, in town for business and lunch. A few men in business suits sat at a front table. Several tables were filled with women who appeared to work in offices in town or ladies who simply liked to eat lunch out. The patronage was timeless, in a way. I'd seen the same types of people at Millie's Café for most of my life.

In the booth across from us, there were several neatly dressed women who didn't look like office workers.

"I think they may be church ladies," Tinkie said. She had an eye for such things.

Before the food arrived, I walked over and introduced myself. The women were polite but didn't meet my gaze. I told them the truth about our case and then asked, "Do you ladies know Danny Anderson?"

They looked down at their plates. Were they timid or were they hiding something? It was hard to tell.

"I know Danny," one said. "He comes to our church sometimes. Nice man. He's helped a lot with drives to feed underprivileged families and kids. He's even taken some of the Sunday school classes out to his place to show them how a real farm operates."

"From all I've heard, he's a very good man," I said, which wasn't a lie. "I heard he worked with Mrs. Wingard a lot."

That was the wrong statement. Even though they hadn't finished eating, they scooted out of the booth and stood. "We have work to do. Pleasure to meet you."

They were gone before I could think of a reason to stop them, but their behavior had told me plenty. The church protected the Wingards, no matter what the gossip might be. That had both a good and negative edge. The bottom line, though, was that it didn't help our investigation.

Tinkie spoke with a few customers who gave the Wingards and Danny glowing reports of decency. We finished our food and headed for Zinnia. I needed to talk with Coleman before I took on a meeting with Micah Wingard.

5

The next morning, I slept past Coleman getting up to go to work. I took my time, drinking coffee and playing with the dogs and Pluto the cat. Poe, the wild raven who had taken up with us, was giving the cat hell. Tinkie had a doctor's appointment with Maylin to get a few vaccinations, so I was on my own for now.

Coleman was out of the office, so I stopped to chew the fat with DeWayne and Budgie, the Sunflower County deputies. Coleman hadn't been able to give me a lot of detail about the Wingards or the Anderson family. The deputies might be a better source of info. DeWayne loved my horses and all the animals at Dahlia House, and Budgie had a real talent for internet sleuthing. I enjoyed both of them.

"Do you guys ever hear anything about Danny Anderson and the Leflore Savior Church?" I asked.

Budgie shrugged. "Nothing bad. I taught in the high school at Greenwood for a year when the math teacher was hurt in a car accident. The kids were all good. Pearl's younger sister was in the class. A very nice family."

"Were they . . . churchy?" I didn't know how to ask the question.

Budgie laughed. "No snake handling that I could tell."

I knew he was teasing me. "That's not what I meant. It just seemed she developed a relationship with the church later in life, after high school. But that's an assumption on my part."

Budgie shrugged. "Back then folks didn't wear their religious convictions on their sleeves like they do now. It was a private thing. Folks attended church or they didn't. Churchgoing wasn't an identity. More of a live-and-let-live time, I guess."

"But she wasn't overtly religious?"

"Nope. Just a nice, decent young woman who happened to be great at sports. Went to Ole Miss on a scholarship. Pearl had an athletic scholarship to Delta State but she didn't go, as I recall. I never thought to ask the students about their religions, and they didn't ask me."

It was true that people could find faith or spiritual beliefs at any time in life. Some came to it late or after a tragedy. And others sometimes walked away. Life was all about flux and change. "Does anything about the Beeson family stick out to you?" I knew Pearl's maiden name from the yearbooks.

Budgie frowned, then answered. "Salt of the earth. Hardworking. Involved in community events. Helped those less fortunate. They were just good people who worked hard."

"And the Anderson family?"

"Danny is the only kid, and he was older. I never taught him, but kids remembered him from his football years. He was a high school standout. Got a scholarship to Mississippi State and got a degree in agriculture, from what I remember. But it was awhile back and what I know comes from high school students' chattering. I was just a substitute teacher, so you should double-check with folks who were on a more inside track."

"Will do." But the gossip about both the Anderson and Beeson families indicated they were just normal people living the best life they could. If I expected to learn anything different, I was going to have to dig a lot deeper.

I left a note for Coleman and told him I was headed to interview Reverend Wingard. I'd already checked with the church secretary, and the reverend was there working on his Sunday sermon. I thought it would be a good time to catch him away from his wife or congregation. Delicacy was called for, and I hoped I was up to the task.

The church was picturesque, to say the least. Nestled among a grove of pecans about twenty minutes from Zinnia, the little white chapel looked like a painting from a Thanksgiving card. There was even a bell in the tower. I instantly felt an attachment. My aunt Loulane had been a religious woman whose church, though in downtown Zinnia, had been simple and focused on the good word and good deeds. A pang of loneliness hit me as I got out of my car and entered the church. The smell of sandalwood was comforting. And furniture polish. I saw a woman leaning down, oiling the wooden pews.

"Can I help you?" she asked.

"I'm looking for Reverend Wingard."

"Is he expecting you?"

"No, ma'am." I couldn't have lied in that church if I'd wanted to.

"He's in his office. Go past the altar and take that door on the right."

She didn't bother to ask my business, which I really liked. I followed her directions and found myself facing a beautiful old oak door. When I knocked, I heard a man call out, "Come in."

I stepped into a room filled with lovely light from a stained glass window. Behind a desk, a man stood up and extended his hand. "Pastor Wingard. How can I help you?"

He was a slender man with kind brown eyes, and for a moment I didn't know what to say. Tinkie should have handled this. She was so much better at the social graces. "I'm here about Danny Anderson." I just blurted it out.

"Danny?" He came around the desk and helped me into a chair. "What's going on with Danny?"

Not exactly the reaction of a man who may have murdered his competition. He seemed genuinely concerned for Danny, and for me.

"Are you Danny's relative?" he asked.

"No, I'm a private investigator."

His eyebrows drew together. "Is Danny . . . involved in something?"

Oh, brother, I was going to have to draw him a picture. "That's what I wanted to ask you."

"The Anderson family aren't members of my congregation, but they are good people. Every one of them. Danny attends services here every once in a while."

Was the reverend oblivious to all the gossip around the county? Surely he wasn't that out of touch. "Danny Anderson is missing. A family . . . friend hired me to find him. They're very worried."

He laughed. "Danny will be home soon enough. He takes his responsibilities seriously. He isn't a man to gallivant around. He probably had a business meeting and forgot to let everyone know."

"That's possible, but I have to make sure there isn't a . . . darker reason for his absence."

"And why are you asking me?" He finally got to the place I needed him to be.

"I was hoping maybe you could tell me if Danny has any secrets."

To his credit, he didn't pretend to be ignorant of the implication I was making. "You think I would know where he is?"

"Do you?"

"No." He walked around and sat behind his desk, putting a symbolic barrier between us. "Danny sometimes attends the church here, as I said. As far as I know he's a good man, dedicated to his farm, his family, and his community. That's all I know."

I could have pushed it, but I didn't. I'd save that gambit in case I needed it later. His behavior told me plenty. He wasn't truly threatened by Danny.

"I spoke with Mrs. Wingard before I came here."

For the first time anger sparked in his soft eyes. "I hope you'll keep in mind that Pearl is a fragile woman."

"Fragile? How?"

He sighed. "Pearl is tenderhearted to a fault. She worries about everyone." He leaned forward on the desk. "Protect her emotions, Ms. Delaney. The world needs people like Pearl. She doesn't judge anyone."

"Was there a reason to judge Danny Anderson?"

He shook his head. "Not that I would know. Or that my wife would know. I hope you find him safe and sound." He walked to the door of his study and opened it to let me out.

As I passed by him, I paused. "I was up on the Tallahatchie Bridge earlier. There was a dark-haired woman in a long white dress. Do you know who that might be?"

The minister frowned. "Can you give me more details? There are a number of young brunettes in my congregation. The river is a draw on a hot summer day, even for those who know it can be dangerous."

I actually couldn't give more details. I'd only caught a glimpse of the strange woman and then she was gone. "This is going to sound ridiculous, but are there any stories about the bridge being . . . haunted?"

He laughed then, and the tension left his shoulders. "I would have pegged you for a skeptic, Ms. Delaney."

"Funny, I would have, too."

"This woman you saw on the bridge. She was . . . walking?"

"No, she was standing at the railing, looking down into the water. I saw her the other morning when I was going for a drive."

"And she . . . disappeared?" He wasn't laughing at me, but he was coming close.

"I know, it sounds ridiculous. But she was there one second, and then gone. No trace of her. My dogs and I searched along the bank for a short distance, but we didn't find any footprints or anything."

"That bridge . . . It's inspired songs and stories. I'm sure you know the history."

"I do."

He stared into my eyes. "Stories and songs, good for entertainment but not a shred of truth in most of them."

"I reported the woman on the bridge to the Leflore sheriff. He said he'd check into it."

"And I'm sure he did." The minister held out his hand, a signal that I needed to depart.

"If you hear from Danny, would you let me know?" I asked.

"I will. And please, don't upset my wife anymore. Like I mentioned, she's tender, and this will worry her."

"The Anderson family is very upset, Reverend. Keep that in mind. The best thing would be for Danny to show up at his home."

"I agree. Should it become necessary to search for him, you can count on me and this congregation. Like I said, he isn't a member of the church, but he's still part of the community. We look after our own."

There wasn't a good reason to linger, so I headed back toward Zinnia, via the Tallahatchie Bridge. It was a little out of the way, but I was drawn there. There was no traffic and I drove onto the bridge slowly, taking my time, aware of the swift waters beneath the bridge. When I got to the top, I saw a bundle of wildflowers left on the railing. A light wind ruffled the leaves and petals of the flowers.

There was no evidence of a human, but someone had to have picked the black-eyed Susans, coneflowers, and asters. Before I could get out of the car and retrieve them, a brisk wind kicked up and the bouquet fell, end over end, into the muddy waters of the Tallahatchie River.

6

The bouquet floated past the bridge and down the river, finally swirling out of sight.

The sun was hot on my shoulders and sweat was trickling down my spine, but a chill took me. I hated to admit it, but the flowers had creeped me out. Where did they come from?

The narrator of the Bobbie Gentry song concluded the tale by saying she spent a lot of time up on Choctaw Ridge, picking flowers and throwing them into the river. The thought that it could be more than a coincidence was unnerving. Was some ghostly entity playing with me?

I almost jumped out of my shoes when my cell phone rang. Only the day before, I hadn't been able to get reception on the bridge. Now I had three bars. I answered the phone as I was hurrying back to my car.

"Cece wants to meet us," Tinkie said. "She may have something helpful. She wants to get some lunch. Budgie told me you were in Leflore County. Can you get back here in time to eat?"

"I'm on the way. Give me fifteen or twenty minutes."

"Are you hungry?"

"No, but let's meet at Millie's." I sighed heavily. "Order me a fried green tomato sandwich anyway." It was impossible to go into Millie's Café and not order food. It was just that good.

I texted Coleman to see if he wanted to meet us for lunch. I felt like lately we were ships passing in the night. He'd been working on a fraud case, and I'd been worrying about Gertrude. And now, I was consumed with finding a missing farmer. I felt like it had been ages since we'd shared a meal. Unfortunately, he responded that he couldn't get away in time for lunch. The fraud case demanded his focus.

When I cleared the bridge, I pressed the gas pedal and streaked toward Zinnia. It was another perfect June day—a little too hot for my taste, but with the top down on the convertible, I felt like a teenager again.

Driving through the open fields of cotton, I forced my thoughts away from my parents and their deaths. Gertrude, damn her to hell, had brought all of those hard things back into the forefront of my brain. Things I'd worked for years to push back. She'd committed many cruelties, but dragging the past back to life was one of the meanest. Somehow, I would find her and make her pay.

I pushed aside thoughts of revenge as I pulled into a parking space at the café. My best buddies, including Tammy Odom, my grammar-school chum who was better known as Madame Tomeeka, psychic medium, were waiting for me. I grinned big as I walked into the delicious smell of Southern cooking.

Millie brought iced teas all around and took a seat with me and Tinkie for a moment. The café was busy, but she could spare ten minutes to see what we were up to.

"We're hunting for Danny Anderson," Tinkie told them. "He's dropped out of sight and his family is worried."

Cece nodded. "I heard some talk last week about how a lot of the farmers are barely hanging on. This weather is killing them. Depression is high."

I didn't say anything, and Tinkie flushed. She and Oscar both were suffering for the role the bank played in the hardships facing the farmers. But the farmers had to have the loans to keep planting. It was a vicious cycle. Oscar gave the farmers the biggest breaks he could, but he couldn't give money away, no matter how much he might want to. Ultimately, he was accountable to the board of directors and the investors.

"Have you seen Danny recently?" I asked Millie.

She thought for a moment. "About three days ago. He started to come into the café, but he was stopped right outside by Pearl Wingard. They chatted a few minutes and he left. She left, too, but not with him." Even as Millie talked, she realized she was painting them with adulterer's red. It sounded like a meeting to schedule an assignation. She stopped talking.

"Danny's missing, and folks are worried." Tinkie took a deep breath. "Oscar told Danny he had to pay back his loan or the bank would foreclose."

Silence greeted her remark until Madame Tomeeka spoke out. "This is not on Oscar or any banker. When money is borrowed, terms are set. The bank has investors and stockholders. It isn't up to Oscar, or even Mr. Avery, to decide who has to pay a loan back and who doesn't."

Cece pulled out her notebook, tapped her pen against it, and then spoke. "This makes me sick. Danny is such a nice man. Most of the farmers have been grumbling about being unable to pay their loans back this year. Some are carrying debt over from last year. Did you know there was a buyer in town last week? I heard he was going around to various farms offering to buy out the locals."

My jaw clenched. "Who is this buyer?"

Cece shook her head. "I didn't get a name, but I will. The farmers I spoke with were upset. Scared. I didn't press them." She slapped her notebook on the table. "I should have. I just had a moment of being a softie." She looked up as the bell on the diner door jangled. Two men in jeans and boots came in and took seats.

"I heard the same thing," Millie said. "A couple of farmers were in here drinking coffee. They were talking about some man who was visiting all the farmers with big debts, offering to buy their property. They were angry. Folks develop hard feelings for out-of-towners who come in and try to capitalize on the bad fortunes of others."

"A lot of these jumped-up buyers with fat rolls of money represent foreign interests, too," Cece said. "If you think there are herbicides and chemicals dumped on crops now, wait until foreign concerns own the land. Every week Congress knocks down regulations that would protect us, the consumers. They work hard to make the regulations look like an oppression of rights instead of safeguards. And the politicians are lining their pockets to sell us out."

I knew things were tough for a lot of farmers now, but I hadn't heard of the land buyers coming in already. I called them the modern-day carpetbaggers—folks who only cared about profit and not about protecting the land or the people who worked it.

"Do you know anyone who might know the name of the buying agent?" I asked Millie.

"No, but check the bulletin board when you go out. A lot of folks will stick a business card up there if they're looking to buy or sell land or equipment. He could have come in when I was in the kitchen."

"We'll do that," Tinkie said. Her lips were pressed into a thin line. "Oscar will do whatever he can to help the locals keep their property."

"We know that," Millie said, touching Tinkie's hand. "This is hard on everyone. I just keep hoping the weather will turn, the farmers will catch a break, and everything will go back to normal."

I wasn't that optimistic. But there was another avenue to investigate. "Madame, are you picking up anything from the spirit world?" I asked.

Tammy closed her eyes and listened. "No. I'm not. It's as if everything is suspended. Very peculiar."

That could be either good or bad. At least she wasn't hearing gunshots and seeing carnage in the streets. Yet. "Maybe this summer the weather will ease off. Maybe we'll have an early fall. Maybe the farmers will be able to plant a fall crop and an early spring crop and make up the money they owe." Boy, did I sound like a Pollyanna or what?

I needed to find out what buyer's agent had been working Sunflower County. A word with him might give me a lead on Danny. If Danny had been approached to sell the Anderson property, that might have been enough to send him running. Or if he'd gotten into a heated argument with a land agent, it could even have gotten physical.

Raised voices drew my attention back to the two men who'd just entered and taken seats at a table in the corner. One of them stood up so abruptly, his chair tipped over. The men glowered at each other.

"Who is that?" I asked Millie. She knew everyone.

"Taller one is Todd Jenkins. He has a small landholding in Tallahatchie County. The other is Wylie Moulton. Not sure of his story." She picked up her order pad and pencil. "I'll go take their order and make sure they don't start any trouble. Tempers are hot right now." She went over to talk to the men in her normal, cheerful way. Jenkins returned to his seat after righting his chair, and the moment seemed to pass.

We finished our lunch, but the mood had soured. We were all worried. We paid our tab and filed to the café door. I stopped at the bulletin board and looked. Sure enough, there was a business card pinned right at eye level. Levi Butler, purchasing agent for Farmland Inc. I knew the company. They'd bought up farms from Nebraska to Mississippi. I didn't know if they were owned by foreign interests, but I was going to find out. And then I was going to track down Mr. Butler and see if he'd spoken to Danny.

Because I was unsettled and struggling to control my anger at the idea of foreign interests controlling Delta land, I went home to Dahlia House and my critters. The afternoon had turned muggy. I bathed the three horses, smiling at their antics with the hose. They all enjoyed a bath, but Reveler loved it the most. He splashed in the water, and when I set him free, he rolled in the dust just to show me who was boss.

Sweetie Pie and Avalon were stretched out in a damp spot in the shade of the barn. Pluto the cat and Poe the raven perched on the wooden fence by the barn. They weren't the best of friends. Dive-bombing Pluto's head was Poe's specialty. Pluto had a wicked left hook with his claws, but he never caught the raven. He could have, I was certain. But he had no real desire to harm the aggravating bird.

I played with the dogs and walked around one of the pastures, checking the fence to be sure it was secure. It was something that needed to be done periodically. The sun was going down and the heat had finally begun to abate. Sweetie Pie and Avalon frisked together, and my thoughts returned to the day back in February when I'd found Avalon chained up at a place where dogs were kept for fighting and bait. We'd saved all the dogs there, but rings of dogfighters were everywhere. They were brutal people who I sincerely believed would have no qualms about hurting a dog or a person.

At last, when I knew the fences were good, I headed back to the house. From my vantage point on a slight rise, I saw Coleman coming home in his truck. My heart did a little flutter. Some women would have made it a point to have a good dinner ready, but I decided to order takeout, for everyone's good. My cooking was better than Tinkie's, but not much.

I jogged the rest of the way home and arrived just as Coleman was slamming his truck door. I hurled myself into his arms and he caught me with a laugh. "I'm glad to see you, too," he said.

"Any news on Danny?" I asked.

He put his arm around me. "As a matter of fact, there is."

"Tell me. I have someone I'd like you to check out for me, too."

"Let's make a drink and porch sit for a few minutes." He had something to tell me, and he wanted a moment to consider how best to do it.

"Is Danny okay?" Patience was never my strong suit.

"Yes, as far as I know. It isn't that. Let's get that drink."

I made us both a Jack on the rocks while Coleman put his gun in the safe and took off his gear—handcuffs, radio, etc. In ten minutes, we were on the shady porch sipping our drinks with the animals around us.

"You've heard that there are land agents buying up properties in the Delta?" Coleman asked.

"Yeah, I heard."

"There's a fellow—"

"Levi Butler?" I asked.

"That's him. He's putting some pressure on farmers like Danny. Those that owe big bank loans. I had two farmers call me today and complain about his high-pressure tactics."

Anger crept up my face and I could almost feel the heat radiating off me. "Can you stop him?"

"So far, no. He hasn't overstepped the law, but he's come mighty close."

"Do you think he upset Danny so much that Danny has . . . fled?" I couldn't bring myself to voice the other possibility.

Coleman rattled the ice cubes in his glass as he thought through his answer. "Danny never struck me as a man who would run from his problems. So, no, I don't think this Butler drove Danny away."

But he did think something unpleasant about Levi Butler. I could read it in the rigidity of his spine. I waited for him to continue. Coleman would tell me in his own time.

"Butler made an offer to Danny to pay off the bank and take nearly half of the Anderson farm."

"But that's a crap deal!" The Anderson farm was worth a whole lot more than what Danny might have borrowed.

"I know. But Butler isn't after a fair price, he's after taking all he can. He's a modern-day barbarian."

"Where can I find this Levi Butler?" I asked Coleman.

"You're going to love this. He's staying at Gertrude's old bed-and-breakfast. The new owners have renamed it Evergreen Park."

It seemed no matter what I was doing, I couldn't escape Gertrude Stromm. But at least it could wait until daylight. I sighed and focused on Coleman, rocking beside me. I stood up and took his hand. "I meant to order dinner, but I never got around to it. What say we skip the meal and go straight to bed?"

"Suits me." Coleman scooped me into his arms and took me up the stairs to the bedroom.

7

I had already fed the horses and other critters when Tinkie pulled up in her Caddy the next morning. We had a date, not with destiny but with a creep. Tinkie had spoken with the land agent and set up an appointment. Levi Butler was meeting us at Millie's Café. The idea of tracking him down at the B and B held zero appeal for me. Gertrude Stromm's presence still haunted the place—and me.

As an added bonus, I'd arranged for Cece and Madame Tomeeka to be in the café waiting. Millie would make sure Butler was seated where Cece and Tammy could overhear the conversation. My plan was a thing of beauty.

The big rush of farmers and businessmen had come and gone at Millie's. I saw my friends, but I ignored them. A handsome man was sitting at a table right beside them. I walked over and held out my hand. "Levi Butler?"

"In the flesh," he said with a charming smile. His looks would work well for him in the profession he'd chosen—fleecing people out of their property. "Please, ladies, join me and tell me how I can help you."

"Like I mentioned on the phone, Sarah Booth may want to sell off some of her acreage," Tinkie said, never missing a beat.

"Oh, really. Now that's a shame, but farming has become an erratic gamble, hasn't it?"

"Too rich of a gamble for my blood. The mortgage is getting too heavy to carry," I added, looking crestfallen. "But it is family land, so I would like to seek alternative routes, if possible." I cleared my throat. "I heard you were making some offers to other farmers to help them out. Maybe a loan?"

He was wary but interested. Greed sparked in his eyes. "How much money do you need?" he asked.

"About three hundred thousand. Just until I can get the fall crops planted and bring them in. I owe the bank, but I'd pay you back first."

"Where is your property located?"

He was smart. He wasn't going to offer cash for a pig in a poke.

"It's terrific farmland," Tinkie said, jumping into the conversation. "Sarah Booth's family has owned and farmed it for generations. They've taken care to rotate, allow the land to lie fallow, and not overfertilize. It's some of the best farmland in the Delta."

"You're lucky to have such an enthusiastic cheering squad," Butler said. It was clear he viewed Tinkie as an annoyance. He wanted what he wanted and nothing more. And what he wanted was the fertile Delta land. "Now, where is the property?"

I gave him a location, and he looked it up on an app on his phone. "Yes," he said. "Yes, I see. Dahlia House. Are you wanting to sell the house, too? It's lovely, but upkeep on a place like that is backbreaking. We'd try to sell the house as a separate piece. Maybe to someone who has horses or wants to graze a few head of cattle. They wouldn't need more than ten acres for that. Just understand, if we can't find a buyer, we'd likely tear the house down to open up the entire acreage for farming. That's the only way to really get ahead in this game now. No houses, trees, or impediments."

He was a hideous human being. I smiled big. "I understand. The house is old and drafty. I know I'd be happier in New Orleans or maybe New York, a city that offers a social life and activities for someone like me with an artistic bent."

Tinkie gently kicked my shin under the table and never lost her smile. She was warning me not to overplay my hand.

"Exactly," Levi said. "I'm so glad you understand. Some people develop unrealistic emotional attachments to places. Property is meant to be turned over, bought, and sold." He was so busy looking at his phone that he didn't see the death stare Cece was leveling at him.

"I don't really want to sell, but . . ."

He finally looked up. "Better to sell and save your credit than to go deeper in the hole, right?"

"She'd prefer a loan. Can you float her one?" Tinkie cut in. We didn't want to sound too eager.

"Let me look at the property."

This was going to be hard. Even pretending to sell Dahlia House made me ready to take his scalp. I didn't want the likes of Levi Butler to touch the sacred ground of my home. But we'd started this gambit, and we had to see it through.

"Let's meet there at nine," Tinkie said, tapping her watch. "Sarah Booth, let's go pick up all that naughty underwear you leave around the house." She smiled sweetly at Levi. "Sarah Booth jumps right out of her clothes in this summer heat. And, lord, if she takes a lover, it is Katie, bar the door. The things I've found under her sofa!"

I snatched Tinkie by the arm and hauled her out of the

café. Levi half stood, his face registering shock and consternation. Behind him, Cece and Tammy turned away to hide their laughter. I was going to get even with my bad friends at the first opportunity.

Tinkie laughed the whole way to Dahlia House, and I finally had to join her. She'd gotten me good—no denying it. And Butler's face! I would remember it with joy.

I did pick up some clothing Coleman and I had dropped along the staircase in a moment of passion. Tinkie knew me far too well. And I was reminded of a scene from Hell when Tinkie had caught us both naked on the stairwell when she'd burst through the front door. I'd just started seeing Coleman, and we'd all three frozen on the spot. Looking back, it was hilarious. And I had yet to get even with Tinkie for that moment.

When Dahlia House was tidy, Tinkie and I went to sit on the porch with Pluto, Poe the raven, and all the dogs except one. The dog she'd rescued from our last case, a severely abused pittie she'd renamed Zelda, was doing better each day. She'd been at the groomer for a bath the last time I was at Tinkie's, but soon, Zelda would be joining us on our cases. Right now, I was curious to see how these critters would react to Levi Butler. They did not disappoint.

The dogs began to growl softly when Butler got out of his car. Pluto went to the top step and hissed, clearly a warning of razor claws to come. The best, though, was Poe. The raven flew a circle around Butler's head and then cut loose. Bird poop splattered on his shoulder.

Tinkie and I managed not to laugh, but Sweetie Pie let out a howl that could only be called joyous. I was convinced my animals acted in league with each other. And I loved them for it.

"Could I borrow your washroom?" Butler asked, his face beet red.

"Sure." I had to force myself to be gracious.

"Do you think Coleman would mind loaning him a shirt?" Tinkie said. She turned to Butler. "Her current beau is the sheriff of Sunflower County. Lord, the men just come and go around here." She assessed him. "Coleman's got a lot more muscle than you, but I think we could repurpose an old shirt for you."

"No, thank you. Just the washroom."

I pointed to the front door. "Second room on your left."

Tinkie and I rocked in unison. We didn't dare look at each other or we'd bust a gut laughing. Ten minutes later, Butler came out, his shirt soaked. The worst of the bird poop was gone. Butler was eager to get down to business and get away from us.

"Would you like to see the property now?" I asked.

"Yes."

"How about on horseback?" Oh, I knew I was being a devil.

"Sarah Booth has three divine horses," Tinkie said. "You're wearing boots, so you'll be fine. Of course you ride, don't you?"

She didn't give him a chance to answer before we headed to the barn to saddle up. I gave him Lucifer and an Australian stock saddle because it had a horn. Lucifer could be frisky, but Reveler was a devil. Miss Scrapiron would carry Tinkie safely.

The day was hot, but once we were moving it was actually pleasant. We rode the boundaries of my property. I hated to admit that it bothered me to even show this man my land. I had no intention of selling, but watching his face shift from greedy to calculating made me a little sick. It was clear he liked the property and knew he could make a profit. I felt like he was trying to cook my firstborn child.

We were headed back to the house when I saw Tinkie pick a switch from a tree we passed under. She wouldn't hit one of the horses, and I hoped she wouldn't hit Butler, but I couldn't be sure. A minute later I had my answer. She used the switch to tickle Lucifer between the back legs. He didn't really buck, but it was enough of a jump to unseat Butler.

The land agent went forward onto Lucifer's neck, and then over the side, landing on his back in a fresh pile of Reveler's poop. It was classic. All I needed was for Roscoe to appear and do the thing he did best—pee on nasty people.

As if Jitty were listening to my thoughts and conjuring up exactly what I was thinking, I heard Sweetie Pie howl, and down the trail came Roscoe, at a gallop. Pumpkin, the devil dog in training, was right behind him. Roscoe never slowed when he saw Butler on the ground. He went straight for him, hiked a leg, and cut loose on Butler's fancy boot. Pumpkin pranced around the fallen man and when he started to say something, she stuck her tongue down his throat.

I couldn't help it. I laughed long and hard, even as I was dismounting to help Butler. Tinkie, too, jumped off Miss Scrapiron and lent a hand to pull Butler to his feet.

"You know I could sue you for injuries," he said, and he wasn't kidding.

"Sure, you could. But there's not a farmer in the Delta who would have respect for a man who couldn't sit a horse and then tried to sue because of it," Tinkie said. She held up her phone. "Here, let me get a picture of you. I'm sure our friends at the paper will love this. I'll bet it goes viral."

Harold came walking down the path and joined us, but he made no attempt to round up the dogs. It was too late for that. He took one look at Butler and the evidence of bird poop that remained on the front of his shirt and the horse poop on the back. "I've heard of a poop magnet, but I never met one in the flesh," he said.

And that was it. Butler picked up his horse's reins and started walking toward the house. Clearly, he was in a bad, bad temper.

8

Levi Butler left in a huff. I was only a little worried he'd sue me, but Tinkie was quick to point out that he'd fallen on a public road, not on my property. And it wasn't deliberate—at least not exactly. And his manly pride might not allow him to own up to falling off a horse that had been, for all practical purposes, standing still.

"Have you heard anything from Danny?" I asked Harold. I was hoping against hope he'd come out to Dahlia House to let us know Danny was safely home.

"Not a peep. I've called a few of the other big farmers and asked." He sighed. "Danny has disappeared off the face of the planet. No one seems to know a thing."

I told them of my meeting with Reverend Wingard. "I just don't see him as someone who would harm another human being. Not even for the honor of his wife. Wingard seems like a gentle man." That was the best way I could describe him.

"I've known him for years," Harold said, "and I agree. One time he even took up for Roscoe in a pretty bad situation."

One look at Harold's face told me he was proud of the Satan dog. "What did Roscoe do?"

"It was a church 'dinner on the ground' and I was attending as a guest. I was trying to help the church secure a loan for some renovations that were desperately needed." He tried to hide his smile and seem disapproving, but it didn't fool me at all.

"What did that naughty dog do?" I asked again.

"He stole Eden Welford's special rum-spiked ham. He just snatched it from the picnic blanket and ran off. The ham was nearly as big as he is."

I could see it play out. Pandemonium would've ruled as people tried to catch the dog and retrieve the ham. "Did he eat the whole ham?" I asked.

"No. Not all of it. I found him about a mile from the church in a ditch with the remainder of the ham and the bone. He was in a food coma."

"And you defended that dog, didn't you?" Tinkie asked Harold.

"He is my only child. Heir to my fortune."

"He is your evil twin," I said, but I had to laugh. Harold forgave Roscoe no matter what he did. And now Roscoe had little Pumpkin that he could teach how to be incorrigible. The two of them were going to get Harold shot! But I knew better than to caution Harold. He loved Roscoe to the moon. And Pumpkin, too, from what I could see. I just hoped that Jody decided to let Harold keep Pumpkin. In the weird way the world sometimes works, Jody had suffered an injury while traveling through Europe—the gossip was that she'd been dancing on a tabletop in a rowdy bar. Her return home had been delayed, and Harold would be keeping Pumpkin until Jody was fully healed. "How did Roscoe escape with his life from that situation?"

"Wingard told the congregation that Roscoe's theft was the work of angels sent to protect the congregation from eating things that were bad for their cholesterol. It worked. Roscoe was spared."

We laughed as we led the horses to the barn, untacked them, and turned them out. Lucifer was tied to a rail at the barn, none the worse for wear. Harold untacked him and turned him out with the others. The horses bucked and snorted and farted—their signature moves—as I watched them with a full heart.

"Want some coffee?" I asked my friends, and we went in the back door to the kitchen where I put on a pot. We settled around the table. At last Harold was ready to reveal the real reason he'd shown up here in the middle of a workday.

When we each had a cup of coffee, Harold wrapped his hands around his mug and bit his lip. "Tinkie, please don't tell Oscar I came here."

This did not sound good, but I didn't interrupt.

"I'm worried about Oscar," Harold said. "He's taking this business about Danny being missing to heart. He believes he is at fault here."

We'd all tried to make Oscar see he was only doing the job he was required to do—by the ethics of his profession. It was clear Oscar hadn't heard a word we'd said.

"What can I do?" Tinkie asked.

"I know you're looking for Danny under every rock. Have you found any hopeful leads?"

"Nothing promising," I told Harold. "We hope to find facts that show Danny left for reasons that had nothing to do with the bank loan."

"I wish I could believe that," Harold said.

"But you don't." Tinkie's voice was flat.

"No, I don't. Danny wouldn't worry his family over a romantic peccadillo. He would face the music. I'm afraid someone has harmed him. Did you find any evidence he might have gone to . . . the wrong people for a loan?"

I honestly hadn't thought about Danny doing business with loan sharks. But there were predatory lenders around Sunflower County just as there were everywhere else. Loaning money to desperate people was always a good way for thugs to get their hooks into a decent person. And it was an avenue for Tinkie and me to pursue.

"We'll check into it," I told Harold. "We will. We're going to find Danny and he is going to be okay." But I had another question for Harold. "Do you know anything about the Tallahatchie Bridge being haunted?"

He gave me an amused look. "There are stories."

"Really?" Tinkie and I asked together. We both loved a good ghost story.

"After the old bridge burned and the new one was built, several reports of strange happenings on the bridge began to surface."

The flesh along my neck and arms began to crawl. Whatever Harold was about to say, I suspected it had some validity. "Tell us."

"We should ride out there tonight and take a look," he said. "Folks tend to avoid that bridge in the dark if they can. But we can take a look. I've always been a little curious."

"It's a date," I said. "I'll see if Coleman can come, too."

"Good plan. I want to see him cuff a ghost."

"You are too full of yourself," I said to Harold. "Please leave the devil dogs at home." It would be just like him to set Tinkie and I up to get a bad fright, and those dogs would be willing participants.

"If you're lucky," Harold said, standing up. "Now, I have to get back to the bank. See you when the full moon rises."

We were in luck that the moon was full and the traffic scarce as we parked beside the bridge abutment on the Tallahatchie River. Without the sun beating down on us, the evening had cooled to a pleasant temperature. It was almost midnight, and Coleman and I had brought flashlights so we could make our way through the brambles to the riverbank. All for the love of a good ghost story.

While we waited for our friends, we picked up dry limbs to make a small fire on the damp, cool sand. My watch showed midnight when Harold pulled up with Oscar and Tinkie in his fancy truck. When Tinkie, Coleman, and I were younger, we'd often built bonfires on riverbanks and sat around to drink a few beers and talk. Oscar had gone to a private school and Harold wasn't from Sunflower County. But we shared so much in common, and on this night, we were looking for the past—and one missing farmer—by means of a spooky tale.

Coleman lit the fire and Tinkie brought out some red wine for us and beers for the men, and we settled back in the cool sand for a good yarn. The river swept by, and I thought of the bouquet that was likely down to Vicksburg by now. On the other side of the river, an owl hooted, setting the scene.

We talked for a while. Oscar played some of the songs of our youth on his phone. When he reached back into the past and played the Kris Kristofferson love ballad, "Help Me Make It Through the Night," Coleman and I danced so closely that Harold and Tinkie catcalled us. It was a perfect evening, blending nostalgia with the here and now.

At last, we gathered close to hear Harold's tale.

"One of my cousins grew up on the river here," Harold began. "He used to camp on the Tallahatchie all the time. You know, it was the typical campout. Some beer, some tall tales about big fish, some brags about the girls they'd kissed. And more." We all chuckled because we knew.

"It was all good fun until he and his friends saw a woman on the bridge. She scared them so badly they stopped coming here."

And the story was off to a roaring start. Harold was most likely making all of it up, but we didn't care. We were there for the thrill, not accurate history. But I had to ask. "Did this really happen, or is this just for fun?"

"It happened," Harold said. "I know you've been looking into the history of this bridge and folks seeing Pearl, or some other woman, up here. Seemed like a good time to share this story."

"If it was Pearl," I said, "she certainly hasn't admitted to it. But please continue."

"One night Robert and Frank, those are my cousins, were waiting right here on this riverbank for their friends to join them. It was a crisp October night, right after the Leflore County High School football game." He took a swallow of his beer. "Some of the young people had split off in couples, but a group was on this sandbar talking and listening to music."

"What kind of music?" Coleman asked, just to devil Harold.

"Good music. Folk and country," Harold said.

"Like Dusty Springfield?" I hadn't meant to say it out loud, but Harold laughed.

"Probably more like Savage Garden," Harold said. "Robert was a big fan of 'Truly Madly Deeply.'"

"Continue with the story," I requested.

Harold began talking again, but I heard something else. A

low murmur of an acoustic guitar seemed to come from the river itself. The music was soft, muffled. I thought I was imagining it. I leaned back on my elbows and listened more closely. A vocal kicked in. Female. I looked at the faces of the others and awareness slowly dawned on everyone. We all heard it. Was this some magic trick Harold had put in place before we arrived at the river? I couldn't say. My questions would have to wait.

I couldn't distinguish the words of the singer, but the chill bumps that danced over me were very real. Even Coleman sat up. He put his beer bottle in the sand and got to his feet.

"What's up?" Harold asked.

"Do you hear that?" Coleman asked. His posture was tense, and I saw his hand go to his hip where his gun would normally be. But he hadn't brought a weapon. Everyone knew you couldn't shoot a ghost.

"Yes! I hear it!" Tinkie was all but in Oscar's lap.

Harold walked to the edge of the water and froze. "Where is that music coming from?" he asked. "It can't be coming from the river."

No one had an answer.

"What's going on?" Tinkie said. This was more than either of us had bargained for. We'd wanted a pleasant chill, not to be scared out of our wits.

"Put the fire out." I got up and started to kick sand on it.

"We should pack up and head out of here," Harold agreed. "That music is probably from kids on a sandbar up or down the river. Noise carries differently here. Or it could be someone up to no good." He listened for a moment to the minor-key singing. "Whoever it is, this place holds a lot of sadness."

The Tallahatchie River had always carried a load of grief. There were plenty of real potential ghosts on the river, not just the fictional ones of Bobbie Gentry's song.

I stood up and gave Tinkie my hand to pull her to her feet. She was anxious, and so was I. The ghost story didn't seem like fun any longer.

"What is this?" Coleman had his flashlight out and was examining the ground farther down the sandbar.

"What?" I joined him. He was staring at a hole in the sand. Someone had been digging.

"Oscar, come take a look," Coleman said. There was an edge in his voice.

I pushed in closer, though he tried to stop me. In the bottom of the hole was an old doll. The thing looked pitiful—filthy, disfigured, and broken. "Let's get out of here." I only wanted to get back to the truck, get inside, and lock the doors.

Harold, Tinkie, and Oscar walked over to examine the bedraggled baby doll. Half of her hair was missing, and one eye. Coleman pulled it from the grave and offered it to me, but I didn't want to touch it. The thing reeked of bad juju. I didn't like dolls—or clowns—on a good day with bright sunlight. This ratty doll left in a sandy hole on a riverbank was not anything I wanted to have in my life.

"Bury it back and let's go to Dahlia House," I said to the group. My feet were itching to kick sand as we made a hasty retreat to the vehicles.

"Look!" Harold's voice, as loud and crisp as a thunderclap, made me freeze.

I followed the direction he was pointing to see a woman standing on the bridge. She was balanced on the railing, her long white dress flowing around her in a gentle breeze. Her dark hair floated on her shoulders. My breath caught in my throat. She sobbed once and then disappeared. There was a loud splash!

"Run!" I pointed downriver under the bridge. "Run!" Maybe we could pull her out before she was swept downriver.

We took off along the bank, which was not easy traveling. Riprap meant to stop erosion, natural boulders, and fallen trees blocked our path. We were too slow, too slow. She'd be gone.

"Run!" I turned back to find Harold, Oscar, and Coleman standing on the sandbar. They were laughing. Only Tinkie was with me, and she looked terrified.

"What?" She looked at me and then turned to look at the three men. Harold was doubled over with laughter.

"What?" she said again, but this time the single word had an edge to it.

"Bastards!" I thought the top of my head would pop off! Tinkie and I had been set up. The men had ganged up and pulled a mean prank on us. They'd made us believe someone had jumped into the river.

Tinkie started back toward the men. Oscar rushed over to the fire and made sure it was completely out, then he started through the woods toward the vehicles. Harold and Coleman were hot on his heels.

"Run, you cowards!" I called after them. "Run, because when we do catch you, you are going to pay!"

They kept laughing. And running.

"I'm leaving a key in the ignition of my truck," Coleman called back to me. "I think I'll ride back with Harold."

"Maybe you better stay at Harold's place," I yelled.

"Yeah," Tinkie said. "You'd better stay there, too, Oscar."

"I think they're mad," Oscar said with a tiny hint of worry in his voice.

I looked at Tinkie and we burst into laughter. They'd really scared us, but we both knew we would have pulled the same prank if we'd thought of it first.

"Come on, girls," Harold said. "You have to admit, it was a beautifully executed prank."

"It was," I agreed. "And you should know that payback is going to be delicious."

We finally caught up with the men at the vehicles. They were laughing and chuckling at their cleverness. I was waiting for a chance to repay the favor. "Where did you get the doll?" I asked Coleman.

"I guess Harold or Oscar got it. That wasn't part of the original plan. I just saw the hole and the doll happened to be in it."

"Where did you find that awful doll?" Tinkie asked Oscar.

He shook his head. "It wasn't me."

"Harold?" Tinkie said.

"Not me."

In the moonlight, he did look sincere. But I wasn't going to take a bite of that apple twice. "Spill it, or you boys will have a long walk home."

"It really wasn't me," Harold insisted.

"Not me," Oscar said.

"It wasn't me," Coleman said, and he looked worried.

"Who else knew what you were planning?" I asked.

"Only Ellen Moore, a teller at the bank," Oscar said. "I hired her to wear that white dress and stand on the bridge. She threw a heavy limb over the side of the bridge to make the splash and then she ducked down and ran to the car where her husband was waiting, but we didn't talk about a doll."

"I'm going back to get the doll," Coleman said. "Hang on."

He crashed through the underbrush, and I followed his flashlight as he made it to the flat bank and then started back. When he got close to us, I noticed his hands were empty, except for the flashlight.

"The doll?"

"It's gone," he said.

"It couldn't be," Harold said. "Maybe you weren't looking in the right place."

"Our footsteps in the sand were all around the hole. The doll is gone."

"Let's get out of here," Tinkie said. "I don't like this."

I wasn't going to argue. My blood was running cold, and tightness in my chest made it difficult to breathe. "Let's talk about this at Dahlia House."

"I'll come back here tomorrow and check the riverbank, just to be on the safe side," Coleman said as we loaded into the vehicles.

9

The next morning neither Coleman nor I was in any hurry to get out of bed. As sunlight filtered through the gauzy lace of the curtains, we snuggled and talked.

"You know Tinkie and I will have to pull out all the stops to get even with you guys," I said.

Coleman only laughed. "You can try."

I merely smiled to myself. There was no one better at revenge than Tinkie. Or maybe Madame Tomeeka. Or possibly Cece. Or Millie. The good thing was that all of them were playing for my team. The men would pay!

"I think I'm going to the riverbank first thing," Coleman said. He lightly danced his fingers across my bare back, knowing it would drive me wild.

"I'll go with you," I said. It would be good to have Coleman with me. The whole doll business was creeping me out. There and then gone. The half-finished burial, all of it was just making my skin crawl. "Coleman, tell me the truth. Did you plant that doll? I don't want to waste my time trying to figure that out if it isn't part of my case."

"We didn't. Now if we'd thought of it, we would have. But we didn't."

"Who could have been right there, watching us, to steal the doll back?"

"That troubles me. I won't lie to you. I know you're itching to get back to the riverbank."

Indeed, I was. "I'm glad you're going with me, too. The whole thing is just . . . disturbing."

Coleman sighed and pretended he was getting up, only to snuggle into my neck and tickle me. When he had me about to wet the bed, he finally let me up and sprang into action. He had the shower turned on and was beneath the spray before I could grab him. Oh, he had a load of payback coming.

I made coffee and jumped in the shower when he was done. We were dressed and ready for our day when his cell phone rang. He took the call and then looked at me. "We have to postpone the river. We have a burglary at the drugstore. Someone broke in and took a lot of Schedule three narcotics."

"Oh, no." I put some bread in the toaster. "I may go on with Tinkie. We'll be careful. It's daylight and no more ghosts. Or fake ghosts!"

"I wish you'd wait, but I know you're working on a case, too. Oscar told me last night how distressed he is about Danny's disappearance."

"Tinkie says he isn't sleeping."

"Just be careful. Take your guns. Don't shoot any innocent fishermen."

"Ha ha, very funny." Tinkie was a great shot, and I was moderate. After the scare we'd had last night, it's true that we might be a little trigger-happy.

I kissed Coleman goodbye—a kiss I hoped gave him something to think about—and he was off. I whistled up the pups and Pluto and headed for Tinkie's. I called her on the way to let her know where we were going, and to be sure she wanted to trek back to the river. The night had been cool and pleasant, but the daylight would bring sweat, mosquitos, yellow flies, and other nuisances. Of course, she was gung ho.

We brainstormed revenge plots against the men as we drove to Leflore County and the river. We had three pretty good ideas, but we needed to research all of them to see which would be the most effective. When we pulled up to the bridge abutment, we got out of the vehicle and sprayed ourselves with mosquito repellent. We'd both worn boots—as we had done last night—in anticipation of ticks.

When we made it down to the water, we froze. In front of us, all along the sandbar, someone had been digging holes—just like the one that had contained the baby doll. There were now dozens. Someone had been desperately looking for something.

"What the heck," Tinkie said. "I guess we have to look in the holes."

I wasn't keen to see dozens of abused baby dolls, but we had to look. We started with the holes closest to us, working our way toward the one that I thought originally held the doll. The holes, thank goodness, were empty. As we examined them, I took photographs of some footprints in the damp sand.

"Does this look like a woman's size?" I asked Tinkie. She was more of a shoe connoisseur than I was.

"More like a woman's than a man's," Tinkie agreed. "But look at these. They're bigger."

She was correct. "Maybe there were multiple people." I instantly thought of Danny and Pearl. But where would they have been hiding while we were on the sandbar? No vehicles had been parked near the bridge.

"They could have been in a boat," Tinkie said, answering

my unasked question. "They could have been upriver and just quietly floated down here. There's a ramp to get boats out not too far from here."

"But why?" I asked. "Why would they be digging around in the sand?"

"Buried treasure?" Tinkie suggested. "That's about the only thing I'd dig for."

I had another, darker thought. What if they'd buried something here? Something that had been thrown into the river. A change of heart. A bundle. I couldn't shake the ominous words of the Gentry song—the implication of a baby thrown from the bridge.

"You think they were digging up the body of an infant?" Tinkie said it quietly and with the same dread I felt.

"I don't know, Tinkie. I really don't know."

"You think someone knew about a dead baby and left that doll for them, but we found it first?"

"That's another question I can't answer. Let's check the rest of the holes." I wanted to leave as soon as possible. A burden of sadness had fallen over both of us. It was more suffocating than the sun that burned hot and humid.

We finished checking every single hole—all empty—before we went back to my vehicle. I sent the photos of the footprints to Budgie—and yes, I had phone reception again. The ghost from last night had proved to be a practical joke, but something really was off with the bridge, music, and our cell phones. Where was Dusty, aka Jitty, when I had a question about the spirit world?

"Maybe we can look at it as a good sign," Tinkie said. "If it was Pearl and Danny, at least Danny is alive and okay."

She was right. Funny, though, that it didn't seem to make either of us feel better.

We'd made it almost to the trail to get back to the car when I saw another mound of sand. This looked like a hole that had been filled in. I nudged Tinkie and edged her in that direction.

"How did we miss that?" she asked.

"It's back here and the shadows of the trees fall over it." That seemed reasonable to me, but at the same time goose bumps began to dance along my arms. Tinkie and I both slowed our rapid walk to more of a dawdle.

There was nothing for it but to explore the mound of dirt.

I dropped to my knees and used my hands to scoop at the damp sand. Tinkie knelt on the other side and began her own excavation. We were like kindergarteners playing in a sandbox—one that held the possibility of Pennywise. Neither of us wanted to be the one to dig up that clown—or anything resembling a baby.

We were up to our elbows when I felt some type of material in the hole. Tinkie felt it, too. Together we pulled up what could only be a christening gown. The smocking and embroidery were exquisite, the material airy, and it had clearly once been white. Along with the gown were tiny crocheted baby booties and little ribbons.

I felt like someone had sucked the marrow out of my bones.

"Do you think we can ever find out who this belongs to?" Tinkie asked. She put the little shoes on the sand by the gown.

"I don't know." I snapped a photo and sent it to DeWayne in the sheriff's office. He might have a way to check the source of these baby items. I rocked back on my heels, uncertain if I wanted to know the truth about our discovery. Experience told me this would bring only heartache and pain.

DeWayne called instead of texting back. "Maureen, the dispatcher, says that's a very expensive christening gown," he said. "I'll send these photos over to the high-end stores in Memphis to see if anyone can identify it."

"That would be really helpful. We have to keep in mind that sometimes these gowns are handed down from generation to generation, or from one family to another." Looking at the bedraggled, dirty gown, I could still see the exquisite detail. Someone had spent a lot of time creating this little gown meant to be worn only once. Someone had clearly loved the baby the gown had been intended for. So why was it in a hole along the bank of the Tallahatchie River? The answer to my question would likely open wounds.

I took more photographs and hiked up to the vehicle to get a plastic bag for my sandbar finds. Technically, they should have gone to the sheriff of Leflore County, but I was taking them back to Sunflower County and Coleman. At least I knew he would push to find answers. And along the way, I'd make a couple of stops and ask my own questions.

Tinkie only looked at me when I didn't take the most direct path back to Zinnia. Instead, I swung by the Anderson farm.

We knocked on the door and when Mrs. Anderson answered, her face fell. "You haven't found Danny, have you?"

"No, ma'am." It was an admission of defeat. "But would you look at a photograph for me?"

"Of what?"

Instead of answering, I brought out my phone and showed her the picture of the gown. "Do you recognize this?"

"No," she said. "It's lovely work. But it's so filthy. Why?"

"We found it on the riverbank near the bridge."

Her expression grew wary, but not hard. She took the phone from my hand and examined the picture. She paged through the photos and stopped on the shoes and ribbons. "I don't know anything about this christening gown. You know they're out of vogue now in many places." She sighed and looked past us down the road. "I always dreamed of having a grandchild. I would have made a gown for that baby. Each stitch taken with love." She looked up. "But this one is truly lovely."

It was clear to me that Mrs. Anderson would not have cared who Danny loved or married or created a child with. She would have loved the baby—and the mother—with every ounce of heart she had. A lump climbed from my heart into my throat, and I thought I'd squall. I'd done a cruel thing, brought a reminder of what might have been to a woman already mourning the loss of her son. Maybe not a permanent loss, but I couldn't say that with the facts I knew today. All I had learned about Danny was that he was a good, responsible, and well-liked man. That, and he seemed to have vanished from the planet. Or at least from Leflore County.

"Mrs. Anderson, we're still looking for Danny."

"I heard," she said. "Asking that preacher's wife, I hear."

"Yes. We follow every lead and ask all the questions we can."

"Pearl is a sweet woman."

"And?" I prompted.

"And once upon a time I thought she and Danny might make a couple. But that was back in high school. That time passed."

"You're positive of that?"

The question caught her up short, and I saw the hesitation. Did that stem from the facts or from her hopes and dreams?

"Danny isn't a man to bust up another man's marriage."

I looked at Tinkie, who had come up as we talked. I'd let her field this one.

"Mrs. Anderson, I'm a married woman, and I love my husband. But there have been times when I was tempted. I didn't, but it could have easily happened. Life can get very complicated very quickly."

"You can say that again," she responded. "But as to your original question, I don't recognize the christening gown. Now, I have a cake in the oven and I need to check it."

"Thank you," Tinkie and I said in unison before we left the porch and got in the car. I still had one more stop to make before I left Leflore County.

10

The small clapboard cottage with green shutters looked sad. The house—once a cheerful fairytale dwelling with neat flower beds and an air of loving care—now gave off a vibe that dark magic was at work. I pulled up in the front yard, taking note of the weedy flower beds and bedraggled plants needing water. Someone wasn't tending the garden. The touch of love was gone. And it had happened so swiftly.

I didn't really have to wonder why. Everything about the once-neat little cottage spoke of depression and despair. No matter what Pearl said, it was clear she was no longer taking pleasure in the nurturing activities she once enjoyed. Was it grief or fear? Maybe I'd be able to suss that out today.

I knocked on the door as Tinkie joined me. She was eager to get back to Zinnia; she had a date with Maylin at the splash pad in the park that Harold had donated to the city. Pauline would take Maylin if Tinkie was busy, but Mama Tinkie wanted to do it. I didn't begrudge her those wonderful moments of motherhood and the special magic of childhood.

I would never in a million years admit this to Jitty, but watching Tinkie see the world anew through Maylin's eyes was one of the most profoundly joyful things I'd ever been party to. To Maylin, the beauty of a cardinal or the wonder of a mud puddle were life altering. Such a shame that most humans lost that innocence. How lucky was I to be able to share it, even a little, through my friend and partner?

Pearl came to the door, took one look at us, and stepped back. "I have nothing to say." She started to close the door.

"We don't care about your relationship with Danny. We're here on something else," Tinkie said quickly. She nudged me. "Show her the photos."

I'd hoped for a gentler entrée to the pictures. As a mother, though, Tinkie didn't have the patience for anyone who might harm a child. I brought my phone from my pocket and pulled up the photos of the christening gown. I didn't have to say a word. Pearl went white and stepped back from the door. She motioned us inside.

It was noteworthy that she didn't ask where we got the photos. Or where we'd found the gown. She took a seat on an upholstered sofa that looked like it came from the Victorian era and waited.

"You recognize that baby's gown, don't you?" Tinkie asked. The bulldog in her had risen to the surface. "We found it buried in the sand on the Tallahatchie River near the bridge."

"Why can't you just leave things alone?" Pearl asked. Her voice was soft but strained. "Please, just stop. It's bad enough that Danny is gone. Why can't you back off so at least his family's memories of him won't be tainted?"

That was almost a confession, but of what? "Where is the baby?" I asked.

"What baby?"

"Pearl, we know that you and Danny were having an affair. Did he leave, or harm himself, because of a guilty conscience?" Tinkie asked.

Pearl burst into soft laughter. "What?"

"Did you two . . . dispose of a baby?" Tinkie was definitely playing bad cop.

"What?" Pearl aggressively leaned forward. The shock of the photos had worn off. She was on the offensive. "Are you seriously asking me if I *disposed* of a baby? Like maybe I was under the spell of Bobbie Gentry's song and *threw a baby* off the bridge into the river?"

Rut-roh. Tinkie had awakened the dragon. "She didn't mean that," I said.

"Yes, I did." Tinkie wasn't backing down.

Strangely, her blunt frankness seemed to mollify Pearl. "I would never harm a child. Never. Not your child or a stranger's child or my child. It is an affront for you to even ask that."

"I'm sorry. I didn't mean to offend you, but right now, the truth is much more important than your feelings."

Right on, Tinkie! For the Queen Bee of Delta society and a woman with more manipulative tricks in her pocket than a carny sideshow magician, Tinkie could win an award for firehosing the truth out there.

"I agree," Pearl said. "And I told you the truth. I don't know why you try to connect that gown with me in any criminal way. I have no idea what you think I did to Danny. Or what you think Danny and I did together. But you are thinking wrong."

"You recognize the gown?" I asked.

She nodded. "I do. It's my very own christening gown."

That was unexpected. "Yours?" Maybe I had misheard.

"Yes, mine. My mother was a talented seamstress. She

made the gown for me when I was christened. Then she gave it to me for my own children."

"How did it come to be buried on a sandbar on the Tallahatchie River?" Tinkie asked.

"I have no idea. I didn't realize it was missing. I haven't had a reason to look at it because I wasn't pregnant. I think you can understand that a woman who isn't pregnant wouldn't be looking for christening gowns."

I did understand, but I also had more questions. "Who would have taken it?" My thoughts jumped instantly to her husband, Micah. Could the preacher have been angry enough at his wife to attempt to frame her for infanticide?

"The gown has been in the attic for the last five years. Ever since Micah and I married. I brought my belongings to this house and stored most of them in the attic. Come up and take a look."

Her openness spoke of her innocence, but I was going to look. "Tink, why don't you talk to Pearl while I check it out? The attic is going to be a sauna."

"I'll come with you," Pearl offered.

"Come and sit down," Tinkie finessed. "Let Sarah Booth work. She'll be quicker by herself and it's hot as Hades up there. I'll get some iced tea for all of us. Sarah Booth is going to need it if she stays up there longer than ten minutes."

"Certainly." Pearl was all graciousness. She certainly acted innocent.

"Call if you need me," Tinkie said as I pulled down the ladder to gain access to the attic.

I didn't have a flashlight, but I had my cell phone and that was good enough. As I made my way into the attic space the heat washed over me in waves. Great. The attic was full of boxes and furniture. This was going to take a lot of time.

We couldn't leave, though. Pearl had been alerted. If there was something here, she'd remove it before I could come back with help. I considered calling DeWayne or Budgie, but this was Leflore County. They had no jurisdiction and if we did find anything, their presence and participation would only compromise what we discovered. No, I would soldier on by myself.

Moving carefully around the attic—I didn't completely trust the flooring, which was warped and a little bumpy—I found an open box in the corner. That seemed the logical place to start, so I braced my phone to steady the light, sat down cross-legged on the flooring, and began to sift through the box. It was an interesting assortment of memorabilia, clothes, and at last a silver baby rattle and brush. Heirloom items traditionally passed from one generation to the next.

There were also tissue papers where something had been carefully wrapped and then removed. Likely the christening gown. I had started unfolding the thin papers when I heard the thrum of a bass guitar. It was coming from right behind me. A blues guitar kicked in, and then a sax. A low baritone voice began to sing, "I tried to leave you."

I spun around to see a tall slender man in a black suit and a fedora. His voice was electrifying. But what was he doing in this attic? Why was he singing about a love that could never be abandoned? I realized it was Jitty in the persona of one of my favorite folk singers, Leonard Cohen. The man had heart, and his music could bring me to tears.

"Stop it, Jitty. I'm working. I don't have time to listen to you."

"Love is the only thing worth having," Leonard said. I knew it was really Jitty talking, but it struck me hard, nonetheless. Cohen always spoke in a poetic voice.

"I don't disagree, but now isn't the time." I spun back around to the box and began going through it again. My focus was finding a missing man, not a conversation about romantic love with a noncorporeal entity.

"What is time?" Jitty/Leonard asked.

"You don't care about time. Eternity isn't on the clock." I couldn't help my snippiness. I was roasting in that attic. "What do you know about a missing man or a baby's christening gown? Talk about that or go away."

"So many answers are in the music of the folk singers, Sarah Booth." Leonard slowly faded and Jitty was standing in the attic in hip huggers and a crop top. She would have rocked the 1960s.

Like it or not, Jitty was correct. On this case, I was trapped in a time warp with Gentry, Leonard, Dusty, and who knew who else would appear. The Tallahatchie River bridge, bundles and bouquets falling into the water, a farmer disappearing—it was as if a folk song had come to life.

"Do you know where Danny Anderson is?" I asked her. "Plain and simple. Do you know?" Of course she knew, but would she tell?

"It's against the rules, Sarah Booth."

"Is he alive?"

"All will be revealed."

"Now that is an annoying thing to say." I unfolded the tissue and only a little white ribbon remained as evidence that the gown had been nestled there. But who would know to come to this box to find it? Who would have a reason to remove it, other than Pearl?

Jitty had taken a seat on top of a camelback trunk. "Sarah Booth, there's your timeline, and then there's the timeline of the universe. Ever wonder why you're always banging your head against things? There's your answer. And you say I never tell you things."

I rose to my feet. I was going to choke her. Sure, she was dead, but if I could get one good lick in . . .

"You got a murderous look in your eyes, missy." Jitty sniffed. "Spoiled a bit, aren't you?"

"Oh, just go away." I picked up the tissue papers and the ribbon. If I didn't get out of that attic, I would pass out from a heatstroke. I moved toward the sketchy ladder stairs. Descending would be much trickier than ascending. To my relief, Tinkie was standing at the foot of the stairs looking up.

"Who are you talking to?" she asked.

Once again, Jitty had put me in a tight position where lying was the only choice. If I told the truth, I might never see Jitty again. And I needed her. She was the connective tissue between me and all the family I'd lost. "No one. I'm just trying to figure things out. I talk to myself when I do that."

"No, you don't." Tinkie wasn't as easy to fool as she'd once been. She knew me too well. "You're getting older, Sarah Booth, but you aren't at the point where you talk to yourself in grocery stores—or in attics. Not yet. What's going on with you?"

"Sometimes, when I go over the facts of a case, I imagine that I'm talking things through with Coleman."

Her blue eyes called me a liar, but she didn't say it. If we kept working together, eventually she'd overhear enough to put two and two together. Then I might lose Jitty. I needed to have a long conversation with my haint to explore possible solutions to this dilemma. Not right now, though.

"I found something." I had to distract her. When I got to the foot of the ladder, I showed her the white silk ribbon.

"That came from the christening gown." Tinkie knew her fabrics, trim, accoutrements, and jewels.

"I thought so, too. The box it came out of had layers and layers of tissue paper. Something had once been protected in them."

Pearl joined us and took the little ribbon from Tinkie's hand. "My mother ordered this ribbon from New Orleans, back in the day. She told me all about creating the gown and how it was one of the most beautiful things the people in the Delta had ever seen on a baby. I was her pride and joy. Ballet, tap, I took all the classes. Piano, guitar, I learned to play those, too. Growing up, I felt I had the whole world at my feet. I should have left the Delta. I should have followed my dream to perform."

"Who knew the gown was in the attic?" Tinkie asked her.

"No one. Except me. Micah put the boxes up there, but he wouldn't remember what was in them. In fact, he never even asked."

"But you told him?" Tinkie pressed.

"I'm sure I did. When we got married and I moved in, I didn't bring a lot of things with me. Micah had the house fully furnished. I had my clothes, some kitchen tools, a few knickknacks. Not a lot. Things were hard when I was growing up. Paying for all of those lessons for me meant sacrifice for my entire family." She shrugged one shoulder. "That gown was so treasured because every stitch was made with love."

"Micah wouldn't remember that?" I pressed gently.

"Men." She smiled. "What matters to Micah is the actual christening. To prevent Satan from taking an innocent soul. What a baby wears has no bearing on the success of the christening." Her face lightened, and she laughed. "Micah is a simple man without the greed and need of many others. Plain is good enough. It's one of the things I love about him."

"Pearl, other than you and Micah, who would know about the baby gown?"

She slowly shook her head. "I may have mentioned it at church." A blush crept up her cheeks. "I try hard not to, but sometimes I'm prone to bragging. When I first came to the church, I was overly proud of that gown. I meant for my baby to wear it when the time came." Her voice cracked, and she was precipitously close to tears. She managed to blink them back and regain control before she continued. "Every woman lives a certain fantasy in their hearts. Once I gave up on being a performer, a baby girl to christen and love was my secret daydream. I never even told Micah."

Her vulnerability made me feel like a jerk, but I had to press on. "If you didn't tell Micah about the fantasy, who did you tell?"

She looked me dead in the eye. "I told Danny."

Tinkie inhaled sharply. "Why? Why Danny and not your husband?"

"As I said, Micah is all about plain. He believes that simple is what God wants from us. I just couldn't let go of that fantasy of the beautiful gown, the perfect baby girl, the church with a choir singing. Silly, I know. Maybe even ridiculous. But it was *my* fantasy, *my* dream and I had a right to it. To dream it and to want it."

"And Danny shared that with you. He didn't judge it. He just accepted it and wanted that for you," Tinkie said.

"Exactly. Danny had big dreams, too. He didn't want to farm. He wanted to be a marine biologist. His great love was the ocean and the animals that lived there. He wanted to do things to save them because pollution is killing so many species. We'd both given up our dreams to live the lives we had."

Pearl's bravado was abandoning her, and soon she would be in tears. "It isn't disloyal to Micah to want that," I said.

"Danny gave up a lot to protect his family's land and heritage. Did he know the gown was in the attic?"

She shrugged. "Maybe. I don't know. He never saw it. I only told him about it. About how my mama sewed it just for me, saving up the money for the fine fabric. Growing up, this story is what made me special in my own eyes. Like Dolly Parton's 'Coat of Many Colors.'"

"And everyone needs to be special in their own eyes," Tinkie said softly.

Tinkie got it. Oh, she got it. Sometimes, life's lessons were easy enough to comprehend. Tinkie had never felt special. She'd had everything money could buy, but not her mother's love and attention. That was the only thing she really craved. Now, though, she was healing that wound with her love for Maylin.

Tinkie's understanding gave Pearl the courage to square her shoulders. "Look, I haven't done anything wrong. Neither has Danny. What we share is the death of a big dream, the loss of our individual fantasies. That's not wrong. Micah doesn't believe we've sinned in any way. He knows Danny and I are close, but he sees nothing evil there. Trust me, he'd say so if he thought it. He's a man who lives every minute by the rules of the Bible."

I didn't doubt her, but I also had read a lot of books and knew that mankind's darkness could never be underestimated. "Where would Danny go if he left of his own volition?" I asked. "Down to the coast? To Biloxi or maybe along the coast of Florida?"

"He's not off chasing his dream of being a marine biologist. He'd have to start over to get a college degree. He doesn't have that kind of money. Or time. But he has a camp on the Tallahatchie. He also might have gone down to Greenville or

Vicksburg to check the prices of grain at the port." She sighed. "Seems like everything has been against farmers for a long time. The weather, the prices, the way those huge corporations are controlling seeds. Fertilizer is through the roof and everyone knows it's killing the soil. Farmers are damned if they do and damned if they don't."

She wasn't wrong about that. "Do you believe Danny is alive?" I asked.

"I have to believe that. Anything else is unacceptable."

"Who could have gone up into your attic and taken that gown?" I asked.

"What I really think is that someone remembered me bragging about that little gown. Someone who maybe wanted something special for their baby. So, they went looking to borrow it."

"So, someone from your church."

"I have work to do, ladies. I'm sorry, but I need to get busy."

I nodded at Tinkie, and we made our way to the door. We didn't have a solid lead as to where Danny might be. And Pearl hadn't given us any information about the baby's gown and how it had gotten to the riverbank. But I knew we'd gotten all we were going to get on this day. To stay longer might tip her off.

11

Tinkie and I agreed that I'd take her back to Zinnia so she could make her date with the splash pad and check on Chablis and Zelda, the dog she'd rescued from our last case. The big gentle red pittie was fitting right in with her family. Zelda was now heartworm clear, spayed, up to date on all shots, and living the life of a Delta princess.

Once I dropped off Tinkie, I'd wheedle Coleman into going back to the river with me. That had been our original plan—until life intervened. Now, though, if my man's schedule was clear, we could have an adventure. Something about those holes still troubled me.

I said goodbye to Tinkie at her house and called Coleman on the way to pick up the dogs and cat. I figured the critters would enjoy a romp along the riverbank, and the dogs might prove valuable in digging up some clues.

I dialed Coleman and greeted him with a naughty, joking suggestion. "Let's go back to the riverbank and re-create the surf scene from that famous movie *From Here to Eternity*."

When he didn't chuckle, I knew something was wrong. "What's going on?"

"Can you pull over for a minute?"

This wasn't going to be good. I did as he requested. "Okay, I'm not driving."

"I was going to tell you tonight, but since you called, the Leflore County hardware store out on the highway north of town was robbed last night. The store owner has tentatively identified Danny Anderson as the thief."

That took the wind out of my sails instantly. "What? Danny?"

"I'm sorry, Sarah Booth. I know this blows up your case of a simple missing person."

"The store owner is positive?"

"There isn't a one hundred percent identification. It's not my case since it's in Leflore County, but from what one of the deputies told DeWayne, they have the thief on camera. The footage shows a man that fits Danny's height and build wearing a ski mask."

I exhaled. "So it isn't one hundred percent positive." I didn't say it out loud, but the good news was that at least Danny was alive and well if he was robbing stores.

"Close enough that the law is looking for Danny now and not just as a missing person."

"How much was taken?"

"Over ten thousand dollars."

That was a lot of cash for a farm supply and hardware store. "I didn't realize stores kept that kind of money on hand."

"They'd just had a big sale on farm equipment. And Sarah Booth, it isn't the only burglary around there. The drugstore burglary is part of it. The Leflore law thinks it's the same man who robbed the feedstore, the pharmacy, and now the farm supply and hardware store."

I could understand that Danny might be desperate to save his family farm, but robbery?

Since I was already planning on going to the river, I decided to stop by the Anderson farm again first. "Want to meet me at the river later?" I asked Coleman.

"I'll do my best."

"Talk soon." I hung up and dialed my partner to give her the bad news. I'd leave it up to her whether to tell Oscar or not. He'd hear the gossip sooner or later, though. When I had Tinkie on the phone, I told her everything I'd learned.

"Come back and pick me up. I'm going to the river with you."

"But what about the splash pad?"

"I can go another day. I don't want you on that river by yourself."

I wanted to argue, but I couldn't. I wasn't afraid to be on the river by myself, but we could cover twice as much ground together. I was only five minutes down the road, so I was back at Hilltop in a flash. Tinkie climbed in the front seat.

"Should we get Chablis and Zelda?" Tinkie asked, then answered her own question. "No, I'll leave the dogs at home. Chablis just had her hair glitzed and that river water might stain it."

Tinkie was still Tinkie, no matter how bold her heart. Appearances mattered. "Good plan." We swung by the farm, and I opened the vehicle's back door for Sweetie Pie, Avalon, and Pluto to hop in. Then we were off.

On the way to the riverbank, we passed the church that was at the heart of Danny and Pearl's relationship. The minister's car was parked by the office area of the church, and I pulled in beside it.

"What are you going to ask him?" Tinkie asked.

"If he buried the christening gown on the riverbank."

"Do you think he'll tell you the truth?"

I didn't have a clue. "Maybe he'll tell me something unrelated that blows this case wide open."

"I never took you for an optimist," Tinkie said.

I only grinned at her and led the way to the door that opened onto the suite of offices.

The door to Micah's study was open, and I watched him tapping away at his computer before he realized Tinkie and I were standing at the threshold.

"Pearl said you'd likely stop by," he said, never looking up from the keyboard. "I don't know anything about that baby's gown or how it got to the river."

"Do you have any suspicions?" I asked.

That question stopped him short. "Are you asking who I suspect has been in my attic rummaging through Pearl's things?"

"That's exactly what we're asking," Tinkie said. "Who might have had access to your house?"

"The parsonage belongs to the church," Micah said, "so it could have been any of the directors or church employees. Folks run back and forth all the time. The ladies in charge of Sunday lunch when we host it at the church are always borrowing pans and pots. Then they bring them back and put them away. And there are tables and folding chairs up there that we use often. Sometimes a kind soul will come over and help with some of the chores like washing or sweeping. Pearl and I don't lock the door."

He was definitely living in a time long gone. Back when I was a child, almost no one locked the doors of their homes. Now, folks had camera systems, dead bolts, and the most sophisticated locks that money could buy. The truth was, I'd just installed cameras at Dahlia House—or rather Coleman had set them up. And that was only after Gertrude Stromm, my nemesis and a woman who wanted to see me suffer and die, had set a fire in the front foyer of the house. I hadn't noticed that the little cottage where Micah and Pearl lived didn't have a security system. But in a way, it made sense. Church property. Once upon a time, that would have been sacrosanct. No one except the lowest of outlaws would have violated the property.

"Who would you name as your top suspect?" I asked.

"I can't point a finger of blame at someone when I don't have any proof," he said.

"But you do suspect someone?" Tinkie was keenly reading between the lines.

"That's all I can tell you. If I find proof, I'll call you. I promise. You should know that it disturbs me that someone took advantage of our open hospitality to plunder through things they have no need to touch. Pearl's mama made that gown for her. It's a keepsake, a treasure from a childhood short on such things."

His righteous indignation rang real for me. He was upset by the violation. "I'm sorry this happened, but a name could go a long way toward helping us sort this mess. I'm not a lawman. Nothing you tell us could result in any legal action. We're simply trying to find a missing man."

"Where did you find the gown buried, exactly?" he asked.

I told him as clearly as I could. He pondered the information.

"People are peculiar. They do things you'd never suspect. Vera is a good woman. Stalwart. Always ready to help the church, but she's been jealous of Pearl since we married. I thought it would get better, but it seems to have gotten worse. The things she says in Sunday school, or at some of the social gatherings." He put his hands on his keyboard and sighed. "The things she says to me. She was in the house a few weeks ago. Up in the attic. When I asked her what she was doing, she said looking for a platter to put some food on for the Wednesday social. But she was over where we'd put the boxes that belonged to Pearl."

"What's Vera's last name?" Tinkie asked.

"Volt. Vera Volt. Sounds like a comic book character, doesn't it?" He tried for a smile but failed.

"And Mrs. Volt lives nearby?" Tinkie asked.

"Ms. Volt. She isn't married."

"And she has a huge crush on you," Tinkie said.

"Pearl believes she does. Pearl finds it sweet, but it makes me very uncomfortable. Vera is . . . unstable. I'm not accusing her. I'm only telling you what you asked for. She says wildly inappropriate things. Sometimes they're sexual, but sometimes they're dark and violent. I've worried she might lash out at Pearl one day."

"Why would she take that baby gown?" I asked.

"Pearl mentioned the gown at church several months back. It was clear Pearl loved the gown and was proud of it."

"And that would be enough to send Vera off the deep end?"

"I really don't know. Maybe. Maybe I'm just looking for an answer because I'm desperate to figure out if someone really wants to harm my wife. And if they've harmed Danny Anderson."

"Why would they harm Danny?" I asked.

"We've been over this ground, Ms. Delaney. Danny and Pearl have known each other since high school. Some people, like Vera, read into a simple friendship too much. I don't consider myself a great catch. I'm barely scraping by financially. But Vera got it into her head that there was a relationship with me. There isn't. There never was. But she's . . . delusional. She told me flat out that Pearl was cheating on me and that she was ready to step in and treat me the way I deserved to be treated."

"Would she hurt your wife or Danny?"

"I can't say." He pulled a list of names from his desk drawer. "Here are the members of the congregation. Give them a call or a visit and ask them. You'll get a more impartial answer than you will from me. Now, I have work to do."

12

Rather than continuing on to the river like we originally planned, Tinkie and I headed back toward our PI office at Dahlia House, eager to examine the congregation list. I was shocked at how small the church membership was. It wouldn't take long to cull the ones with alibis.

"It's a wonder Micah can make a living preaching there," I said. "Unless a few of these people are millionaires, the Wingards are on a tight, tight budget."

"Micah may pick up another church on Wednesday night. A lot of preachers in the small rural churches serve more than one congregation. Like the old circuit riders. I've read statistics that show church membership among young people has radically declined. A lot of churches are having trouble making ends meet."

It made perfect sense, and for a person dedicated to preaching, it would be a solution to the monetary problem. The smaller churches were struggling. Nationwide, so many younger people had abandoned churchgoing. I couldn't point any fingers; I'd gone to Sunday school and church only when Aunt Loulane made me.

At thirteen, I'd been angry, rebellious, and determined to set my own boundaries. Church was off my list. Aunt Loulane didn't push the issue. The devastation of losing my parents changed everything about my life. She understood. She said I'd been taught right from wrong and exposed to religion. Either it would take, or it wouldn't. I wish I'd appreciated my aunt's wisdom when she was still alive. She'd sacrificed so much for me.

Once Tinkie had gone over the list and eliminated people she knew who were either too old, too ill, or out of the country—information she was privy to as grand marshal of Delta society—we were left with a much shorter list. We split it in half and started calling to ask questions. If the person had information, we scheduled a face-to-face interview.

On my list was Vera Volt. Tinkie refused to call her. They'd had some kind of set-to a couple of years past over the purchase of Christmas decorations for Zinnia. To be honest, I wanted to talk to Vera. In the last few years, I'd come to enjoy taking on people who thought they were the ethical gatekeepers of the community—or world. The hubris they exuded was amazing. They never doubted their own narrow views. I had a sense that Vera might be this type of person.

I dialed the local number and waited.

"This is Vera." She answered with a sultry voice and a hint of laughter.

"Ms. Volt, this is Sarah Booth Delaney. I'm calling in regard to a case I'm working. Do you have a minute to answer a few questions?"

"A case? Now that sounds fascinating, sugar. What kind of case?"

She was hooked. I'd engaged her nosy gene. Excellent! "I'm sure you've heard that Danny Anderson is missing. Delaney Detective Agency has been hired to find him."

"You'd better get the water search and rescue then. He's probably at the bottom of the Tallahatchie River."

The bad thing about the phone was that I couldn't see her expression or body language. I wasn't as good as Coleman at reading those physical signals, but I was getting better with each case. On the phone, I missed all those cues, drat it.

"Most folks say Danny would never harm himself."

"You don't have a clue what a person desperate for love will do."

I'd been lovesick and disappointed in the past, but I'd never harmed myself or disappeared. Danny was beloved by his family and respected in the farming community. He was a leader, and from what I knew of him, he'd never shirk those duties. "I don't think Danny was desperate for love."

"Oh, honey, he had it bad for Preacher Micah's wife, Pearl. They'd had a fling in high school and broke up, but in the last year, the fire was rekindled."

"Are you a confidante of Pearl's or Danny's or Micah's?" I asked.

"Micah talks with me."

"Has he said his wife was cheating with Danny Anderson?" I was curious what she'd say.

"Not in so many words, but the man is in pain. You can see it if you look. He loves his wife, and his wife loves Danny."

I let the silence stretch and was rewarded with an angry response.

Vera snorted. "Pearl should be tarred and feathered and run out of town. She's a temptress. A homewrecker."

Vera Volt pulled a wagonload of spleen behind her. I was

curious about why. "Have you ever been in the parsonage?" I asked.

"Of course. Every member of the church has been in and out of that house on a regular basis. I was there a lot before Micah married Pearl."

Oh, that implication was too big and mean to ignore. "Were you and the reverend lovers?"

"No."

The one-word answer was both caustic and bitter. Whoa. In my mind I pictured Vera as a coiled rattlesnake. She was shaking her rattle as hard as she could, and she was ready to strike. The target she wanted more than anything to hit was Pearl Wingard.

"Vera, could I buy you a cup of coffee or maybe lunch? It's a little late, but I'm hungry." I would have offered her a drink, but I didn't know if she was a teetotaler and I didn't want a lecture from Vera. She was the type who'd definitely take joy in whanging on and on about my failings.

"Why would you offer to buy me lunch?" she asked.

The way she asked let me know she was wary of a trap. That told me something. "My partner, Tinkie, and I will be in Leflore County close to lunchtime. I figured it would be easier to meet up in a restaurant. Up to you, though. We can meet anywhere."

"The Shady Rest at one thirty."

I didn't know the place, but I could find it on the internet. And that was a good thing since Vera hung up on me before I could say anything else. When I filled my partner in on what I'd learned, Tinkie was thrilled with the meeting. She was eager to see me battle Vera, and I planned on giving her a good show.

We had some time left, so we continued down the list of congregants, making more calls. We set two appointments with other church members who seemed to have information we could use. We'd do those first, on the way to the Shady Rest diner.

We entered Leflore County and stopped at the Collins farm, which abutted the Anderson land on the north side. Gary Collins was a regular at the small church Wingard pastored. "If the doors are open, I'm sitting in a pew," he told us when we caught him riding the soybean fields in his pickup.

Collins embodied the Delta farmer to me. Dressed in blue jeans and boots, he was lean, wiry, and neat. He worked hard—physically hard—every day of the week, every week of the year. It was no joke that farmers were up before dawn and working until last light. And that was just the physical work. The nature of farming—the big gamble—claimed an even heavier emotional and mental price as farmers tried to triangulate weather reports and planting crops. One wrong decision could bring ruin.

"You grew up in the church where Wingard preaches?" Tinkie asked him.

"Yes, ma'am, I've been going to that little church since my mama had me christened there. 'Course there was another preacher there up until Micah came to the area. I think the world of Reverend and Mrs. Wingard—the whole congregation does. Good people. And before you ask, Danny, too. I know a lot of people are saying bad things about Danny, but don't believe them. I know you're looking to find him." He frowned as he propped his boot on the running board of his big pickup. "I'm worried about Danny. Have you found any clues as to where he might be?"

"I'm afraid not," Tinkie said.

I nodded at my partner, encouraging her to keep Collins talking.

"Since you knew Danny, where do you think he might be?" Tinkie asked.

"Oh, that boy knew his way around the Delta *and* the big cities. He represented the farmers' coalition at the national conferences. A lot of the big chemical companies courted Danny's favor. They wined and dined him, trying to get him to endorse their products. Danny couldn't be bought, though."

This angle hadn't even been on my horizon. Could one of those corporations have had it out for Danny? "Did Danny endorse any of those chemicals?"

Collins snorted a laugh. "Danny hated those companies. He was fighting to keep the herbicides, glyphosate-ready crops, a passel of chemicals, and some of those dangerous fertilizers from being used all over the Delta. Farmers—and the people who eat the food—are being poisoned, and Danny said it plain and simple. He'd made a lot of people angry."

If this was true, Danny was stomping all over the chemical companies' Christmas pie. It would be an excellent reason for them to want him gone. And they had the money to hire someone to take care of Danny. *Take care*—as in permanent removal.

"Was there any company in particular who might be glad if Danny . . . left the scene?"

"A couple." Collins pulled out his phone and sent us websites. "Check those places. They hated Danny with a passion."

"Did Danny ever mention that he thought someone was watching him, or following him?" Tinkie asked.

Collins thought a minute. "Back in March, when a lot of folks were prepping to plant, something was going on with Danny. He and Todd Jenkins got into it at the stadium while they were watching a spring scrimmage."

"About what?" Tinkie asked.

Collins slowly shook his head. "I don't know. They were shouting and both red in the face, but Wylie Moulton broke it up before it came to blows. It was distressing to see."

"What do you mean?" I asked.

"Danny was acting weird. He had been for a while. On edge. All nervous. That was when he was taking meetings with some of the giant chemical companies. Some of the big-wigs came down to the Anderson farm, and Danny also went to Washington to talk with some senators who were opening investigations into the chemical companies and the USDA. Danny thought someone at the governmental oversight group was taking kickbacks."

Tinkie looked at me and I could read her mind—she wanted to know why no one had mentioned any of this to us before now. I had the same question. The motive for murder was much clearer framed with these facts. Had Danny found out something and stepped on toes?

"Mr. Collins," I said, "did Danny receive any threats?"

"Not that I know of. But Danny kept his cards close to his chest." He frowned as he pulled his hat a little lower on his head. "Danny never believed people would hurt him. There was right and there was wrong. He was on the side of right, so he felt like he wouldn't be harmed."

"That's a bit naïve," Tinkie said.

"Very," Collins said. "But that was Danny. He never wanted to hurt anyone, but he did love the land and the people who work it. Standing up to protect the land wasn't a controversial stance to Danny. It was just the right thing to do."

A man who didn't value money and would never think that grave harm would come to someone because of money—was he naïve or just moral? The reality was that if Danny had stepped between some people and a payday, he could very well have been murdered. It might be years before his body was found, if it ever was.

"This case just got a lot more serious, and a lot more dangerous," Tinkie said softly.

"I know." I didn't want to talk further. Gary Collins seemed like a trustworthy, likable guy, but I didn't want to bet my life, or Tinkie's, on that fact. I was eager to check out the two websites that he had given us.

"When was the last time you saw Danny?" Tinkie took the interview to safer ground.

"I saw him the day he disappeared. He was at the local feedstore." Collins sighed. "He was stirring up trouble."

"What do you mean?" I asked.

"He was arguing with old man Rutherford about carrying some of those herbicides. Danny wanted to ban them in the Delta."

Oh, I could see how that would aggravate not only the companies that made the herbicides, but a lot of the farmers, too. Farming was hard work; the defoliants and plant-specific weed killers had lightened the workload. Farmers had been assured that the chemicals were safe. In fact, they were still being told that, even when the incidence of cancers drastically rose among those who farmed or lived on land being cultivated with the use of those poisons.

"They need to make those chemicals illegal." It was simple enough for me to see the right action to take.

"That won't happen," Collins said. "Farmers need those products."

"Even knowing the potential danger?" I asked.

"Even so," Collins said. "They may be dangerous, but living without them is too hard. Especially with all the other environmental struggles farmers are facing now."

The man who leased my land didn't use any of the chemicals, environmentally dangerous fertilizers, or seeds that required dousing with herbicide. Billy Watson did his best to protect the land and the people who worked it. But Billy farmed a number of smaller parcels of land. He wasn't planting and plowing the tens of thousands of acres that some Delta farmers kept under cultivation.

"Farmers are in a real predicament. They'll lose their land if they can't make it productive, and making it productive with those chemicals will kill them with diseases." Tinkie summed it up nicely.

"That's the facts," Collins said. "Now, I hate to break up a good conversation, but I have to get to work."

And we had miles to go before we slept. We thanked him and waved goodbye as we drove to the next person we wanted to interview.

13

Florence Smallwood was a tiny woman with black hair that curled around her face. She had the look of a pixie about her, and I surreptitiously checked her ears to see if they were pointed. Drat! Her hair covered them. Her husband, Thomas, was the size of a road grader. They were an odd couple, but the affection between them was clear when she invited us into her house.

Tinkie and I took seats at the kitchen table in the clapboard house that was filled with color and personality. Wonderful watercolors depicting familiar scenes of the Delta covered the walls. The person wielding the brush had a load of talent.

“Florence painted those,” Thomas bragged.

“Honey, no one cares about that,” Florence said.

“They’re terrific, and we do care,” Tinkie and I responded in unison. We weren’t blowing smoke.

“Do you ever show your work?” I asked.

Florence chuckled. “No. I paint for joy. If others started criticizing me, it would make me unhappy.”

I completely understood. Art for art's sake was the purest of motivations.

"Thomas is a good provider," she added. "I'm lucky."

We talked about a few of the paintings—places I recognized and could name. The beauty of nature was featured in each one. At last, I nodded at Tinkie, and she brought the conversation around to Danny Anderson.

"That young man has everyone in the county worried about him," Thomas commented.

"You indicated on the phone you might know where he'd gone," I reminded them. Tinkie had talked to Florence, who said she knew Danny's routines. But it was Thomas who answered. He cast a worried glance at his wife.

"Danny spent a lot of time near Memphis," Thomas said. "He had business dealings there."

"What kind of business?" I asked.

"Farming, working on new USDA regulations to control the use of poisons. He was very involved in that." Thomas looked a little uncomfortable.

"That sounds a little dangerous," Tinkie noted. "Wouldn't the chemical companies be furious?"

"Yes." Thomas stood up from the table and walked to the foyer. "I'm sorry, ladies, but Flo and I have an appointment at the hospital in Zinnia. She's having some tests done."

I didn't believe him for a minute, but I respected the fact that he was worried. Pressuring him would yield nothing new. "Thanks for talking with us. Would you have a guess where Danny might be?" I asked.

"Not really. Danny covered a lot of ground when he chose to. He's always in demand as a speaker. Maybe he's away on business."

"Do you know anyone who might want to hurt him?" Tinkie pressed.

"Look, the farmers are upset over the changes in the climate," Thomas said. "They're all about to lose their shirts. Danny was making it even harder for some of them by calling out the chemical companies and a host of others he labeled as polluters. He's right about the chemicals and poisons, but now isn't the time to take on that fight. Not when so many are on the verge of losing their farms."

"Good point," Tinkie said. "Did Danny have a girlfriend?"

Flo stood up, walked over to her husband, and motioned us toward the front door. "I don't know anything about a girlfriend," Flo said. "If I hear anything, I'll be in touch."

"Thanks." I pasted on a smile and let the Smallwoods nudge me to the front door. At the screen, I waited for Tinkie, who was still talking to Florence. I took a moment to look at a watercolor in the foyer and stopped. The scene was clear in every detail. It was the small church where the Wingards served. Beside it was the big oak tree, and beneath the oak was a picnic on the grounds. A couple with their backs to the viewer looked like Danny and Pearl. The woman in the painting was very pregnant. No mistaking that.

"Florence, who are these people?" I asked.

"Just people I painted into my picture," Florence said, but she was nervous. She knew more than she was telling, but I didn't think I could drag it out of her with her husband guarding her so closely.

We'd been ricocheted from poisonous chemicals as a motive right back to extramarital affairs. Danny Anderson had a finger in a lot of pies. Business, environmental, romantic—any combination of those elements made for a brew of motivation to hurt Danny.

As soon as we were out of the house, Thomas closed the door. I heard the lock slide into place. We might get more out of them at a later date, but not today.

Now it was time to take on Vera Volt.

We pulled into the diner parking lot at one thirty on the dot. The restaurant had a large picture window that gave a great view of every table and the lunch counter. I picked out a slender woman with glossy brown hair and bright red lipstick. Vera Volt.

Tinkie walked right up to that booth. She made the introductions, and we slid onto the bench seat across from Vera. She carried herself like a model, and she had the looks to support that idea.

"Have a seat, dear ones," she prompted, waving a red-tipped hand. Her hands were beautiful, and the red polish on her fingernails drew attention to them. She sure knew how to highlight her assets. "I hear you're the official search party for Danny Anderson." Her smile revealed perfect teeth. She'd had some work done.

"Do you know where he is?" I asked.

"I don't keep up with the local farmers," she said. "I respect the work they do, but it never ends. I don't need a man who works that hard. So no, I don't know where Danny might be. I'm just glad he hasn't flown the coop with Pearl Wingard. That would break her husband's heart and lead to nothing but pain and judgment."

And I had a pretty good idea who would be casting the first stone in Pearl's direction. Vera had means, motive, and opportunity to make Pearl's—and possibly Danny's—life a living hell. Something about the tension around her eyes told me she was a spiteful woman who wore her proclivities like a royal cloak. So far, her comments about farmers and Pearl only confirmed my gut reaction. Stranger Danger for sure.

"Did you ever date Danny?" I asked. The alternate verb I could think of would be offensive. Vera reminded me of a praying mantis who would pop the head off a lover and suck the brains out.

"No, Danny wasn't anyone I dated."

She made it sound like it was her choice, but I wasn't so sure about that. "He's a very handsome guy. You know that old saying, 'Wrangler butts drive me nuts.'"

"I wasn't aware there was a name-brand butt slogan."

"You need to hang out with a more erudite crowd." I could see that steamed her, and Tinkie gave me the death stare. We were there to get information, not trade barbs.

"Who has Danny been dating?" Tinkie asked with a gossipier tone. "He is cute. I'll bet the girls are all after him."

Vera frowned. "Other than the preacher's wife?" She left the question dangling.

"Pearl is a beautiful woman," I chimed in. "But it couldn't be her. I mean all the vicious gossips in town watch her every move." I yelped in pain as Tinkie spiked my foot with her stiletto heel under the table. I swear she had X-ray vision to even be able to see my foot.

"Pearl and Micah seem to have a solid marriage and a lovely home," Tinkie said. "But someone has been stealing things from the parsonage."

I was curious how far Tinkie would take this, so I zipped my lips.

"What do you mean?" Vera asked, eager for something juicy.

"Oh, some of Pearl's personal things have gone missing."

"Like what?" Vera leaned in closer.

"I'm not at liberty to say." Tinkie pulled back, knowing it would piss Vera off. She'd dangled the lure of gossip and then snatched it back. "The law is handling the situation."

"You tease me with something and then fail to deliver. I can do the same to you."

"Do you really know anything about Pearl or Danny?" Tinkie asked, leaning to meet Vera halfway across the table. "I'll trade if you have something worthwhile."

"Pearl supposedly took savings out of the church account to give to Danny. He had a big payment on the land due."

This was not what I anticipated—and it was serious. Embezzlement was a felony. "Do you have any proof?"

Vera looked at me like I might have grown a third eye. "I don't have to have proof. I'm not a lawman or a bank official. Tinkie can get the goods from Oscar if she wants to have proof." She turned away from me. "Now, Tinkie, spill it."

"Someone stole some antique clothes from the parsonage attic. It was something highly prized by Pearl."

"Antique clothes—like Halloween costumes. This is not equal to what I told you."

Tinkie sighed. "I'll make it up to you, Vera. I promise. I don't have anything else on Pearl, but what about that old biddy Clara Watkins?"

I didn't know Clara Watkins, nor was I interested. This was just a Tinkie diversion.

"What about her?" Vera was hooked.

"She had her husband arrested two nights ago for drunken caterwauling outside their home. Waymon is still sitting in the Sunflower County jail. He'll be arraigned later this week."

"Did he really serenade her?" Vera asked.

Tinkie shook her head. "I don't know the details, but I heard the neighbors all filed complaints. He had an air guitar and was doing a suggestive dance. Check the docket and attend the arraignment when it's scheduled and you can get the real scoop. No one else knows about this except the law. They're keeping it quiet."

"Thanks!" Vera was happy with her nugget of information.

The waitress came to take our order, but Tinkie suddenly scooted out of the booth and stood up. "Sarah Booth, I forgot all about my dental appointment." She checked her watch. "I have twenty minutes to get there."

"But . . . lunch!" I'd seen the plates of piping hot Southern cooking coming out of the kitchen and I wanted to give the Shady Rest a try.

"I'm sorry, Sarah Booth. You have to take me back to Zinnia. I can't miss this appointment. I've been waiting four months."

A big, dark storm settled on Vera's forehead.

Tinkie waved the waitress over, pulled some folding money from her purse, and handed it to her. "Please give Vera whatever she wants. The change is yours."

Vera's forehead cleared. "Thank you, Tinkie. That's very generous."

"Happy to do it, Vera. Next time, maybe we can actually have lunch and talk." Behind her back, Tinkie crossed her fingers.

"Let's go, Hannibal Lecter," I said. "Gotta get those choppers in working order."

We left before Vera could catch on that we just didn't want to stay in her company any longer than necessary.

14

Skipping lunch at the Shady Rest made me a bit cranky, so Tinkie and I drove to Millie's Café in Zinnia. We needed to set a plan of action in further pursuing what had happened to Danny Anderson.

Vera Volt was a troublemaker and a terrible gossip, but I had to wonder if she knew a lot more than she'd let on. I wondered if she'd respond better to Oscar or Harold questioning her—or maybe even Coleman if it looked like she was involved in illegal acts. She had a thing for the male of the species.

"No." Tinkie was looking at me.

"No, what?" I waved Millie over.

"No, Vera does not know anything worth telling. No, my husband can't talk to her. She's a vamp of the worst type."

"Vera Volt?" Millie asked as she took a seat. She made a *pffft* sound and waved a hand. "That woman is pure venom. That's what I call her: Vera Venom. If she can say something bad about a person, she'll kill herself doing it."

Obviously, I wasn't up to speed on the local pariahs. "Why is she so mean?" I asked.

Millie shook her head. "Only you would ask, Sarah Booth. She's mean because she has a boil on her butt, and she loves to spread the pain."

It was some description, but it did fit Vera. She took pleasure in cutting others down to size. Or what she perceived as size. I had a sense she didn't feel the need to stick to facts and preferred vicious gossip.

"Has Vera ever been involved with—"

Millie cut me off. "That woman is a home-wrecker."

"Odd, that's what she says about Pearl Wingard."

Millie arched one eyebrow. "I don't keep up with Vera's conquests, but she sure had a hankering for Micah Wingard. She did nothing to hide it. I heard from one of the congregants that Vera made a shameless play for Micah. He managed to evade her, but my source told me Vera made a fool of herself. She's probably still smarting from that."

Micah had modestly told us the same. Vera was projecting onto Pearl exactly what *she* wanted to do. Peculiar how common projection was. I'd seen it play out in national politics where elected officials accused each other of crimes that they themselves were committing. Why? Why telegraph the crime? I didn't understand people.

Tinkie folded her menu. She was ready to order.

"As far as I know, Pearl is a decent person." Millie wasn't going to give an inch. "The same can't be said for Vera. Sarah Booth, did you ever talk to that land buyer, Levi Butler? He was back in here."

"We did."

"Sarah Booth's horse dumped him in the middle of the road." Tinkie didn't bother to hide her glee. "He holds a grudge," she warned all of us.

"How well do you know him?" Millie asked Tinkie.

"I don't really, but I mentioned him to Oscar. He's been in

the bank a few times. Oscar told me about him," Tinkie said. "The bank doesn't have to work with him, but some of the farmers don't have a choice. For some, it's either sell to him, or someone like him, or go into foreclosure, which is awful."

"When he was here, he was talking about the Tallahatchie River," Millie said. "I tried to eavesdrop, but I didn't catch everything. Only that he thinks the bridge is haunted."

That perked my ears right up. "I think so, too." I told them about the woman I saw on the bridge. There and then gone. I couldn't talk about Jitty, but this bridge ghost was fair game to discuss. And I mentioned the music I'd heard. It had sounded as if it came from beneath the water. Even talking about it gave me goose bumps. "Speaking of the river, I want to go back and check out that sandbar. All of those holes. What is going on with that? I'm just not satisfied with what we found."

I turned to my partner. "Tinkie, I insist that you take Maylin to the splash pad. It's hot and I can handle the river. I'll take Sweetie Pie and Avalon. I'll be fine."

"Are you sure?" Tinkie was torn between loyalty to me and the real need to be with her child.

"I'm positive. Now, take that baby to play! I insist."

"What are you hoping to find?" Millie asked.

I considered my answer. "I want to find the reason someone is digging up the sandbar. We found that christening gown, but the other holes were empty. But why dig them? It's bothering me."

"Are there any stories about buried treasure along that stretch of the river?" Millie asked.

"I don't know." I looked at Tinkie and she shrugged.

"I'll call Cece and ask her," Tinkie volunteered. "If there's anything to know, she'll know it." She gave Millie a sly look.

"I would think you might have a theory or two. Something from the *Globe* or *Enquirer*."

"I get my info from a better source now," Millie sniffed, but she couldn't hold the grin back. "One of the big national papers has a new section on fake news! It's loaded with the dumbest conspiracy theories, but some of them are delicious."

I didn't want to ask what she was talking about. I was ready for the dogs, the river, and maybe even a wet T-shirt moment. Better yet would be skinny-dipping, but only if Coleman was with me, and that wasn't going to happen. He was busy.

"Do you have cell reception on the river?" Millie asked. "I don't want you there by yourself if you don't."

"That's a funny thing. When I saw that woman on the bridge, I didn't. Then when I was back there the next time, I did."

"Are you implying that a ghost woman knocked out your cell service?" Millie was thrilled.

"I'm open to other explanations." I did believe that a supernatural element was at work, but I didn't want to verbally commit. I already had a reputation for being a little woo-woo. Tinkie had caught me talking to empty air one too many times, and it was clear she suspected that I wasn't being truthful about what I was doing. There were only two conclusions she could draw—I was nuts or I was haunted. It could go either way.

"Go on," Tinkie urged. "That way you can get back well before the day is over."

I didn't need much encouragement. I didn't want to be on the river after the sun set. I wasn't exactly afraid—but I was a little spooked. That was a position of weakness. Going into any situation with your nerves on edge was always a danger.

Because of Jitty, I knew ghosts were real. But I also knew they couldn't really hurt me. Still, that did nothing to calm my jitters.

I dropped Tinkie at Hilltop and picked up my pooches. When they were comfy in the back seat of the SUV, I headed toward the river. I was just driving up onto the bridge when the radio clicked, clacked, and "Ode to Billie Joe" came over the speakers. This was a repeat of my first experience on the bridge. Instinctively I slowed. Again, the bridge was empty of traffic. Almost as if a spell had been cast, precluding other vehicles from driving on the span over the river. I crested the bridge and slammed on the brakes.

A woman in a long, flowing white dress was balanced on the bridge railing. She was barefoot, and seemingly unaware that I approached. I could only see her profile, not her face. Her dark curls whipped around her face in the breeze. Who was she? Or who had she been? If she was a ghost, she was once a living person. Why was she haunting the bridge here? The old bridge—the bridge of Gentry's song—had been burned in the 1970s. Looking at the dress the figure wore, I couldn't tell if it was modern or vintage. She could easily have been a hippie from the 1970s, or she could be a modern woman. Her dark hair surrounded her face, giving me only a glimpse of her profile. Her total focus was down at the water. Was she okay? Was she contemplating jumping?

I pulled as close as I dared, then parked and got out. When I looked up, she was gone. Vanished. I rushed to the railing and looked down. Nothing. The river flowed by, calm on the surface but hiding treacherous currents. In the distance, a boat came into view with two fishermen in it. They were casting toward the sandbar. When they saw me on the bridge, they waved.

I waved back, jumped in my car, and drove down to park near the abutment. I nearly tripped half a dozen times, briars and weeds grabbing my pants and shoes as I rushed to the riverbank. I was just in time. The fishermen were abreast of the sandbar when I ran out onto it.

"Excuse me!" I called out to them.

They both had paddles and there was a small trolling motor on the aluminum boat. They angled toward the sandbar, and I waded out to catch the prow of the boat and guide it onto the sandbar. Sweetie Pie and Avalon took that moment to appear out of the woods like canine apparitions.

The men almost fell back in the boat. They weren't old, but they weren't young and spry either.

"They're my dogs," I said as I extended a hand to the men. "Sarah Booth Delaney, private investigator."

Their names were Bob and Jim Parnell, two brothers who were also farmers. I was in luck.

"Did you happen to see a woman up on the bridge?" I asked.

"No," Jim said. "We haven't seen anyone. Been slow, but that's good for fishing."

"I'm trying to find Danny Anderson. Do you know where he is?" I asked.

"Rumors are flying all over the county that he jumped off that there bridge," Bob said, nodding to the span.

I looked up, half expecting to see the woman in the white dress. But there was nothing. "Why would Danny jump?"

"Same reason we're out here fishing," Jim said. "Between us we have over six thousand acres under cultivation. We're going to lose our shirts, and today we just couldn't confront the reality. I heard Danny was in the same situation. More debt than income."

"I'm sorry." I didn't have to fake sympathy. These farmers,

and hundreds more just like them, were facing the end of a way of life. Their solution was to go fishing on a hot summer day and I applauded them. If only Danny was with them. "If you don't mind, would you tell me what you know about Danny?"

The brothers looked at each other before they answered. "Good man. Excellent farmer. Smart and hardworking. But none of that matters when the weather goes against you."

"Do you really think he'd take his own life?"

"To speak honestly," Jim said, "it's something we've talked about. All of us. Our families have farmed this land for over a hundred years. We bought more land when we could, always growing, putting more and more acreage to the plow. Now, we're going to lose it. Folks don't understand a lick about climate change. People want to ignore it because they're hard-headed fools. The price is going to be steep, and it will hit the workingman the hardest. Rich folks can move at the drop of a hat. We're here, where the land has always sustained us."

My heart was close to breaking for them. They weren't complaining. They were stating simple facts.

"There's no such thing as weather insurance," Bob said. "Even if there was, I have to wonder if the companies would pay out. A lot of folks suffering from natural disasters aren't getting any help from the companies that insured their homes or businesses. A number of farmers have considered finding a way to kill ourselves that wouldn't invalidate our life insurance. As far as I've heard, life insurance is still paying out."

I felt a sharp pain around my heart. These men weren't afraid of danger or hard work. But failure was more than they could handle. "You would think there would be insurance for crops."

They both laughed—and not just a chuckle. It was a full belly laugh. "Oh, there is crop insurance, but it helps the corporate farmers more than us. Up until recently the federal government sometimes came to the rescue. Basically, we're on our own. You think the insurance companies care if we kill ourselves?" Bob asked.

"No, they do not," Jim said. He'd had enough and was ready to talk about it. "The land is a lot more valuable than anything we owe. If we default on our loans, the banks get the land and then they'll turn around and sell it for a huge payday. Foreign investors have the cash. I'm tired. I'm worn out. Each year it gets harder and harder to figure out what to plant and when to plant it. The government tries to tell us what to plant, and that's a problem, too. Depletes the soil and no crop diversity. Maybe it's time to let it all go. I could teach agriculture at a trade school."

Teaching was hard work, but not as hard as farming. And not as risky. But teaching was not the job these men loved. They were farmers. They lived by the seasons. They planted seeds and watched them develop into corn, cotton, soybeans. As my daddy used to say, "Farming is a job filled with hope. And hope gets you through a bad day." If these men lost their land, it would be devastating.

"Maybe this will be a better year for farming." It was more of a wish than anything else.

"Maybe so," Jim said, but his heart wasn't in it.

I changed the subject. I had no sunny predictions to offer them for the future. I needed to focus on my case. "Do you know who's digging all these holes in the sandbar? Or what they're hoping to find?"

"There are always treasure hunters along most rivers. There's still the hope of De Soto's gold or jewels or doubloons from some of the French and Spanish explorers who came through here. The foreign men who came through here claiming to discover this continent believed they'd find cities of gold." He laughed. "We could use some of that gold, couldn't we, Bob?"

"Yep," his brother agreed. He picked up his paddle, signaling he was ready to get back to fishing. "Folks are desperate. Looking for leprechauns and a pot of gold, or treasure buried on the river, are the only hope some folks have."

"Have you seen anyone digging on the sandbar?" I asked.

"Nope, not lately," Jim said. "But we might all be out here soon, looking for buried treasure. We all need some magic to save our farms. Right now, I'd like to believe in a fairy godmother. That was one thing about Danny. He believed in miracles. Maybe it was because he was such good friends with Pearl Wingard. Maybe her faith rubbed off on him."

"What do you mean?" I asked.

"They used to come here and dig around on the riverbank. When I asked him one day what he was doing, he said he was looking for treasure. He and Pearl. He said they'd split it like partners." Jim laughed, but it was a sad sound. "I guess we all still believe in happy endings, or we'd pack up and sell out today. That Levi Butler man is offering pennies on the dollar to buy my land. Maybe it's better than losing everything."

"By the way," Bob said, fishing rod in hand, "Danny was down at this sandbar the day he disappeared." Bob motioned for me to push them off.

"Why was he here?" I asked.

Bob shrugged his shoulders. "Beats me. Ask him if you find him."

"What time was he here?"

Bob shook his head. "The hours slip by me."

"Has anybody ever found any treasure?" I asked, trying not to show my disappointment.

"Nope," Bob said. "Not that we know about. Now, do you mind pushing us off?"

I had more questions, but I could track them down later if I needed to. I gave a mighty heave on the boat. "Good luck fishing," I said as they paddled back into the current. In a moment they had disappeared around a bend in the river.

15

I romped with the dogs on the sandbar. Sweetie Pie loved the water, and Avalon was willing to share her enthusiasm. It did my heart good to see the two hounds fly past me, kicking up sand, and then rushing to the water to jump in. The joy of my hounds made me profoundly happy, and for a moment the dread that had taken root in my heart was quelled.

I ran and tumbled with them until I was panting. I stopped to stare into the river, mesmerized by the passage of the muddy water. I looked south to see the trees hanging over the water in places. Magical. My state held such beauty it was almost unbearable at times.

I sat down on the sandbar, where I had a view of the water. The river was so calm on the surface but turbulent beneath and filled with sorrow and tragedy. It was a perfect metaphor for the history of my state—beauty and horror; calm and turbulence; good memories and tragedy.

Birds flitted through the leafy canopy of trees and small creatures rustled and scampered through the dense foliage.

For a moment I was back in the grove of old oak trees with my mama.

I closed my eyes against the bright sun and slipped into the past. Mama is curled in a nest of oak limbs, reading a book; I am playing in the roots of the trees. I hear a faint rustle of leaves, and I jump to my feet, ready to greet the elves and fairies. I feel the sunshine on my shoulders and smell the green of the canopy of leaves. I am living a perfect moment of memory. And then it's gone.

Sweetie Pie dove into the river, swimming out and circling back, and I was returned to the here and now. For a time, I believed in magic. I was convinced my special place among the oaks was visited by the brownies, elves, and fairies. When my parents were killed, I gave up my belief in any magic. No amount of wishing, dreaming, begging, or praying could change the fact that my parents were dead. I lost my ability to believe. I understood one thing—that I was the only thing I could believe in. But when I returned to Zinnia—and Jitty—I found myself relearning that there was more to life than what lies on the surface. So much more.

Jitty's first appearance made me a believer in ghosts in a hurry! It's a miracle I hadn't died of fright. She'd been so excited to get one over on me! Now, I wondered if she could clue me in to the truth about fairies, elves, and brownies. I saw them when I was a little girl. I'd find their secret places in the roots of trees and the grassy hillocks. Some might say it was my imagination or a fancy, but I remembered them in great detail. Maybe I just needed to believe again.

I wished Pluto was with us, but the cat had no use for sun, sand, and water. He kept himself immaculate and didn't like to be gritty. Or hot. No, he was happier at Dahlia House.

I walked down the sandbar. The dogs helped me excavate

some of the holes—which were already filling up with sand again. We didn't find anything of interest. I wasn't satisfied with my search, but I was hot and tired. Mosquitoes feasted on my arms and legs, and I was about to be cranky. I wanted to go home and take a hot shower. Maybe Coleman would grill when he got home. I was learning to make some interesting vegetarian menu options. Coleman wasn't really a hard sell on changing our diet—it was just something we both had to master. He was happy to let meat and dairy go as long as we had something tasty to eat.

"How about some grilled black bean burgers?" I asked Sweetie Pie. She gave me the most mournful look and howled. Well, I had some chicken for her and Avalon. The new dog, who was coming along like the champ she was, would eat whatever I put in front of her. But Sweetie was the princess, and I'd always give her exactly what she wanted. She'd saved my life more than once.

When the dogs were tired of swimming and digging in the sand, I whistled them up to go home. On the way, I called Coleman to see if grilling was an option or if he was brave enough for me to cook something. Maybe a salad—I could make a really good salad.

"Grilling is fine," Coleman said. "I do have to talk to you."

Oh, I didn't like the sound of that. "What's up?"

"We'll talk when I get home. And I'm headed that way in half an hour."

Perfect timing. I'd pick up some veggies at the grocery and meet Coleman at Dahlia House. I hustled the dogs into the vehicle, and we were off.

I'd just put the groceries away when Coleman walked in the front door. He came back to the kitchen and pulled me into a wonderful hug, topped off with a kiss. Coleman was the best kisser I'd ever met.

"Let me get the grill going and then we need to talk. Make us a drink?"

"Sure." I smiled, though I wanted to tug at his sleeve and ask him what was going on. I restrained myself.

I made the drinks and met him out on the slate patio where the grill was set up with a table and a few chairs. Coleman and I had plans for a pergola with cross vines to create a shady place to sit while grilling in the summer. But those plans would have to wait until next year.

Ice clinked in his glass as he swirled the bourbon around and looked at me. "I have some bad news about Danny."

"You found his body?"

"No! Not that bad. But Danny's in some trouble. Legal trouble."

"What?" I knew Coleman wasn't talking about a bank loan.

"I was called over to Leflore County by the sheriff there to help with another burglary scene at a drugstore."

"'Help'?" Why would a sheriff with his own department need the Sunflower County sheriff to help him? Something wasn't right.

"'Help' isn't the right word," Coleman said. "I think he wanted me to know the details in the hope that I might be able to tell him something."

"About what?" This was like pulling teeth.

"About the feedstore burglary here. Mr. Rutherford wouldn't talk to them. He may be protecting Danny."

"Are you sure it was Danny?" My heart was breaking. This wasn't a good or smart thing if Danny was stealing. The stores and businesses—who relied on the farmers spending money there—were struggling, too. Danny was only sharing the pain if he was stealing.

"It sure looked like Danny. We don't have all that fancy facial-recognition software and besides, he was wearing a ski mask. But the sheriff is going to see if the feds can't help us out. I think the Leflore County sheriff was just hoping I might be able to make a positive ID. I didn't because I wasn't absolutely sure, but if it is Danny . . ."

"When will you know something?"

"Maybe tomorrow."

"And if it is Danny?"

"They're going to alert the authorities all over the South."

"Did he have a gun in the video?"

"I didn't see one," Coleman said.

"How much was taken?"

"More than ten thousand at the feedstore, but I'm not sure about the other locations. Either way, it's a felony. And the feedstore will likely go out of business. They hadn't made the deposit from the week's sales. It'll ruin them."

"There have to be some answers," I told Coleman.

"I agree. Now, let's get the grill fired up so I can cook some of those vegetables you bought. Tinkie said you missed lunch."

"These cabbage steaks are going to be divine," I told him. "Let me refresh our drinks." I sighed. "I hope it wasn't him. I hope he isn't breaking the law. This is all too much. Apparitions on the bridge, Danny disappearing, Pearl involved in goodness knows what, and add Vera Volt into that mishmash. I need a vacation from this case."

"At your service," Coleman said. "Bring us another round of drinks, then we'll eat, and I'll make you forget all of your worries and woes."

Oh, that was a big brag! "How are you going to do that?" I asked.

He leaned down and whispered in my ear, "Magic." He caught me up, pulled me against him, and kissed my neck until I squealed. That man did know how to rock my world

But as much as I adored my time with Coleman, I couldn't completely shut out my worry for Danny Anderson and his family. If Danny was breaking the law, Coleman would have no option but to arrest him. It wasn't the outcome I wanted for this case. But it wasn't anything I could change on this late summer afternoon.

16

The next morning Tinkie had a spring in her step. Spending the afternoon with Maylin was just the elixir she needed. I was on the frisky side myself.

We were in good spirits as we got ready for the day. Tinkie recounted Maylin's fascination with the splash pad and how Chablis and Zelda had played with the baby in the water—to the consternation of one other mother, who said something about the dogs being dirty. Not the wisest course of action. Tinkie was indeed Mama Bear. And her grizzly defense applied to Chablis and Zelda as much as Maylin. Tinkie used her heel to step on the squirt nozzle and shot water into the complaining woman's face—then pretended it was an accident. Tinkie! She did it all with honey in her voice and a smile on her lips.

We were still laughing about it as we drove to the feedstore that had been robbed. I filled Tinkie in on my afternoon on the river. When I asked her about Florence Smallwood's painting, she hesitated. "I saw it, Sarah Booth, and now that you mention it, the couple did look like Pearl and Danny. But I didn't think that it might be Pearl until you mentioned it. Maybe it's just the power of suggestion." She bit her bottom lip. "I don't want to believe that Pearl did something to a baby."

"Maybe she just put the child up for adoption," I said. "There's no evidence that she did anything nefarious. And maybe the painting wasn't of her. Let's put this aside until we talk with the store owner about the robbery. Coleman showed me the footage from the store camera and it sure looks like Danny, but you can't clearly see his face. He's wearing a ski mask and a hoodie."

"Why would . . . ?" Tinkie let her question fade away. We knew why. Danny was desperate for money. Ten grand wouldn't even put a dent in what he owed the bank, but it would give the Anderson family a chance to fight for a few more days.

The parking lot of the drugstore was covered in pickup trucks. I parked around the corner and Tinkie and I went in together. We meandered our way to the pharmacist's platform, where a cluster of people had gathered to wait for their prescriptions to be filled. We were able to get close without being seen. We were discreet as we eavesdropped on conversations that had grown too familiar—the hardships of farming with a rapidly changing climate and the high cost of living for families. Most of the residents of the Delta were intricately involved in farming on one level or another.

I listened for a mention of Danny's name, but none of the folks there seemed inclined to gossip about his disappearance. When the pharmacist came over to talk to a client, one customer patted him on the shoulder. "I hate what happened. You've been good to all of us. Really good. We were talking, and we'd like to host a fish fry to raise some funds. It won't generate the amount that was stolen, but it may help a little."

"Thank you." The pharmacist, touched by the gesture, cleared his throat. "That's mighty generous."

"We have to stick together. We can't get by without the local drugstore, and you can't run a store without the community."

Several of the people agreed.

"Was it Danny Anderson who robbed you?" a fellow in the back asked.

"I don't know." The pharmacist looked down at the floor. "I can't believe that. I've known Danny since he was trotting along at his daddy's knee. He was always a good boy. A good man."

"We heard they caught him on the store camera," the same man said.

"I saw that footage and I can't swear it was Danny." The pharmacist's mouth had gone white. "Let's just leave it up to the law to find the guilty party. Until then, I don't want to hear any talk about Danny. His family is hurting bad right now. Let's not make it worse."

"Make what worse?" Levi Butler came up to the counter. The customers scattered, several muttering under their breath. Even if a person didn't have a farm, the word was out that Butler was a snake trying to take advantage of people in a bind.

"Mr. Butler, don't let the doorknob hit you in the ass," the pharmacist said. "This is my place of business, and you're very bad for business."

"I'm only here to see if any of these men have come to their senses. I know you aren't all farmers, but you know the local guys. It's time they realized that it's better to sell before you get foreclosed on," he said, speaking loudly. "Come on, men, I'm not your enemy. I had nothing to do with bad crops and bad decisions. I can make it a little easier, though, if you'll let me. Farmers can walk away with something instead of nothing."

Beside me, Tinkie tensed. We'd both turned away from

Butler, but Tinkie was about to spring into action—and it was not going to be pretty for the land buyer. If Levi Butler saw us, he would surely make an issue of it. He'd hurt his pride when he fell from the horse.

I grabbed my partner's hand. "Let's go."

We edged away from the pharmacist counter and ducked behind a shelf with hair dye, vitamins, supplements, and grooming tools. We could still hear the conversation, but we were out of sight.

"Has anyone found Danny Anderson?" Butler asked the handful of people who remained near him.

"Leave Danny alone," someone said. "And his family, you bloodsucker."

"Ha ha ha. That's rich. I can offer Danny or any of the leveraged farmers a way to save something of what you call your land. It's not really yours, though, if you've borrowed against it. But have it your way. If you see Danny, let him know that my offer expires tomorrow at noon. That goes for the rest of you, too."

"Please get out of my store." The pharmacist's voice was hard. "Now. I won't ask again."

"You men know where to find me if you want to negotiate."

Tinkie and I waited until we heard Butler go out the front door. It was as if everyone exhaled all of a sudden. We were about to leave when the door swung back open. Two men hustled back to the counter. "Mr. Taylor, Mr. Taylor, did you know about Todd Jenkins?"

"What about Todd?" someone asked.

"He was found dead about an hour ago on a sandbar on the Tallahatchie River."

"What?" Everyone was as stunned as Tinkie and I. "Found dead? What happened?"

"The sheriff is saying his death was suspicious," one man said.

Tinkie and I peeked out from behind the shelves. Mr. Taylor, the pharmacist, was ashen and the other men were in a dither.

"Please don't jump to conclusions," Taylor said. "Let the law investigate this."

I looked at Tinkie. "Who is Todd Jenkins?" I asked.

"Local guy," Tinkie said. She was frowning. "He was in Millie's Café the other day. He has a hot temper and a bad reputation. A few years back he was supposedly dating Vera Volt."

"Well, that's not a good enough reason to die. Do you think Vera killed him?" I was half-teasing, but Tinkie took it as a serious question.

"I told you she was a praying mantis," Tinkie said with bitter irony. "We need to check on this. Todd was a member of the Wingards' church."

"You want to talk to Vera again?" I asked her.

"I'd rather drink arsenic, but I guess we have to do it."

"Let's get it done. After we talk with Mr. Taylor."

We found the pharmacist perched on a stool behind the counter. The customers had picked up their prescriptions and dispersed.

"Mr. Taylor, can we ask a few questions?" Tinkie asked.

"You're those detective ladies trying to find Danny, aren't you?"

We nodded. "Danny's family is sick with worry," I said.

"You're the Delaney woman, and you're the banker's wife," he said.

"We are." Tinkie looked at me. "My husband is distraught over Danny's disappearance."

"Oscar has gone out on a limb to help more than one farmer," Taylor said. "Oscar helped me get the financing for this store." He looked grim. "No one likes to foreclose on a friend or neighbor."

"Was it Danny who robbed your store?" I asked.

Taylor sighed. "I think it was. It looks like him on the store video, but it doesn't make sense. Danny knew all about the cameras and where they are. He could have avoided them if he'd wanted to."

"Why would he know that?" I asked.

"He helped install them. Not physically, but he was telling me how to do it. He had a knack with electronics, and he helped me order them."

Mr. Taylor was making a very good point. Why would Danny rob a place and walk in front of the cameras when he could have easily avoided them?

"What do you think is going on?" Tinkie asked.

"I don't know, Mrs. Richmond. You know a couple of folks have reported seeing a woman on the Tallahatchie River bridge. You heard anything about that?"

I almost choked. Tinkie answered while I coughed. "No. We haven't heard anything, have we, Sarah Booth?"

"We had a picnic on the sandbar recently," I said. "We were telling ghost stories about the bridge being haunted." That's as far as I could go without violating the rules of the Great Beyond. Maybe I was being overly cautious, but I didn't want to risk losing Jitty. "Those old stories have been going around for decades."

"Lots of good, creepy tales about ghosts on that river," he said. "I guess that's par for the course for Mississippi. Lots of tragedies and lots of ghosts, if you believe in that sort of thing."

"You don't believe?" I asked.

"Two farmers I wouldn't suspect of being inclined to the

paranormal said they've seen a woman in a white dress on the bridge." He looked at me as if he knew I was dodging the truth. "You haven't heard anything?"

I ignored his questions and offered one of my own. "Do they know who this ghost might be? Or who she was?" It was hard to know whether to talk about ghosts in the past or present tense.

"Oh, some say she's the woman Bobbie Gentry wrote that song about. 'Ode to Billie Joe.' Mighty good song. It captured the feel of a hot summer day here in the Delta."

He was right about that, and about the ghostly figure of a woman in a white dress. But I wasn't going to cop to anything about seeing ghosts. "Do you believe they're seeing an apparition?" I was pressing him, and I wasn't certain why. Except that the woman on the bridge had creeped me out more than once now. I had to accept she was ephemeral. But it was a relief to know that others were seeing her, too.

17

We left the drugstore, heading toward the Wingard parsonage beside their church. To get there, we'd have to cross the Tallahatchie River. I wanted to see if Tinkie picked up on anything supernatural.

"Call Coleman and see if you can get an update on what happened to Todd Jenkins," I suggested to Tinkie.

She made the call and put it on speaker.

"I'm calling for Sarah Booth," she told Coleman when he answered. "Any updates on Todd Jenkins?"

"Not in my jurisdiction," Coleman said, "but I have some gossip. Budgie said his cousin was with the river rescue when they found him. Looks like he drowned, but they're not ruling out murder. He had a head injury but it could have happened after he drowned. The autopsy will tell us more."

"Don't you find this a bit strange?" I asked Coleman.

"More than a bit. Todd was a strong young man. It doesn't make sense that he would drown."

"Was Todd in any financial distress?" Tinkie asked.

Coleman hesitated. "I don't have any official word, but the talk is that he was in deep debt at a Memphis bank. Just like so many other farmers. He was caught between a rock and a hard place."

Tinkie paled, and I knew she was thinking about Oscar and the people who owed money to the bank he ran. "Any other news?" I asked.

"No word on Danny. Where are you?"

"Tinkie and I are going to talk to Pearl Wingard. Again. Do you know where on the river Todd was found?"

"A bit upriver from the bridge," Coleman said. "I don't have the exact location because I'm not involved in the case. Just be careful. Something unusual is happening on that river."

"Something like a ghost?" I couldn't help myself. I didn't get a lot of chances to tease Coleman about spirits and such.

"I don't care what it is or what you call it as long as you and Tinkie are safe."

"We'll be very careful. I promise."

"Call me when you're headed back to Zinnia."

"Will do," I said and ended the call.

"Do you believe in ghosts, Sarah Booth?" Tinkie asked.

The urge to tell her the truth—all of it—was powerful. But what if I opened my mouth and somehow prevented Jitty from visiting me? I would be bereft. No, it was better to shut up and play it safe. But I did have a partial answer I could share with her. "I believe that all life is made of matter. Matter can't be destroyed. So when someone dies, it makes sense to me that energy is converted or changed, but it doesn't go away."

"Is that a yes or no to ghosts?"

"It's an 'I don't know.' I'm open, but I don't know how all of that would work. None of us do."

Tinkie's expression was pensive. "I want to believe that I'll always be around Maylin, to make sure she is loved and happy. I know I physically won't be able to do that, but I need to believe that I'll be right there with her, in one form or another."

"Then believe that," I said softly. "I know my parents are still around. At times." I smiled. "I'm glad they aren't always around!"

"Yeah, you'd scandalize them for sure," Tinkie teased. But she understood what I was saying. "Have you ever seen a ghost, Sarah Booth?"

I kept my eyes on the road as we approached the Tallahatchie River bridge. "I have."

"Did it scare you?"

"At first. But now if I see a ghost, I find it comforting." I was on thin ice—getting too close to the truth. I needed to change the focus of the conversation. I didn't want to prejudice Tinkie into seeing a ghost because I had suggested it.

We were at the river, and Tinkie was leaning forward, looking ahead and to her right.

I glanced back up at the road and gasped. A woman in a white dress once again stood balanced on the railing. Her hair blew around her face, but I knew who she was—Pearl Wingard. This wasn't the apparition I'd seen before. This was a flesh-and-blood human who might be in danger.

Tinkie saw her, too. "Drive!" she commanded.

I hit the gas pedal and shot up the incline, but I was too slow. Pearl looked at the approaching car. She made a motion with her hand, almost as if she were asking for forgiveness. She jumped from the bridge, the white dress flashing in the sun.

"Crap!" Tinkie called out. "Drive, Sarah Booth. Hurry!"

I roared across the bridge and down to the parking spot that led to the sandbar. We had to get to Pearl before she drowned.

I called 911 and asked for paramedics and then I parked and jumped from the car. Tinkie went a bit upriver while I crashed my way through the brambles and shrubs to fight to the river's edge, south of the bridge.

"Can you see her?" I yelled back to Tinkie. I swept the river with my gaze, but I didn't see anything that resembled a human body.

"Yes! Yes! She's coming around the bend now. Grab her, Sarah Booth. She's drifting close to you on the sandbar."

The light on the water was blinding, but I used my hand to protect my eyes. I was able to make out an arm rising out of the river as Pearl rolled over onto her back in the muddy water. The fall likely knocked the breath out of her, if not something worse.

She was only about fifteen feet from the shore, but the current was strong and she was clipping along. "Pearl!" I called out to her. "Pearl! Try to slow down so I can grab you."

She lifted her head and shook it slowly.

She didn't want to be saved. She was going to allow herself to be swept away.

I did a shallow racing dive into the water at an angle that I hoped would allow me to intercept her. As the river curved and turned along, there were areas where the bank was steep. I wanted to avoid that and stay near the sandbar. If I was going to be able to save her, I needed to pull her body up on the sand.

I swam with every bit of strength I had. The current was strong, even though it was June and the water levels were slightly down. "Tinkie!" I called out.

"I'm on the bank, following. I found an old rope and I'll throw it out to you."

Thank heavens for Tinkie.

I came up on Pearl, who seemed to be in a stupor. I grabbed

her arm, spun her, and caught her up in a fireman's carry before fighting to get back to the sandbar. We were moving downriver too fast. If I missed this sandbar, would there be another in time for me to save her?

"Call for help. Someone with a speedboat," I yelled at Tinkie.

"Sure," she said, but instead she waded into the water. She tossed the rope at me, and by some excellent luck, I caught it and held tight. Tinkie began to haul me toward the shore.

Pearl was bluish white. I couldn't tell if she was alive or dead. I didn't have time to check. Tinkie and I were fighting the river with everything we had in us.

When at last my feet found the bottom, I hauled Pearl around and began dragging her toward the shore. She had to be alive. She had to be.

18

By the time I dragged her up onto the sandbar, I was exhausted. Luckily Tinkie took over chest compressions and mouth-to-mouth until Pearl coughed, gagged, and finally started breathing on her own. She had a whole lot of explaining to do.

When she was sitting up, leaning against a tree trunk, I asked her, "What were you thinking, Pearl?" There was heat in my question—I was angry. She'd scared me badly and almost killed herself.

Tinkie put a hand on her shoulder. "What in the world, Pearl? You would have broken Micah's heart."

Pearl looked down at the damp sand and began to cry. "No matter what I do, I hurt someone. I don't want that. I never wanted to hurt Micah or Danny or anyone else. I just want all of this pain to end."

"And you thought jumping in the river would do it?" I sounded harsher than I intended. The fact that another body had recently been recovered from the river was heavy on my mind. "Look, folks are upset over Danny. No one knows where he is or if he's okay. If you disappeared in the river, what do you think would happen?"

She shook her head. "You're right. I just didn't see another way. I knew, as I was falling, it was the wrong choice. But it was too late." She put a hand on Tinkie's arm and looked at me. "Thank you both for saving me."

"Why?" Tinkie asked. "Why did you try to . . . Why?"

"No one is to blame. No one but me. It was just . . . Vera stopped by and she said Danny was certainly dead and that it rested at the doorstep of someone who had betrayed him. She looked at me like I had been spit straight out of hell. She made me believe everyone would be better if I was dead. That because of me, Danny was dead."

That was a mighty high pile of poo-poo-ca-ca that Vera was distributing. Thank goodness for Tinkie. She knew how to deal with the fallout from the Veras of the world.

"No one should make you feel that way," Tinkie said. "Vera is meaner than a cornered snake, but it's on you not to buy into her cruelty."

"I know." Pearl sounded defeated, but she sat up a little straighter.

"Bullies are everywhere, Pearl. You have to be strong enough to ignore them. If they don't get a reaction, they won't keep it up. But you have to be in charge of your own future happiness. Vera is jealous of you and that's why she targeted you for this. But you can't let her win."

Tinkie was putting the truth on Pearl, and I could only hope that it would give the young woman a sense of worth.

"Did you really mean to kill yourself?" My question was indelicate, but it wasn't meant to be judgmental.

"I don't know," Pearl said slowly. "I don't think so. I—" She inhaled deeply. "I hope not." She looked up at both of us. "Can we keep this to ourselves? I mean, I know you have to report it. Besides, you've already called an ambulance. But please, can we just say I stumbled and fell in the river?"

In the distance I could hear sirens on the way. I didn't want to lie. What if she did it again and no one was around to see it? But on the other hand, if the gossip started, it might break her marriage with Micah. Not to mention throw Danny Anderson's family into additional turmoil. I looked at Tinkie. She nodded slightly at me.

"We'll lie for you, Pearl, under one condition. You tell us the truth about you, Danny, and this bridge."

Pearl lifted her chin. "Okay. Deal. There's not that much to tell, but I'll tell you everything. Just see if you can stop the ambulance. Send them back. Those paramedics need to be helping people who need them. I'm fine now. You saved me."

"I'd feel better if you got checked out. In fact, I'm taking you to the hospital." The hospital in Zinnia was her destination whether she liked it or not. I could put a bug in Doc Sawyer's ear so he could evaluate Pearl to be sure she wouldn't try a stunt like this again.

"Okay." Pearl was wise not to argue.

"I'll meet the ambulance on the bridge and explain to them that you accidentally took a fall and are going to Zinnia to get checked out at the ER." I also wanted to pull up some of the images Coleman sent me from the feedstore camera. I was hoping Pearl could identify Danny.

"I'll wait here with Pearl," Tinkie said, putting an arm around the distraught young woman.

I hustled up the embankment and was standing in the road when the ambulance arrived. While the paramedics were glad no one needed emergency care, they were a little annoyed that they'd been called out for no reason. It took a bit of finessing, but I worked it out with them. On the way back to Tinkie and

Pearl, I grabbed my phone from the console in my car. Coleman had sent the images in a text.

By the time I got back to the sandbar, Pearl was up and walking toward the abutment. I realized then, she had no vehicle. "Where is your car?" I asked.

"I walked from the church." She was young and healthy and it was only a mile or two.

"We'll give you a ride home, after you see Doc in the ER," Tinkie said. She was clearly worried. It would seem Pearl had thought to disappear into the river—she'd made certain not to leave her car on the bridge. She seemed to have planned ahead, and that was disturbing.

When I was beside the river again, I pointed to a fallen tree. "Let's take a seat." I had questions and I intended to get answers before we left the river. And it would also give Pearl and me a chance to drip dry. It wouldn't take long in the June heat.

"I am sorry," Pearl said. She was more herself, and embarrassment was setting in. "I took a cowardly action. You saved me from myself."

I waved a hand in the air. "I'm just glad you're okay. That's all that matters."

"Exactly," Tinkie chimed in.

"Pearl, take a look at this photo." I passed over my phone, which had the image pulled up. "Do you recognize this person?"

Pearl inhaled sharply and tried to give me the phone back.

"Do you know who that is?" I pressed.

She shook her head. "You know it looks like Danny. But I can't be certain. The image isn't clear. I don't recognize the background. His face is hidden. Why are you showing me this?"

"Because the hardware store in Leflore County was robbed," I said slowly. "If this is Danny Anderson, we need to know."

"I can't say one way or the other. Heck, both of you know Danny. Is it him?"

The truth was, we couldn't say for certain either. "You know him better than we do."

"That's true," Pearl said, "but this person has his face concealed. Could it be Danny? Yes. Could it be someone else? Yes. I'm sure if the law could make a positive ID, they would do so and a warrant would be issued for Danny's arrest. Has anyone done that?"

"No." Tinkie spoke clearly. "That's why we're asking you, Pearl."

Pearl stood up. "If this is Danny, and he is robbing businesses, then we need to stop him. And why would he do this? Ten grand is nothing compared to what he owes. What does he hope to accomplish by stealing from the people who are suffering just like he is?"

She had some good points that Tinkie and I had already discussed. "If that isn't Danny, do you know who it might be?" I asked.

She shook her head. "No. I wish I could clearly identify the person, but I can't."

"Pearl, you almost died. What drove you out here on the bridge today?"

She sighed. "I've hurt too many people. I told you that."

"So, it was guilt?"

She looked at me. "Yes, you could say that."

But guilt at what? "Because of cheating on your husband?"

She shook her head. "Please take me home."

I needed more than that, but Tinkie shot me a warning glance. "Let's take her for Doc to check out," she said.

Doc took over an hour examining and talking with Pearl. Tinkie and I paced the hospital hallway. Waiting was killing us.

"I can take you home," I suggested to Tinkie. "No point in both of us losing the rest of the day."

Tinkie shook her head. "I'm worried about Pearl. I want Doc to reassure me."

The door to the exam room opened and Pearl came out. She met my gaze briefly and shook her head. "I'm so sorry."

"No apologies necessary." I meant it. "Are you okay?"

"Yes." Her attempt at laughter ended in a sob. "I can't even do away with myself without making a mess."

"Stop it." Tinkie got in her face. "Stop that talk right now. You have folks who love and care for you. You owe them more than this."

Tinkie's tough love put a little starch in Pearl's spine and she stood taller. "Will you take me home? I need to talk with Micah."

"Sure. Give me a minute." I ducked in to talk to Doc before anyone could protest.

"How's Pearl?" I asked as he rearranged some instruments.

"I can't talk about another patient."

Sometimes Doc made me mad enough to snort fire. "Look, we saved her, and I need to be relatively certain she won't do something like that again."

"Talk to her," Doc suggested, not unkindly. "She needs a friend, Sarah Booth."

"She's a suspect in a missing persons case that may have turned into a murder."

He chuckled out loud. "You think that slip of a girl did something to Danny Anderson?"

"Maybe. Or maybe it was someone else." I was backed into a corner and unwilling to give up. "Todd Jenkins was found dead on the river today."

That got Doc's attention. "What?"

"A fisherman found the body on a sandbar."

"How did he die?"

Before I could answer, the phone rang. He picked it up, looking at me the whole time. "Okay. Yes. Why don't you bring him here where I have the equipment I need?" A pause as he listened. "Good."

He hung up and shook his head. "They want me to do the autopsy on Todd. They're thinking foul play. They don't want to wait on the state crime lab."

"And there's still no sign of Danny Anderson." I was getting more worried about the missing farmer. A lot was going on in the Delta, most of it centered, seemingly, on the Tallahatchie River. None of it good.

After a slight pause, Doc continued, "Sarah Booth, don't stress Pearl Wingard out if you can help it. She's fragile. I can tell you that without violating my oath."

"Doc, do you think Pearl is capable of harming . . . ?"

"Herself? Yes, I think she's proven that."

"I was going to ask if she could harm others."

"What are you getting at, Sarah Booth?"

I found I couldn't accuse Pearl of killing her baby—or anyone else. The words wouldn't come out of my mouth. There was something about Pearl that made me think she might harm herself but no one else. "There's a lot going on." I couldn't tell him more at this point, but I had another topic. He'd been in the area for a long time and he had patients all over the Delta. "Doc, have you ever heard talk about the Tallahatchie River bridge being haunted?"

He stared at me. "What's going on, Sarah Booth?"

"I've seen some things on that bridge lately."

"You're wondering if some malevolent spirit might have instigated Pearl to jump."

That was exactly what I was aiming at—though it hadn't crystallized in my brain yet. "Do you know something?"

Doc settled onto the end of the exam table. With his nimbus of wild, white hair and in his white doctor's coat, he looked a lot like Albert Einstein. "Over the years, I've heard some things, but I thought all of that hysteria had died down."

Now he wasn't going to get me out of there until he told me. Tinkie and Pearl were waiting on me out in the hallway, but they would have to sit tight. My gut was telling me Doc might have info I could use.

"When you were a little girl, a woman committed suicide by jumping off the bridge."

I wasn't surprised. Sadness lingered on that river. "Do you know the story?"

Doc nodded. "It was truly tragic. Her name was Charline Smith. She was working as a student teacher in the elementary school."

"Did she fall from the bridge?" She was a young woman. I could easily create a scenario where she was on the river with her friends and accidentally fell into the water.

"Her death was ruled a suicide, though I was never certain the fall was deliberate. Still, once the coroner of Leflore County ruled it a suicide, there was no undoing the damage. The local minister of her church refused to let her be buried in consecrated ground. She was buried outside the cemetery fence. Her family was active in their church and they were devastated." Doc sighed heavily. "Two years after her death, her mother had a heart attack and died. Her father died shortly after. He just gave up and slipped away. It was a horrible tragedy that kept claiming victims."

"Why did she jump?"

"She didn't leave a note to explain, but folks thought she

had gotten pregnant by a local circuit court judge. Rumor was that he threatened to send her to prison if she claimed he was the father of her baby. She was in despair. She didn't know what to do or who to turn to, so she jumped."

"Who was the judge?" I was getting a very, very bad feeling.

"The Honorable Mark Truett."

Oh, I knew him. My father had crossed swords with him more than once. I'd always viewed him as corrupt. "Was he the father?"

Doc shook his head. "Her body was sent back to her family. There wasn't an investigation that I know of. It was all hushed up. Folks back then were afraid of Mark Truett. Anyway, the Smiths had a private funeral in their home and buried her just outside the church cemetery."

There was a knock at the door and Tinkie popped her head in. "Pearl is getting antsy."

I walked over to the door. Before I left I turned back. "If you remember anything else, please let me know. But you think Charline Smith is haunting the bridge?"

"That was the story," Doc said. "All folklore and no fact."

But I wasn't so certain about that.

19

The closer we got to the church and parsonage, the more antsy Pearl became. She was about to crawl out of her skin.

"Don't fret, Pearl. We won't say anything. You have our word," Tinkie reassured her.

"I know what I did was very wrong. It's my own guilty conscience eating me alive," Pearl admitted. "What was wrong with me that I did such a foolish thing?" She shuddered. "If Sarah Booth wasn't such a good swimmer, we would both be dead."

I wasn't particularly eager for Coleman to learn about my aquatic prowess. It would worry him a lot to know I was jumping into rivers to save people. Especially after the earlier rains in the Midwest. The runoff had our rivers running fast. "Let's just keep this among the three of us, if we can. Sometimes discretion is the better part of valor. I won't lie to the authorities, but I also won't be running my mouth."

"Thank you," Pearl said. "I'm going to ask Micah to find a good therapist for me. I want to talk to a professional. I never believed I'd be in such despair that I'd consider self-harm. But I did, and I can't let it get to that point again."

That was terrific news to hear. I did have some tough questions for her, now that we were on the road to delivering her safely home. She finally calmed and settled into the back seat of the vehicle. "Pearl, what was the relationship between Danny and Todd Jenkins?"

She didn't hesitate. "They knew each other. They were two farmers who shared a lot of the same issues. I was sorry to hear that Todd had died." She turned away to look out the window to compose herself. I kept an eye on her via the rearview mirror.

"Were Todd and Danny especially close friends?" I asked.

Pearl thought for a moment. "I don't know if 'friends' is the right word. They saw each other all the time around the county and at farmer meetings, but didn't socialize as far as I know. I—" She broke off her thought.

"What?" Tinkie pressed gently.

"I'm going to be totally honest. I didn't care for Todd. He was one of those guys that talked a line of bull a mile long. And he had crazy ideas about how to make money. Ideas that didn't seem exactly honest. Rob Peter to pay Paul, that sort of thing. Danny never got caught up in the schemes, but Todd wasn't what I think of as ethical. He struck me as a man who wasn't above cutting corners. But then I'm a fine one to talk, aren't I?"

"Even the most perfect people fall from grace," Tinkie said. "Cut yourself some slack. You're okay. Sarah Booth is okay. No one was harmed. Just talk to that therapist, like you promised."

"Okay." But Pearl didn't sound convinced.

We crested the bridge again, and I automatically slowed. Someone was standing by the rail looking down into the water. His pickup truck, an older model, was pulled so close to the bridge railing the passenger side was completely blocked. The solitary man stood staring down into the water, as if he were mesmerized.

"Who is that?" Tinkie asked with alarm in her voice.

"That's Wylie Moulton," Pearl said. "He's Todd's friend." I couldn't tell by her tone or expression how she felt about him.

We slowed and when Wylie flagged us down, we stopped. He came up to the passenger window by Tinkie and looked in the car. "Pearl, how are you? I know you must be beside yourself with worry. You and Danny go way back, and as far as I know, he's missing and in trouble."

"I'm fine, Wylie. I'm sorry to hear about Todd. I know you were close."

Wylie was a handsome man with a mustache and dark, quick eyes. "I'm going to find out who hurt him and make that person pay. I just stopped up here on the bridge to pay a little tribute to Todd."

"Did they rule his death a homicide?" I asked.

"Wylie, this is Ms. Delaney and Mrs.—"

"I know who they are." Wylie's voice grew hard. "They were hanging out with that land buyer. I saw them at the café in Zinnia." He spat on the ground. "I got nothing for those parasites who come to feed off the blood of the farmers. They pretend to be all pro-farmer, but it's just a honey-coated trap to steal our land. They're worse than the bankers."

"Wylie! That's no way to treat Tinkie or Sarah Booth. They're trying to help find Danny and they don't have anything to do with that Levi Butler character."

"Drive a man to suicide and then pretend to hunt for him. Great plan." The sarcasm in his voice was thick enough to cut with a knife.

"Mr. Richmond at the bank has done all he can to help the local farmers." Pearl wasn't backing down. "If you'd been in church on Sunday, you would have heard the report on all that's being done. Do you think they want to see foreign investors buy up the Delta?"

"Danny always said you were too sweet and naïve for this mean world," Wylie said. "Better get home so Micah can cover you in Bubble Wrap and keep you safe."

Wylie Moulton was furious. At me, at Tinkie, at Pearl, at Micah, at the lending institutions, and at the church. I understood. His best friend was dead, possibly the victim of foul play. Maybe because of the crushing debt he, too, faced. But I still needed answers. "What happened to Todd?" I asked. "Has the sheriff pinpointed the cause of death?"

"They won't tell me, but they don't have to. Todd was supposed to meet up with Danny to take him some supplies. Just upriver. That's where Danny is hiding out. But when Todd got there, Danny killed him."

"Why? Why would Danny do that?" Pearl's voice was strained. "Danny isn't like that and you know it, Wylie. He wouldn't harm anyone. What's wrong with you?"

"I'm tired of working fourteen-hour days in the heat and cold and ending up owing more to the bank or feedstore than the profit I make from my crops. Farmers can't keep on like this. Who's going to feed everyone if we stop farming?"

He wasn't lying about the cost of being a farmer, but his anger was misplaced. We were all in the same boat. Maybe not Tinkie, because Oscar had long ago sold off his farmland, and Tinkie's folks had been bankers and merchants, not farmers. They weren't linked to the land in the way that I was. Or that the farmers were. But the Richmonds were just as linked to the farm families in the Delta. The web of farming, crops, and money connected us all.

"Todd's body was found upriver," I said, watching Wylie carefully for his reaction. He was volatile. I didn't want him to jump down Pearl's throat again or say more mean things to Tinkie. "Why are you here on the river?"

"I can be wherever I want to be," he said hotly.

I tried to bring him back to reality. "Why would Danny harm Todd? They were friends."

"Danny owed Todd money. He owed everyone money."

"And you think this money was the motive for murder?"

He had the decency to hesitate. His cheeks flushed red. "I don't have any proof, but I know. Danny was frantic. He was desperate to hang on until harvesttime. He thought he was going to make it all up when he sold his soybeans and cotton. But have you looked at the weather? We've had spring floods, a rainy May, then hot temperatures ten degrees above normal. June hasn't been any better. We need rain now. Not a chance of precipitation according to the forecasters. The farmers are screwed. By this time next year, a lot of the huge farms won't be nearly as big as they are now—if they even still exist." I couldn't argue with that.

We'd been lucky to avoid traffic, but I could see a line of vehicles approaching. Time to quit blocking the bridge. "Wylie, we need to move our cars."

He nodded. "Do you know how Todd died?"

"I don't." I could answer honestly. Neither Doc nor Coleman had told me the official verdict.

"I'll be in touch." He jumped into his truck and drove away fast. I got behind the wheel and followed, but at a calmer pace. It wasn't far to the cottage where Micah and Pearl lived, and we had plenty of time.

20

It didn't take long to arrive at the parsonage. As we pulled into the yard, Pearl put a hand on Tinkie's and my shoulders. "Please don't tell Micah," she pleaded again. "He will worry. I've done enough damage. I don't need to make a good man suffer needlessly. Micah's the kind of man who will try to keep me close enough to watch. He'll feel guilty if he needs to visit a parishioner or do his job. I promise I won't try to hurt myself again. I don't want to put that burden on him."

But was it fair to put that burden on me and Tinkie? What if we didn't tell Micah and Pearl took another action to harm herself? Tinkie stepped up.

"We told you we wouldn't discuss this with anyone," Tinkie said. "Don't make us regret this, Pearl. You could really mess up Sarah Booth's head and mine, too."

"I won't. I swear it. On a stack of Bibles." She grinned and at last I felt she'd gotten her feet up under her. "Will you let me know if you find out anything about Todd Jenkins? I know his death is somehow involved with everything else going on now."

"We'll let you know everything we can," I said.

She nodded and opened the car door. The front door of the house opened, and Micah came out. The look of relief on his face made me wonder if someone had told him about Pearl's action.

"Where have you been?" He came up to the car, trying hard to appear casual instead of worried. "I've been looking for you everywhere."

"I was just taking some time to be on the river." Pearl was flustered, but she managed to make sense.

Micah finally seemed to become aware of me and Tinkie and he tried for a smile. "The world can be a dangerous place, Pearl. I worry that you're too trusting."

"You're right about that, Micah. We were telling Pearl much the same thing. The May rains up north of us are still impacting the rivers. The currents can be treacherous," I said.

"Sarah Booth, Mrs. Richmond, thank you for bringing her home." He turned back to Pearl. "Do you mind if I ask why you were at the river?" I was just glad the hot sun had baked us all dry.

"I meant to walk down to the water and sit on the sandbar," Pearl said. "Sarah Booth saw me on the bridge and stopped." She put a hand on her husband's arm. "Have you heard about Todd Jenkins?"

He nodded. "Some of the men came by to tell me. It appears that river is bad luck these days. Tragedy on top of tragedy."

He'd cracked a door that I had to push open. "This may sound crazy, but have you ever seen any . . . spirits on the bridge?" I asked. Why did it feel so wrong to ask a man who believed in God about a spirit?

Micah wasn't a man who took offense easily. He smiled, this time with genuine warmth. "I've heard stories about a woman in white on that bridge," he said, putting his arm around Pearl. "I always thought the ghost stories came from the death of a local woman who drowned in the river. Charline Smith. You know how folks like to take a tragedy and spin it into a story. But I don't know the facts for certain. It happened before I moved to Leflore County."

"Charline Smith." Sure, I'd heard the name and some of the story from Doc, but I wanted to know what Micah knew.

"She killed herself jumping off the bridge, didn't she?" Tinkie asked. "I remember hearing Mother talk about it. Or I should say speculate. Mother didn't believe it really happened, but some folks have said that the Charline Smith story was the inspiration for the Gentry song." Tinkie pursed her lips. "I always thought the whole Charline Smith story was a fabrication. Something the grown-ups made up to scare us kids away from the river, because of the treacherous currents."

"When was Charline supposed to have jumped?" I asked.

"I'm not certain." Tinkie kept the conversational ball bouncing. "I know it was before the 1970s. Birth control had just become available, but only married women could get it. And if this incident was inspiration for the song . . . It had to have happened before 1967. That's when the song came out," Tinkie said quietly.

Pearl had gone pasty white at all the talk of suicide. "That was all made-up foolishness, I think. I don't believe there was ever a Charline Smith."

"Have you ever seen a ghost?" I asked Micah.

He shook his head. "No. Not me. I wonder if it would scare me if I did. I kind of feel sorry for ghosts. They're stuck, aren't they? Unable to move on. Caught between heaven and Earth."

He made a sad point. I sure hoped Jitty wasn't trapped in the in-between. I'd always felt she chose to stay near me. But what if her punishment for staying close to me was to never be able to join Coker, her husband, wherever he was? I had to push that thought away. As much as I needed Jitty, I would never ask her to forgo being with her husband and family.

"Who was this Charline Smith?" Tinkie asked.

Micah waved us to a picnic table under an oak tree. "I've heard the talk and the stories. Now, I'm not saying all of this is true. She was a local woman. It's the same old tired story. She fell in love with a married man, got pregnant, and rather than destroy his marriage, she took her own life by drowning."

"Why is it that the woman always pays the harshest price?" I blurted.

Micah agreed. "It's very unfair that women always bear the burden of guilt. I don't agree with it. It takes two to break a marriage vow. Or make a baby." He put his arm around Pearl's shoulders. "I remember reading *The Scarlet Letter* for the first time in college. Hester Prynne had to wear the 'A' of adultery, but Dimmesdale, supposedly a man of God, got off scot-free. That wasn't right. It's taken decades for mankind to get beyond that point of blaming the woman, and now I see our society slipping backward. It's disheartening."

I wondered how much of his speech was designed to show Pearl she was forgiven for whatever she'd done. There were so many parallels I'd never have thought of with Nathaniel Hawthorne's work of fiction. Dimmesdale was a minister. Hester Prynne gave birth to a child named Pearl. Hester paid the heavy price of her "sin." Micah was a well-read man. Surely he saw those comparisons, and yet he didn't run from them. My admiration for Micah increased, again.

"You grew up in Mississippi?" Tinkie asked Micah.

"Across the river in Arkansas. My parents were sharecroppers on a row crop farm. I have a lot of sympathy for what farmers endure." His expression fell into sadness.

"Micah's mother died when he was ten," Pearl explained.

"His daddy was a good man but he was exhausted at the end of the day. He had to make a living and provide for his children by himself. Micah learned to cook and take care of the other kids while his dad was in the field."

"My heart is always with the man who farms the land," Micah said. "I think that's one reason my little church has done so well in Leflore County. And I love the land and the people of Mississippi."

The parallels between the past and the present were very clear to me. Perhaps there was an answer there that would help me. "I'm very interested in folklore regarding the river," I said. "You seem to be a student of regional history here. Can you tell me anything about the legends of the Tallahatchie?"

"I can't," he said. "Like most folks, I just take it for granted that the river out there is the Tallahatchie. I know it was named for a Native tribe. I understand there were at least twenty-one Native tribes in Mississippi before their land was taken. The Tallahatchie people were a small tribe. That's about all I know, but now I want to know more."

Pearl circled her arm around his waist. "I've often wondered what life was like here when Indigenous people inhabited the area." Pearl sighed. "Before the Europeans began to carve out and claim the land for their own. I think European civilization has done so much damage. Yes, penicillin is grand to have, but if we don't stop cutting down our forests and polluting the oceans and the air, we're going to reach a tipping point that can't be undone."

That wasn't a sentiment I heard a lot of in the rural areas of the state, but I agreed with Pearl. So-called progress was often not a good thing.

Micah pointed at the church. "I have to go work on my

sermon for Sunday. Thanks for bringing Pearl home. I'm glad you got to her before she could take a dip in the river. The rushing water can be dangerous even to wade in."

He didn't look at Pearl, but I couldn't help but wonder if somehow he knew what had happened. But that was between Pearl and her husband.

"Micah, did you know Todd Jenkins?" Tinkie asked.

"I knew him." His voice was flat.

"Wylie Moulton seems to think that Danny Anderson may have killed Todd." I waited for his reaction.

Micah shook his head. "I don't see that, but Danny was under a lot of pressure. Todd didn't always walk on the right side of the law, though. Hard for me to imagine those two having a lot in common. I don't see Danny taking up with him."

"Tell me about Todd Jenkins," I suggested. Micah would give the most objective view of Todd I was likely to get. He struck me as the kind of man who would speak the truth without trying to color things to win approval for his view.

"Todd came to a few services," he said. "I don't think God's word was his real objective. He had something of a . . . fascination with one member of the congregation."

"Vera Volt," Tinkie said.

"Yes, Vera. It's a shame, but Vera likes to toy with people. Especially men who are drawn to her."

"Passion with a praying mantis," Pearl said. Micah tried not to laugh, but he couldn't stop himself.

"That's not very charitable, Pearl."

"But it's true," she said. "Todd was nobody's idea of a grand prize, but I never knew him to be deliberately cruel. I can't say the same about Vera."

"Did they have anything going? I can't say." Micah took a few steps toward the church. "I think Vera was a challenge for some of the men. She was feisty and cruel. They wanted to tame her. Todd was no exception."

"What about Danny?" Tinkie asked. "Was he smitten by Vera, too?"

Micah thought about it while Pearl looked down at her hands.

"For the past two years, Danny was focused on farming. Only farming. He was worried. He knew things were going sideways for him. I know Vera wanted him to make a move, but what went on between them, I don't know. Vera is what I call a 'predator,' and I don't mean that as someone harming young children. She saw all *men* as prey."

"Vera is a woman who likes to chase a man. When she catches him, she's done. If she had anything going with Danny, it had already run its course," Pearl said.

"That sums it up," Micah agreed.

"We talked with Vera," Tinkie said. "I have to point out that she didn't seem interested in Danny at all. She was focused on you, Micah."

"Plenty of the ladies get a crush on Micah," Pearl said. "We just ignore them, and it passes."

"Even with Vera?" I asked and was rewarded when Micah flushed red. "She doesn't strike me as someone who takes defeat with grace." There was something more here. If Pearl was mooning after Danny, was it possible that Micah had acted on the invitation Vera had clearly given?

"Vera is more persistent than most," Micah admitted. "I managed to avoid being alone with her most of the time. But Pearl paid the price for it. Vera is determined to have what she thinks she wants, and when she was thwarted, she took it out on Pearl. I've traced some of the fake rumors directly back to Vera."

"Did you consider taking legal action?" Tinkie asked. "I've known Vera awhile. She's vicious when she doesn't get her way. And she can do damage. It isn't just words."

"Pearl and I talked about it, but Pearl didn't want to press the matter. She believed Vera would grow tired of torturing her and move on to someone else."

"And did she?" I asked.

Pearl's smile was tinged with sadness. "No. I was wrong. But I don't know that making a huge issue out of it would have made for a better outcome."

"Did Vera steal the christening gown from your attic?" I asked.

"I believe she did." Micah sighed. "I saw her coming out of the house with a bundle of clothes. I clearly saw the baby blanket Pearl had saved, and I believe the christening gown was hidden in the blanket."

"Why didn't you say so?" Tinkie asked.

"I had only suspicions. No evidence. I didn't go up in the attic to see what she might have taken." He looked over at his wife. "We didn't want to stir the pot with an accusation we couldn't back up."

"And you think she would have buried it on the river?"

"Now, that part doesn't make any sense to me at all," Micah admitted. "Vera doesn't strike me as a woman who enjoys digging holes on a sandbar."

He had a point there. But if Vera hadn't buried it, who had? Maybe Todd Jenkins had been doing her bidding.

21

Tinkie and I had just driven away from the little church when my phone rang. Coleman was on the line. I put it on speaker as we flew through the fields of cotton and soybeans, the green plants lush in the afternoon sun. On the horizon a bank of clouds looked like two dragons ready to rumble. The beauty of the landscape never failed to leave me in awe.

"What's going on?" I asked. "Tinkie is in the car with me. She's listening, so keep it clean."

Coleman only chuckled. "In your dreams," he said. "But in deference to Tinkie, I won't talk about your kinky sexual preferences."

"Coleman!" I realized too late that teasing him came at a price.

"Tell me! Tell me!" Tinkie chimed in.

They were ganging up on me. "If you say one word—"

"I'm sorry, Sarah Booth," Coleman said. "I did promise not to talk about how you like to eat popcorn from my navel. Tinkie, Sarah Booth says I have the sexiest navel she's ever seen.

And when she goes for that buttery, salty kernel . . ." He gave a low, sexy moan.

"You two! Stop it. Coleman, why are you really calling?"

"Not good news, Sarah Booth. There was another robbery overnight. I'm just hearing about it. Another drugstore, this time in Vicksburg along the Mississippi River. Store video shows a man who looks a lot like the guy who robbed the feedstore here and the drugstore in Leflore County."

Coleman hadn't mentioned the hardware store because there was no video there.

"Is it Danny Anderson?" Tinkie asked.

"There hasn't been a positive identification. He's wearing a hat and a mask, so the facial-recognition programs didn't flag anyone. Budgie says it could be Danny, though. Based on build. And Budgie is positive it's the same man who robbed the feedstore."

"What was stolen?" I asked, hoping it wasn't narcotics.

"Money. And drugs."

"How much money?" Tinkie asked.

"Less than five thousand. The store was closed and the pharmacist had taken most of the money to the bank."

"What kind of drugs?" I asked.

"Oxy and fentanyl."

He didn't have to say those drugs could easily be sold for a nice amount of cash. We were all thinking it. But still, it couldn't be nearly enough money to make a difference in Danny's debt.

"This isn't making sense," Tinkie said.

I agreed. I didn't see the logic of these actions if it was our missing farmer.

Tinkie continued, "If he is in such a dire financial situation that he's willing to steal, why isn't he hitting some place with more money? Drugstores don't keep a lot of cash on hand after closing. Drug supplies are kept at a minimum because of the danger of theft. Danny isn't stupid. He knows this. Something about this isn't right."

"It doesn't feel like a serious robbery attempt." Coleman said exactly what I was thinking. "Remember, he's seemingly working alone."

"What else could it be?" My mind was churning.

"It could be someone attempting to set Danny up." Tinkie saw it before I did.

"That's brilliant. But to what end?" I still didn't have a clear picture.

"Danny is in financial trouble," Coleman said. "If he's also in a legal bind, he can't do a damn thing to clear his name. I'm not saying this is the situation, but if Danny is set up to look like a dangerous criminal, a thief who would rob people who've helped him in the past, he won't be able to fight for a way to save his farm. He'll be forced to remain in the shadows. Without Danny, the Anderson family will be forced to sell out."

"And who would benefit from this?" My question was rhetorical. Levi Butler was the first person who came to mind. He wanted the Anderson land. And he was a man who had no ethical boundaries, as far as I could tell.

"You can make a list. Be sure and include any real estate buyer who can push hard for foreclosure on the Anderson land. Danny's father would sell the whole place before he let it go to the bank. He would salvage what he could from the debt, but it wouldn't be much. They'd pretty much be destitute. That sale would only benefit the vultures who prey on the farmers. Then there are Danny's enemies, and he has a few," Coleman said. "Some folks are jealous of the respect Danny has earned with his work to keep the plight of the farmers before state and federal legislatures. Danny is highly regarded, and that pinches a few people's pride."

"That makes me angry," Tinkie said. "They won't do the hard work Danny does, but they want all the credit."

"Jealous people have always been dangerous," Coleman reminded her. "Danny is a likable guy. But that doesn't mean there aren't people who'd like to see him fail."

Coleman was right. "Whoever is doing this, if it is an attempt to destroy Danny, has planned it for a while. The only thing I can tell you is that it isn't Micah. I'm certain of that."

"Me, too," Tinkie chimed in. "We haven't resolved exactly the relationship between Pearl and Danny, but I can tell you this—whatever it is, Micah wouldn't hurt either of them. It's just not in his DNA."

"I never suspected him," Coleman concurred. "But it is someone close to Danny. And Sarah Booth, we need to find him. Or her. This financial sabotage is just the beginning. A person who would try to frame Danny as a thief and murderer—and Todd Jenkins is most profoundly dead—could very easily do much more damage. Physical damage. If it seems Danny can escape the blame for the robberies and somehow save his farm, the stakes could get much higher."

"Has Doc determined the exact cause of Jenkins's death? He was found in the river so the assumption is he drowned. Is there more?" I asked. Doc would call me—but his first report would be to Coleman.

"I'm going by the hospital now to talk to him. He did say it was definitely murder. I'll get the details. Where are you girls?"

I was a long time from being a girl, but I loved that Coleman viewed us that way. This was the benefit of long-term relationships. Coleman had known me in grammar school, when the "girl" descriptor would have been appropriate. He knew me through my twenties, and now into my mid-thirties. He had a historical sense of who I was, and I had the same bond with him. When I looked at him, would I always catch a glimpse of the sandy-haired, blue-eyed catcher on the high school baseball team tagging a runner out? I sure hoped so. Because even though those times were gone for both of us, I was so happy to still be able to glimpse them in a gesture, a look, or the way the sun struck Coleman's hair. Cherished moments in time. Coleman was a bridge back to a time when I had family.

"Sarah Booth has drifted away from us," Tinkie teased. "She's in la-la land. But I'll tell you we're leaving Micah and Pearl's. Not sure what else is on our agenda today." She looked at me, inviting me to speak up.

"Have you talked to Wylie Moulton?" I asked Coleman.

"Not yet. He's on my to-do list." Coleman sounded a little grim. "He's not one of my favorite people."

"Want us to talk to him?" I asked. Coleman had the power of his badge, but Tinkie had her feminine wiles.

"I'm tempted," Coleman admitted. "Let me—" He broke off and I could hear DeWayne talking to him. Apparently, someone had arrived at the sheriff's office to see Coleman.

"Well hello, Sugar Lips."

The voice was sultry and female, and she was talking to Coleman. Sugar Lips? Who the hell was this woman?

"My word, Brigette, it's been a month of Sundays since I thought about you. How are things in the Big Apple?"

"Exciting, tiring, exhilarating, frustrating . . . I bit off a lot more than I can chew with this modeling business. I needed to recharge my batteries, so I came home. So, where is Danny Anderson? Folks said you were looking for him. Danny isn't the kind of man to disappear. I'm worried enough to come home to help find him."

"What folks?"

"His parents. Oh, Coleman, you're on the phone. Finish your call and then you can take me for something to eat at Millie's Café. You know, there are many nights I dream about Millie's cooking. I can't eat a damn thing for fear of gaining an ounce, but dreams are calorie-free. And I am going to have one fine meal at Millie's before I have to go back on that diet."

"Is she the girl who left Greenwood to become a model?" I whispered to Tinkie.

Tinkie nodded. "Brigette McEachern. She was Danny's first wild love after high school. She left the Delta to be a model in New York. Very successful. And she's back right when Danny may need her most. This is exciting! We should call Cece right away so she can get some photos for the paper."

Tinkie was excited by the prospect of rekindling the flame between Danny and Brigette, though Pearl might not be so happy about it. I was pretty sure Pearl had feelings for Danny, even if she didn't act on them.

"Sarah Booth, I have to go. Brigette McEachern is back in town. I need to talk with her."

I felt a little twinge of jealousy myself. "I hope she has some ideas on where to find Danny. Coleman, why don't we meet you at Millie's? I need to speak with Ms. McEachern as well."

"I'll bring her to meet you and Tinkie there. I ate not too long ago. I have a few questions for Brigette, and then I'll cut her loose so you can talk with her. I only need a few minutes alone with her. I'd rather have lunch with you, but I have work that must be done."

"Perfect." I did appreciate his consideration for my feelings. "I'll see you when you finish up today."

"Anything we need to do before we meet Ms. McEachern?" Tinkie asked.

"Maybe we should check with the Vicksburg police to see if they will share any camera footage of the drugstore robbery."

"Excellent idea. I'll call Budgie and see if they will share it with him. You know they aren't likely to give it to any private investigators."

She was right about that. And Budgie was far smarter with technology than Tinkie or I. She placed the call and a moment later nodded with success. "Budgie is on it. Coleman had already asked him to get a copy of the footage."

I picked up my phone and placed a call to Cece. "Hey, can you help me out with some background on Brigette McEachern? I'll see if I can get her to agree to an interview with you."

"I heard she was in town! When are you meeting her?" Cece asked. "I remember when she left for New York. There was a parade in Greenwood in her honor. It was very exciting. She had been such a standout in high school. And you know she won the Miss Mississippi beauty pageant and went on to be first runner-up in the nation? Folks were calling Brigette the second Mary Ann Mobley."

I didn't know those things. My befuddled look made Tinkie sigh deeply.

"I forget how absolutely out of touch you are with popular culture and society," Tinkie said, speaking loud enough for Cece to hear. "Mary Ann Mobley was Miss America in 1959. She went on to be a television-and-film star and even starred with Elvis in two movies."

"She was a Mississippi girl?"

"From Biloxi. She was the nation's sweetheart. Folks all over the world were saying that Mississippi had the prettiest girls in the world. And now we have Brigette. She's going to be a superstar. Mark my words."

"Well, let's head to Millie's, then. I have to see this world phenomenon."

We set off driving over the speed limit, which was par for the course. I was eager to meet Brigette. Mississippi could certainly use a spokesperson with élan who gave the state some artistry and class. Our elected officials were too often laughingstocks.

22

The parking lot of Millie's Café was packed. Cars and trucks were even parked across the road in a lot that was only used for things like the Christmas parade. The word was clearly out that Brigette was home.

Coleman and a beautiful woman with dark hair and expressive brown eyes were sitting in the back at a table. Folks were not bothering them, but Brigette was the focus of attention for all of the café patrons. Some were snapping photos of her from a respectful distance, and I could see why. She was something special. There were people who had the "it" factor, and Brigette was definitely an It Girl.

We approached the table, and she stood up. "I've heard so much about the detective agency you ladies run. Ms. Delaney, Ms. Richmond, I sure hope you can find Danny." She shook our hands and indicated we should sit.

We talked for a moment before Millie came over to take our order. Cece was right on Millie's heels, and I made an introduction. Coleman indicated I should step outside with him as he said his goodbyes to everyone.

When we were outside of the café, he said, "Ask her about Danny."

I nodded. "Sure. They were an item after high school, I think."

"Get as many details as you can."

"What are you thinking?"

"Whatever went on between Danny and Brigette, it was a decade ago. Don't you find it strange she is suddenly back in Mississippi right when he's missing, and maybe in trouble?"

I thought about it. "I don't know, Coleman. If they were really close, she may not have romantic feelings for him any longer, but maybe just friendship. Or maybe she's decided she'd like a relationship."

Coleman nodded, but it didn't seem I'd really convinced him.

"I'll see you tonight when I finish work. I want to check that footage from the drugstore in Vicksburg. And I need to talk to Doc. He's finished the autopsy on Todd."

"Be careful." A chill suddenly made goose bumps dance across my skin. Or maybe it was an omen. I wanted to tell him about Pearl, but I'd given her my word. What troubled me was a nagging sense of danger. I just couldn't pin down the source of my concern.

"I have a sense Brigette has a motive for her visit home. Try to find out what it is."

I put my hand on his arm. "Do you think she's up to no good?"

He shook his head. "No. It isn't that. It's just that her timing is . . . interesting. She may know where Danny is."

If she and Danny had been close in the past, she might know where he would hole up. And Coleman was right in noting that her appearance at this particular time did raise some questions.

I kissed Coleman before returning to the table with my friends. Brigette was telling Cece about a photo shoot in the snow, and she had everyone at the table laughing about her struggle to control chill bumps. As I listened to her, I thought again of my first love—theater. That was a world where appearances and talent were front and center, much like modeling. My life was so different now. I wore my jeans and boots and dressed for comfort and mobility. I ate what I wanted. And I drank with my friends. The decision to come home to Mississippi hadn't been my first choice, but it had worked out in the long run. I'd come home with my tail tucked between my legs, but I'd found friendships and love that I'd never anticipated. Not to mention my critters. The horses, dogs, cat, and raven made my life all the better.

I settled into a place at the table and gave Millie a smile.

"Your regular?" she asked.

I nodded. It was a good day for fried okra, green beans, sliced tomatoes, and slaw. I turned to Brigette. She really was a beautiful woman. But it was more than physical perfection. She had that unspoken star quality. Plus, the devil danced in her eyes.

"What brings you home?" I asked.

"My little sister is getting married."

"Congratulations to the groom and best wishes to the bride. When's the wedding?"

She smiled. "To be determined."

It was an unusual answer, and I looked across at Tinkie.

"It's hard to find a venue in June," Tinkie said. "A lot of the best places book out early."

"My sister is . . . not thrilled that I'm here. My mother is pressuring her to name me as a bridesmaid, but Donna is resisting. And I don't blame her. This is her day. I don't want folks watching me when the focus should be her. I don't want to be in the wedding party. She has dozens of friends who can do it."

"I thought you might have come home to help us find Danny. Did you?" Cece asked the money question.

Brigette was saved from answering when Millie brought the steaming plates of food to the table. It took a few minutes for us to settle down, but Brigette answered before she took a bite of her food.

"I do hope I can make contact with Danny. I talked with his parents yesterday on the phone. They're worried sick and so am I. Danny isn't like this. When I heard he was missing, I knew something was really wrong."

"I heard you and Danny were an item," Cece said.

Brigette's smile was sunny and whatever her memories, they seemed to be good ones. "We were, for a time. I was a senior in high school and he had just graduated two years before me. Danny loved the land. He knew every kind of tree and plant growing in Mississippi. He knew the best fishing holes. He was elected to the national Farmers for the Environment group and testified in Congress on behalf of changing farming practices to wean farmers off chemicals, herbicides, and dangerous fertilizers." Her eyes teared up. "And Danny also made me believe I could follow my dream and achieve it. He didn't laugh at me or try to hold me back."

"It takes a secure man to support a person who is leaving."

"I know." Her smile was tinged with sadness. "I love Danny. I always will. But he was so bound to the land—which is a good thing. He loves this place and its people. I was suffocating here."

"I completely understand." It was Cece who spoke, and I was reminded of how many offers she'd had for jobs as a journalist. Yet she had stayed in Zinnia. Tinkie, too, could have gone far away. She had the money and the family connections to have led a very different life.

"I do get homesick a lot," Brigette admitted. "But my life is in the city. Danny understood this better than anyone else. Even though he knew I'd leave him, he encouraged me to dream big. That is a generous heart, to give another person the freedom to grow and leave."

She was right about that. Aunt Loulane had done that for me after my parents died. She'd protected me while still allowing me the freedom to decide my own fate. Currently, I was watching Tinkie struggle with that overwhelming need to protect little Maylin but not to the point of suffocation. It was a fine line that she and Oscar walked.

"Why are you home now?" I asked Brigette. "I'm not buying the whole wedding story."

Her smile was crooked and she nodded. "You're right. I'm here because Danny is missing. I booked a flight home the minute I heard."

"Do you have any idea where he might be?" Tinkie asked.

"I've rented a boat. I'm going to check along the Tallahatchie. We spent many wonderful afternoons on that river." Her voice sounded wistful.

Was Brigette the woman Danny really loved? Would Pearl view her as a rival or a friend?

"When did you arrive in the Delta?" Cece asked Brigette.

It was the perfect question.

"I've been here a day or two." Brigette gave one of her movie-star smiles, but it didn't hide the fact that she was deliberately vague about her arrival. Why?

"Danny's been gone for several days now. How did you hear?" I asked. I tried hard to make the question sound merely conversational, but Brigette was no fool. She knew we were grilling her for a purpose.

"I'm still close with people who love Danny." And again, she was vague with her answer.

"Who might that be?" Tinkie followed up.

"People we went to school with. Our class was small, and we developed strong ties."

"Did Danny's parents call you?" I pushed.

Brigette was raising her hackles over the grilling. We tried to keep it light, but she understood exactly what we were doing. "No, I spoke with the Andersons only once, to tell them I was coming home and wanted to help look for Danny. Why do you care who called me?"

It was an opening, if I could finesse my answer sufficiently. "Tinkie's husband, Oscar, has hired us to find Danny. Everyone is very worried. If you know anything that might help, please just tell us." I put it there for her to accept or reject. "Did Danny call you?" I pressed.

"I haven't spoken to Danny," she insisted. "That's the truth. I'd tell you if I had."

"We are worried sick," Tinkie said. "Many of the farmers are in a rough spot. Danny isn't the only one."

"But he's the one who will take it the hardest," Brigette said. "Danny is the most responsible person I've ever met. For him to lose the family land—that will kill him. It would be kinder to put a bullet in his brain."

Tinkie blanched. She turned her head to hide her dismay.

"No one is going to do anything rash," I said. "We're going to find Danny. He's going to figure out how to save his land, and this whole thing will be another legend for the Delta."

I turned to Brigette. “Are there any places you know where Danny might go to hide out?”

“We only want to help Danny,” Tinkie said, “but you have to be honest and tell us if you know where he is. Please, let us help.”

23

The din of the café had quieted, and Tinkie's plea had silenced all of the voices at our table. For a moment, I thought Brigette might stand up and bolt. Anger snapped in her eyes, but she inhaled calmly and didn't leave. Instead, she nodded. "I'll check along the river. My boat rental is scheduled for tomorrow morning. If I see anything, I will tell you."

"Why the river?" Cece asked. She'd been quiet and mostly taking in what everyone else said.

"Like I said, we have a lot of memories together there. Danny had a special bond with the Tallahatchie," Brigette said. "We both did. We came of age on that river."

"Brigette, it might be best if you told us the locations and let a search and rescue team look around first," I tried to persuade her. I wanted to protect her from finding her friend dead somewhere along the river, but it was clear she wasn't going to fully trust me.

"I'm not a fool, Sarah Booth. I know Danny is wanted for questioning in a series of robberies. I know people are saying he killed that scoundrel Todd Jenkins. I can tell you one hundred percent that Danny would never harm another living creature. I mean, he wouldn't even hunt. When we went fishing, he threw the fish back. That's who Danny is, not some crazed killer and robber."

"Did you also know Todd?" I asked. It would be good to set up a timeline of who and what Brigette knew.

"I did. Todd and his constant companion Wylie Moulton."

"And your opinion?" Tinkie prodded.

"Todd was sad and Wylie was mean. But Danny wouldn't forsake them. They went to school together and he had some kind of misplaced loyalty to both of them."

"Who do you think killed Todd?" I asked.

"How was he killed?" she asked.

I didn't have the answer to that, but I would before the day was out. "The autopsy is complete, but I haven't seen the report."

"I assumed he'd drowned." Brigette waited for a response.

"I don't think so," Tinkie said. "Doc is taking his sweet time on the autopsy so we don't have official word. Rumor is that he had a head wound, which could have happened after he fell in the river and drowned. Or it could have happened before."

"Why would Danny want to hurt Todd?" Brigette questioned. "It doesn't make any sense."

I couldn't argue that point. Danny killing Todd didn't make sense, but often murder did not. "Do you know anything about buried treasure on the river?" I asked.

Brigette nodded, and her expression lightened. "Well, I know the legends. The whole buried treasure thing was part of our childhood. We loved listening to the stories, pretending to be pirates, and speculating on what kind of treasure might be lying in the sand. We would camp out on the sandbars and search for treasure supposedly buried by explorers like De Soto. It was a total fabrication—a game we played as young teens, trying to act grown-up. I can't believe folks are still talking about that foolishness. Trust me, we dug up every sandbar along the river for miles. If anything had been buried there, we would have found it. We had metal detectors and about every other tool of the treasure hunter."

"And you found nothing?" Cece had her notepad out and was jotting notes. "Would you mind posing for a photo on one of the sandbars for an article in the paper? It would make my day."

Brigette shrugged. "Sure. I'll let you know when I get back downriver tomorrow. We can meet by the bridge in LeFlore County."

That was exactly the bridge where I'd seen a ghost. I had to ask: "Brigette, have you ever heard of any ghosts on that bridge?"

She laughed, and I was charmed by her open amusement. "I love ghost stories, and there are several good ones about the bridge. Some folks have said they saw a woman in a white dress on the bridge. I've heard she committed suicide but rued her decision to jump, so she returns to the bridge to try to change the outcome. Of course, you can't undo history."

I must have paled, because she looked at me long and hard. "Have you seen anything?"

I wanted to play it off as a joke, but I couldn't. "Yes. I have."

"The woman in the white dress?" she asked.

I nodded. "I saw her just the other day. Just standing at the rail, looking down at the water, and then she was gone."

"Did she look at you?" Brigette asked, and there was something dark behind her question.

"Why?"

"The alleged ghost, Charline Smith, was related to Todd Jenkins. Some believe that if she makes eye contact with you, a terrible fate will befall you. I know people who claim to have seen her spirit on the bridge, but they just drove through her and kept going. Folks are afraid of her spirit. In more recent years, the legend has faded."

"She's related to Todd? That's a new tidbit. I have to say, the irony is bitter. That they both died on the river," Cece said. "But back to the legend. If you make eye contact with the ghost, what exactly happens?"

Brigette looked at me, gauging my reaction before she spoke. "The story varies. Some have said anyone who makes eye contact could be driven to madness and take their own life. Other stories say if it is a healthy young woman, she will conceive. I've heard of women who have gone to the bridge to try to make eye contact with her. They were having fertility issues, and they were desperate."

"And did they conceive?" My whole body had tightened at the idea of a pregnancy. Did I even want a child? Could I bring an innocent soul into a world that was destroying itself with greed? I had big, big issues around having a child in this world that was on fire.

"The three I know of did."

I didn't think she was pulling my leg. She believed what she was saying.

"Would you mind sharing their names?" Cece asked. "I mean, a happy ending is something everyone loves. This will make a fabulous story. I can see that bridge and the ghost becoming like a tourist destination for the infertile. That could really bump the economy of Leflore County, and it also gives that bridge and the river some redemption from some pretty bad history."

Brigette laughed. "Sure, let me ask them first. But what about Mrs. Richmond here? Did you see the ghost? I heard your little girl was a terrific surprise to you and your husband."

I was a little unsettled that Brigette knew about Tinkie's little girl. When Maylin was born, it was a big topic of talk. Most people were thrilled, and so they told the story of the miracle birth. Tinkie had wanted a child for a long time, but her body didn't cooperate. Until it did. But Maylin was old news these days.

"Oh, Maylin was definitely a surprise. The best surprise of my life," Tinkie said. She whipped out her phone and started showing Brigette photos.

"She's gorgeous, and the camera loves her," Brigette said. "I'm doing a photo shoot at Morgan Freeman's blues club. Could I borrow Maylin for a few shots? We'll pay her a professional wage."

Tinkie's face brightened, and I saw the fever of a big idea hatching. "Yes, of course. But what if we did a fundraiser for the farmers? To help them pay their debts. We could let folks bring their babies and have a photograph taken with you. Would you consider it? We could sell calendars, mugs with photos, T-shirts. A whole store of items to help the farmers."

"I'd be honored," Brigette said.

"Great idea." Cece was all over it, and even Millie paused from serving her customers to applaud the idea.

Cece stood up. "I have to get back to the paper. Ed will be looking for me, and he can be a bear if he thinks I'm playing when I should be working."

Brigette checked her watch. "Me, too. I have a fitting for a dress for the wedding. I'm trying to avoid this, but I need to show up for my sister. She's making a huge deal out of this and it's easier to go along."

I hadn't gotten to the meat of my questions. "Have another glass of iced tea," I said. "Please."

"Okay, but only for a short visit. I do have people expecting me."

I waited until Millie went back to the cash register and Cece was gone. I didn't mind them hearing, but I suspected Brigette would be more forthcoming if we were alone.

"Before you go, can I follow up on the ghost?" I avoided looking at Tinkie, who was definitely watching me.

"I'm sure you know the same stories I know, Sarah Booth." Brigette wasn't evasive, but she was ready to go.

"Humor me. Did Todd Jenkins's relative really kill herself?" Growing up in Leflore County on the river, Brigette had access to stories and legends I might not.

"She did drown. That's a fact. Some say she jumped off the bridge hoping to cause a miscarriage but she ended up drowning."

"Is it true?"

"She died. And she drowned. Those are facts. Was she pregnant? I don't know. Was this the inspiration for a song? I highly doubt it. I'm sure Todd's relative isn't the only woman confronting an unwanted pregnancy who took drastic action, *if* that is what happened at all."

"We heard she had an affair with a married man and got pregnant." I felt like I was beating a dead horse, but I had to keep plugging.

She shrugged. "Humans have sex all the time. Pregnancies happen."

"And what about the hidden treasure on the river?" Tinkie followed up. "Do you think it's real?"

"It was fantasy for us. Some say De Soto buried treasures on the river when he was exploring. Precious metals and things he stole from the Indigenous peoples. But there are other tales, too."

"If my life were in danger, I think I'd leave wealth behind," Tinkie said.

"Any reasonable person would." Brigette checked her watch again. She was getting antsy.

"What kind of wealth?" I asked. "The land was the real wealth for the planter class."

"True, but there was still portable wealth, like gold and silver. Jewels. Confederate dollars, which ended up being worthless except to collectors."

"And the rich families decided to flee down the river?"

"Supposedly. It was only a handful, but it was enough that the guesstimates of the wealth they were attempting to move would be worth many millions in today's dollars."

"Did they make it safely to New Orleans?" I asked.

Brigette pondered for a moment. "Remember, this is all local legend. How much is true, I can't say. But according to the stories, they never made it off the Tallahatchie. They disappeared into thin air, and their wealth with them."

One of the things I loved best about Mississippi was the local folklore. The South had, for a long time, been a decade behind the rest of the world. Traditions of family dinners and sitting on front porches shelling peas and butter beans and passing along history and lore were strong in my home state. Or had been in the past. Now folks were hooked to phones or tablets or televisions. The art of good storytelling was fading. But for a time, Mississippi had produced incredible literary talent, and I believed it all stemmed from that oral tradition.

"How did they disappear?" Tinkie asked her.

Brigette shrugged. "I've asked that question a number of times and no one ever gives me a satisfactory answer. Either they were set upon and killed by thieves or they made it down to New Orleans and quietly set up house there, or maybe they went on to Europe. England was a friend to the South and would likely have offered sanctuary. But no one seems to know what actually happened. Or if anything happened at all."

"You're right. The whole tale could be fabricated," Tinkie said.

"Is this the treasure you and Danny used to hunt?" I asked Brigette.

"Yes. We were all starry-eyed about finding the money and building a grand life. We were children. Danny and I have been friends since the sixth grade. We didn't get romantically involved until he was out of high school."

"Someone has been digging along the riverbanks. At least the ones by the local bridge."

"Kids still looking for that treasure?" she asked, amused.

"Maybe."

She read my expression. "But you think it's something more sinister."

"Maybe."

She made an exasperated noise. "Say it plainly, Sarah Booth. I don't have time to play guessing games. If there's something related to Danny, just say it."

I told her about the christening gown I'd found. And hinted at the rumors about Danny and the preacher's wife. She paled and then her cheeks turned red.

"I don't believe Danny would be involved with a married woman. Not any married woman, but especially not a preacher's wife. Even if he was head over heels in love with Pearl Wingard, he would not sleep with her. He wouldn't."

Brigette wasn't a naïve schoolgirl. She was working in a

tough business and she clearly had a good head on her shoulders. She knew exactly how power and wealth could corrupt. And how *lack* of power and wealth could sometimes also corrupt. "What do you make of the christening gown on the sandbar?"

"You think Pearl and Danny did something to a baby?" Brigette was incredulous. "You don't know anything about Danny. I only know Pearl vaguely. We were in school together, but Pearl wasn't that kind of girl. At a time when most girls were having sex and drinking, she wouldn't. I know she was teased about it. And Danny, I'm telling you straight up, he wanted children. He would never harm a child. Especially not his own. So, I assume the christening-gown business is exactly what Pearl said it was. Someone stole it from her attic and planted it on the riverbank to frame Danny and Pearl. Just like they're trying to frame Danny for Todd's murder."

"Who would do such a thing?" I pressed.

"Who stands to gain if Danny is driven away from his farm and his family?" Brigette countered.

"The land buyers and the banks." I said it, nodding at Tinkie when I did. "Oscar was trying to help Danny, but we don't actually know who all Danny owes money to, or how much."

"Are you even certain Danny is still alive?" Brigette asked, and her voice broke. "I want to see him. I want to help him."

"You've put a bug in Cece's ear and she'll put that article about you in the newspaper. Chances are Danny will see it. Is there a place he should meet you or any way he can contact you?"

Brigette nodded. She pulled a card from her pocket. "Here's my cell. Please have him call me if you find him. I have some resources. I can help him. He needs to come back to town and turn himself in. I'm terrified he's going to be hurt. I'm going to be on the river tomorrow, as I mentioned. He can find me if he wants to."

I thought of Wylie Moulton. I didn't trust him at all. I had no doubt he'd sell Danny out if he thought he could profit from it, but he'd been a classmate of Brigette and Danny. "What do you make of Wylie Moulton?" I asked Brigette.

"He and Todd were always close friends. Danny used to go fishing with them. I thought they had a friendship, but I can tell you Wylie is not to be trusted."

"Why do you say that?" I asked.

"If he had Danny's best interests at heart, he'd be on that river looking for Danny. Was he on the river with Todd? Has anyone been able to check it out?"

"You think Wylie would hurt Todd?" Tinkie asked.

"If there was money to be had, yes I do."

Brigette checked her watch again, and this time I stood up. It was time to go to visit Doc and see if the autopsy lent any insight into what had really happened to Todd Jenkins.

"If you learn anything, please let us know," Tinkie said to Brigette.

Brigette nodded.

"Do stop by and see the Andersons," I suggested. "They'll be glad to see you and know that you're in town to help find their son."

24

Doc was in his office at the local hospital. He wasn't shocked when Tinkie and I arrived. He assessed us to see if we were bleeding—he'd seen plenty of that—then patted his wild hair to make sure his glasses were there. "You two look fit as a fiddle, so I'm guessing you're here about the autopsy," he said. "Want some coffee?"

I viewed the coffeepot with trepidation. The brew Doc concocted could probably dissolve bones. "No, thanks. We just had tea at Millie's."

He poured a cup for himself and sat on the corner of his desk. "These autopsy results are reported to the Leflore County sheriff, but I'll share them with you. Todd Jenkins was murdered. Blunt-force trauma to the head. Looks like he was killed and dumped in the river. There wasn't any water in his lungs, so he was dead before he hit the water."

Doc was matter-of-fact about death, but he wasn't unkind. "Blunt force. Could you determine the weapon?"

"Something like a hammer. I can't be more specific right

now. The crime lab in Jackson is trying to help match some instruments with the wound. I may have more information later."

"What else can you tell us?" Doc knew more. I could tell.

"It was a violent death. He was struck on the shoulder from behind, but he tried to get away. The first blow must have prevented any real self-defense or escape—the clavicle and acromion were both broken and the head of the humerus was dislocated from the socket. It would appear he was yanked hard or possibly dragged. The second blow was the coup de grace. It shattered his skull. It wasn't a pretty way to die."

Doc could discover a lot, but he couldn't tell motive. And he couldn't tell me who had wielded the hammer or whatever tool killed Todd.

"Oh, it was a right-handed person, which doesn't really narrow the field of possible candidates much," Doc said. "Let me caution you about being on that river right now. Todd knew the lay of the land as well as anyone in these parts. He'd camped on the river for years. If someone harmed him so easily, you two would be easy pickings."

"Thanks, Doc. If you get more information, please call us."

"I'll call the sheriff." He said it with a stern look, but his eyes were twinkling.

"You do that. Coleman will just tell us anyway," I said.

He laughed. "Do you have any leads on finding Danny Anderson?"

I shook my head. "None. The more time passes, the more I fear that Danny has also been hurt."

"That worries me, too," Doc admitted. "Danny's disappearance has a lot of people upset and worried. You have no indication why he left or where he may have gone?"

"Danny owed money on loans he'd taken out. And not just

from banks. That's what folks think, but we don't know for certain if it's true. It could be any number of reasons."

"Coleman told me about the robberies. Is it Danny?"

"We don't know," I responded. "The video I've seen isn't clear enough for a positive ID of anyone. It could be Grandma Moses for all we can tell." I clapped a hand over my mouth. I was sounding more and more like my aunt Loulane every day!

"No prints or conclusive evidence?" Doc asked.

"None so far."

"What's your next step?" Doc asked.

"I'm going to bird-dog Brigette McEachern tomorrow. If she's meeting up with Danny, I'll find them."

"How?" Doc and Tinkie asked together.

"I'm going to rent a boat and follow her." I didn't see any other way to tail her.

"What about a drone?" Doc suggested.

"That's a great idea," Tinkie said. "And it would be safer."

"The only issue is that I don't know where on the river they might meet up," Doc said. "And I don't have a drone."

"But Harold does," Tinkie said. "He was using it for real estate. Checking out properties when folks came in asking for loans."

I had to hand it to Doc and Tinkie. They were smart. "That's good to know. Will you ask Harold?" I said to Tinkie.

"I will."

"Then when I'm on the river, tailing Brigette, assuming I have a signal, I can text you where I am so you can see if it is within range of the drone. The camera footage would be really helpful."

"How do you plan to get on Brigette's trail? I mean, you need to know where she's going to rent the boat and put in."

Doc was right about that, but I had a plan. "I'll be careful. I swear it."

"And if you find Danny?" Doc asked gently. "What then?"

I knew the right answer to give—so I did. "I'll contact Coleman instantly. Or the sheriff of Leflore County. Law officers can bring him in for questioning."

Doc and Tinkie looked at each other and rolled their eyes. "Like you'd just step back and hand it over to the police," Tinkie said.

"If you believe that, I have some property off the coast of Oklahoma to sell you," Doc chimed in.

"You people," I huffed. "I'm not going to try to arrest him myself." That was the truth. I had no desire to see Danny arrested until I heard his side of things. I just wanted to talk to him and figure out what he'd gotten involved in. "I'll take the dogs with me for extra protection."

"And what about me?" Tinkie said. "Are you dumping me?"

"Of course not." But I didn't want Tinkie with me. I didn't think Danny would harm me, but what if he did something crazy? Tinkie had a baby. "But if you're with Harold, you can help him manage the drone. That would be the biggest help."

She cut a look at me that let me know she didn't believe a word coming out of my mouth. "Right. Because Harold needs my help so desperately."

Doc finally stepped in. "Sarah Booth is correct, Tinkie. Those drones require special skills and knowledge, but if you and Harold are in a boat or even a car, driving to places to launch the drone, he's going to need someone's help. He can't drive and fly the thing."

I wanted to kiss Doc, but I restrained myself.

"Okay," Tinkie agreed at last. "I'm going home now. I'll get with Harold and we can plan this out. Tomorrow, you have to tell us when you're leaving and where you're going," Tinkie said to me. "We can keep an eye on you with the drone."

I wasn't certain that was true, but there was no point in adding to her worries. "We'll work out the details tomorrow, assuming Harold has a drone with the capabilities."

"You know Harold. He'll have the latest, state-of-the-art drone. That's just how he rolls."

"Not to mention the worst dog on the planet. Or worst two dogs on the planet," I amended.

Tinkie rolled her eyes. "Yes, Roscoe and Pumpkin are like Bonnie and Clyde. I wouldn't be surprised if they were robbing banks. Speaking of which, Oscar banned them from the bank." She tried to hold back her smile but failed. "Roscoe peed on Sylvia Roe's tap shoes. She always wears them in the bank and they clickety clack and drive the tellers crazy."

"If I were a dog, I'd pee on her shoes, too," I said.

Tinkie made me laugh as we climbed in my vehicle with the sun still far above the horizon. I drove my partner back to Hilltop. She could spend some time with Maylin and I could get a few snuggles with the baby. It was a win-win.

With the baby loving complete, I headed back to Dahlia House. Instead of going inside, I went to the barn and saddled Reveler. Sweetie Pie and Avalon were with me as I set out down the driveway at a trot. Pluto remained on the front porch, and Poe was perched on the back of the rocking chair. He normally flew with me when I rode. Instead of coming along, he cawed loudly as I left him behind.

It was too far to ride a horse to the Tallahatchie River, which was unfortunate because Reveler would be very useful riding along the river. He could jump fallen trees and plow through the underbrush. The June day was hot, and Reveler was a strong swimmer. He enjoyed the water and could be a real practical joker. He'd dumped me in a creek last summer and then pretended he was going to run off and leave me to walk home. Thank goodness he relented and came back for me. But despite all the bonus points of Reveler, I wouldn't be taking him to the river. It was enough to be out in nature for a short ride on my big boy.

Reveler's swinging walk relaxed me. The gentle rotation of my hips loosened the tightness in my back that came from stress. As my back relaxed, so did my brain. There was an angle to this case I was missing. Danny Anderson had disappeared. That was undisputed. Had he been harmed? Was his absence voluntary? Was he hiding from the law or from something else? Was he gone because of his debts or because of his heart?

Reveler and I crossed the main road—Sweetie Pie and Avalon following like perfectly trained trail dogs. When we struck out across a cotton field, I nudged Reveler into a gentle canter. He could cover miles at this gait and never break a sweat. Sweetie Pie and Avalon raced beside us, darting in and out of Reveler's shadow on the warm, brown earth.

I let him have his head and enjoyed the sun on my face and the sound of birds in the nearby brake that helped control erosion. Billowy clouds moved across the vista. The sky, a perfect robin's-egg blue, reminded me of summer days when I was out of school and able to be my mother's sidekick. Those stolen hours, running the back roads of Sunflower County, were precious to me. It was one reason I kept my mother's old antique Roadster in good shape. It was, in some ways, like a time machine to the past, a tribute to the joy of sharing a ride with my mother.

We made the loop of several fields, covering at least five miles before we turned to cross the highway. I heard a vehicle coming, so I stopped across from my driveway. The dogs, Reveler, and I were standing on the verge by the driveway when I heard the sound of a fast-approaching vehicle. I nudged Reveler back and whistled up the dogs, and just in time. A dark pickup with tinted windows rushed past, towing a fishing boat. It was a nice rig, but it was going way over the speed limit. Even when the driver saw us—and he had to see us—he didn't slow.

I wished for a rifle to shoot out his tires, but I didn't have one, and that was probably a good thing. I'd grown up in a time when folks respected other people. Most farmers would never fly past a horse and rider. It was dangerous for all involved. Slowing was merely good manners and courtesy to a neighbor. But the world of good neighbors, good manners, and good sense seemed to be in the rearview mirror.

My little entourage crossed the road and trotted down the driveway toward Dahlia House. The sycamores, their pale bark so beautiful, flashing among the green leaves, always made me stop. How lucky I was to have this life when rural land was being gobbled up by developers. Would the farmland last into the next generation? I had no answers for that, either.

In the barn I unsaddled Reveler, brushed him good, and returned him to the pasture with his buddies, Miss Scrapiron and Lucifer. As usual, they ran up to the gate to greet him as if he'd been gone for years. Then they performed their signature move and ran away. They did this every single time.

The slant of the sun, fast disappearing behind the horizon, was the perfect illumination for the horses moving in unison across the green pasture. Darkness began to fall before I could make it up the back steps.

Walking into the house, it hit me. Danny had two women in his life who obviously cared for him. Pearl and Brigette.

Brigette had suddenly reappeared in Mississippi. Was it possible the two women were acting together to hide Danny? Brigette was going on the river to "hunt" for him. Perhaps she was going to take supplies or help smuggle him to a safer location.

I hurried in the house and called the sheriff's office. Budgie, just the man I wanted to speak with, answered. "Hey, can you get phone records from Pearl Wingard and Brigette McEachern?" I asked.

Budgie hesitated. "It would take a court order."

"Would you ask Coleman?"

"Sure, but he'd need to have evidence to show a judge to get the order, and remember, this is not in our jurisdiction."

I appreciated the laws that protected folks from overly intrusive law officers, but this was dang inconvenient. "You're sure you can't just . . . snatch the records without telling Coleman?"

Budgie laughed. "What's up?"

I told him my theory, and he didn't laugh. "I'll talk with Coleman. See what he thinks. If he says do it, then the data is yours."

I didn't push Budgie. He was a good friend, and I didn't want to put his job on the line. "Thanks, Budgie. I just have a feeling that Danny Anderson is still in the state and someone is helping him hide. But why is he hiding? Why not come in and defend himself against the accusations?"

"I know Danny acts guilty of something. He does. But hold off on judgment until you see all the cards," Budgie suggested. "Maybe there's more to the financial element. Or perhaps he's protecting someone else. I told you I knew Danny a little, and he isn't a coward or a man who would do something and then run from it. He'd own his actions."

I'd heard that more than once about Danny. And I believed it. So, Tinkie and I needed to burrow deeper and deeper into the motives of who killed Todd Jenkins, why, and who would benefit if Danny Anderson were forced into hiding.

"I appreciate your read on this," I told Budgie. "When you see Coleman, please tell him I'm at Dahlia House. Safe and sound."

I put on a pot of coffee to help me think and took a steaming cup through the dining room, heading for the office. A piercing voice stopped me in my tracks.

"She walks these hills in a long dark veil . . ."

I recognized the singer instantly, and my heart jolted. Joan Baez. Her voice had been raised for protests throughout my mother's life. I'd listened to this album sitting on the floor of the music room while my parents played the songs they loved so much. Joan was a figure of hope, strength, and resistance. But what was she doing in Dahlia House?

Of course I knew she wasn't really in here. Probably another trick by Jitty. But her voice was so true, so perfect, that I didn't care. I just wanted to enjoy the song.

Out of the corner of my eye, I caught sight of someone moving on the front porch. My hand went to my hip, but my gun was in a lockbox in the back of my car. I was armed with a cup of coffee. It was scalding hot, so maybe not a bad weapon, if I needed it.

I eased to the front door, where I pulled back the curtain on one of the side lights. The figure on the porch was female—a woman with her face covered by a veil. From behind me, the music came back up. Baez sang the folk song about a man who allowed himself to be hanged for murder because he refused to give his alibi—he was in the arms of his best friend's wife. And so the cheating wife, who spoke not a word, spent the rest of her days walking the late nights in a long black veil. It was a chilling song, and yet another tidbit from Jitty about a couple cheating on their vows.

I eased out onto the porch, but the black-clad figure was already down the steps and headed toward the grove of oak trees where I'd played as a child. It was the special place I'd shared with my mother. I often went there when I needed to feel close to her.

". . . when the night winds wail," the figure sang. Her voice carried back to me. I didn't have a flashlight or any means of lighting the path, but the moon was almost full, and the path was easy to follow. I almost called out to Jitty, but I held back. Was she leading me somewhere or was I just off on a wild-goose chase? Only time would tell.

We came to the oaks, and the thickly leafed branches blocked out the moon. It was suddenly dark. My guide had fallen silent and blended into the darkness. I had the sense that I was completely alone. And it suddenly felt creepy.

"Jitty?" I spoke softly. There was such a hush about this special place that I didn't want to be loud. But when there was no response, I spoke louder. "Jitty?"

My coffee had grown lukewarm and I poured it out. I'd give Jitty another minute or two to respond, and then I was going back to the house. Coleman would be coming home any minute. If I were a different kind of partner, I'd hurry back to the kitchen and put some supper on. But Coleman wasn't with me because of my culinary abilities. In fact, it was my bartending skills that hooked him. And I felt a sudden desire for a Jack on the rocks.

I scoured the shadowy area beneath the big oaks and tried to find Jitty, but she was gone. Just gone. This was likely her idea of a practical joke. Sometimes she really aggravated me.

I had turned to go home when she popped out from behind a tree and almost made me fall over backward.

"Boo!"

"I'm going to 'boo' you into eternity!" I ran toward her, but of course I went straight through her. There was no punishing Jitty for her practical joke.

Jitty pulled the veil off her face and I could see her teeth flashing in the moonlight. She had a contagious laugh, and I couldn't stay mad for long. I was laughing right along with her. "That was mean," I said.

"Sorry. I couldn't resist. You had that little creepy walk going."

I had been a little spooked by her disappearance. "Well, I followed you here and you disappeared. That qualifies as creepy."

"This is what you want to talk about?" Jitty motioned me to walk with her back to the house.

"Why are you singing 'Long Black Veil'?"

"Isn't it obvious?"

"It's a song about cheaters who pay the ultimate price."

"That's right."

"Are you saying that Danny's disappearance is all about cheating?"

"You forget, Sarah Booth, I'm not allowed to say anything about your cases."

"Or much of anything else." I was a little miffed. She could help me, but she wouldn't. She had access to things in the Great Beyond that I couldn't touch. But there were rules, and I never pushed too hard because I relied on Jitty to be with me. If I demanded her help and she gave it—breaking the rules—I might lose her forever. I could not bear that. "Okay, you can't tell me anything. If I guess, can you say whether I'm hot or cold?"

"You are such a child," she said, but she was amused.

"So, you're pulling out all the songs about cheaters who paid the ultimate price because someone in this case is carrying on an affair?"

"Hot."

"Danny Anderson is carrying on an affair."

"Warm."

That gave me pause. "Pearl is having an affair."

"Hot."

That really stopped me. How could Pearl be hot and Danny only warm? "Is Pearl sleeping with someone who is not Danny?"

Jitty skipped across the yard to the back door. "I can't answer that."

"If you are messing with me, Jitty, I will get even."

"How?" she asked.

That was a dang good question. Jitty answered to no one, as far as I could tell. "Look, if this is a simple case of a couple falling in love but not wanting to hurt people, I get it. But Danny needs to come home. His family grows more desperate by the day. Decisions about settling the bank loan need to be made. Danny's parents need to know he is okay. And if Pearl is in love with Danny, she needs to be honest with Micah."

"I agree."

I was stunned. Jitty never agreed with me. "So, what is the truth?" I asked Jitty.

The front door at Dahlia House slammed and I heard Coleman. "Sarah Booth, where are you?"

When I looked up, Jitty/Joan was gone. It was just the dogs, the cat, the raven, and me.

25

Coleman wasn't thrilled with my plan to boat down the Tallahatchie River in the hopes of seeing Danny. The fact that I was following Brigette made it slightly more acceptable, but only because he believed Brigette knew where Danny was and would lead me there.

"I should go with you," Coleman said. "Danny is a suspect in several burglaries. The Leflore County sheriff is looking for him, as is the Vicksburg police chief."

"If I am lucky enough to find Danny, he'll disappear if he sees law enforcement."

"I know, but he needs to turn himself in. If he's innocent, let's clear his name."

"I'll try to talk to him. If I see him at all." There were a lot of "ifs" where Danny Anderson was involved. It wasn't my favorite plan, but it was the only one I had at the moment. "I know. I see the drawbacks. But I also have to try, Coleman. For Danny's parents, and for Oscar and Tinkie."

"Take the dogs, for sure."

"I wonder how Pluto would react to a boat ride."

Coleman grinned. "Take the cat, too. As bad as those dogs can be, Pluto can be ten times worse."

And he was right about that. Docile, loving, purring-up-a-fog Pluto could take the top of a person's head off if he got pissed. "I'll take him. But you have to make it up to him when I get back. A day in a boat on the river is not going to be Pluto's idea of fun."

"He may surprise you." Coleman put his arm around me. "Now, take a seat on the front porch and I'll make us a libation. I also took the liberty of stopping by Sally Crawford's and picking up some gumbo she made."

"Yum! Thank you." Sally only cooked sporadically, but she was almost as good as Millie—and with certain dishes, like gumbo, she was even better.

For the next hour, Coleman and I sipped our drinks as I told him all about the drone and how Harold and Tinkie were going to follow me as I floated downriver.

"I should just go with you," he said, rubbing the back of his neck. He did that when he felt cornered by circumstances.

"I'll be fine. I swear. I'll get behind Brigette and follow along. If she stops to talk to Danny, I don't think either one of them will harm me."

Coleman nodded. "I agree. But we don't know the circumstances of Danny's disappearance. Has it occurred to you that someone contacted Brigette about Danny because she's a wealthy model?"

"I've wondered what role she might play in this."

"Think about it. If Danny is being held hostage for a ransom, Brigette has a better chance of paying for him than anyone else we know."

That was very, very true. Tinkie, who kept up with such

things, told me Brigette had a house in Italy and an apartment in New York City. She traveled the world, and yet she was still willing to pose with local children for a fundraising calendar to help the farmers.

"Do you know Brigette's family?" I asked Coleman.

"Slater and Linda McEachern are good people. I don't know them well, but I did get Budgie to run a check. Neither has been in legal trouble. The family seems solid."

"Would you ask Budgie to do a little digging into this?"

Coleman nodded. "It sure couldn't hurt. And you promise me that if you see Danny, you'll call. The man I know would never harm a fly, but people change. Desperation can make a person do tragic things."

He wasn't wrong about that. "You have my word. Now let's eat some gumbo and grab some shut-eye."

I awoke early the next morning. Coleman had left a note on the pillow saying he would meet up with me when I decided where to rent a boat. The sun was just coming up, but I had to get busy. Brigette McEachern wasn't the kind of woman to lie around in bed and let the hours slip away from her. And I wasn't wrong. I'd just slipped into my boots and gotten the dogs in the vehicle when my phone rang. Budgie was on the case. He'd been sitting on Brigette's hotel since daybreak, waiting for her to take action.

"She's pulling out now," Budgie said about Brigette. "She's on the move."

"And so am I." I started the car and stepped on the gas.

Budgie talked to me as he followed Brigette and while I rushed along the back roads that took me upriver. I had to get behind her as she came down the river so I could drift along and quietly come upon her. She was not going to be happy with me. I'd decided the simplest way to follow her was to wait until she'd rented her boat and set out. Then I could rent at the same place and stay behind her until she docked somewhere.

Budgie tailed Brigette, and I followed behind, talking to Budgie on the phone as he gave me a blow-by-blow account of the route Brigette was taking. While we drove, we chatted.

"Have you talked to Brigette?" he asked.

"I have." I could hear the awe in his voice. "And you?"

"No, no I haven't. But I sure would like to."

"If Brigette is still in town after we find Danny, I'll try to make that happen," I said. Budgie was starstruck.

"I'd just like to say hello," he said. "Mississippi has a lot of famous people, but I don't think any of them are as beautiful as Brigette."

Budgie was such a sweet guy; I didn't have the heart to tease him about his crush. "Coleman and I will see what we can do," I promised.

"Brigette is headed north toward Fox's marina on the river," Budgie said. "I'm in my personal pickup, so I can follow her in. Once she's rented a boat, I'll rent one for you and you can pay me back."

"You are the best." I wasn't blowing smoke. Budgie was a very good man and a loyal friend.

"I'm going to get off the phone. I don't want to look suspicious."

"Good plan." I didn't think Brigette would find a man talking on a cell phone suspicious, but it was better to be safe than sorry. I sighed. I could almost hear Aunt Loulane saying that in my ear. I was on the verge of needing professional help to exorcise my aunt's addiction to adages.

"I'll call when Brigette takes off down the river. I'll rent you a boat with the same kind of motor. In case you have to pursue her."

Yeah, that was me. The improved Donnette Johnson in a cigarette boat roaring around the rivers. *Miami Vice* would be looking to hire me. "Thanks, Budgie. Hey, is Brigette alone?" It had just occurred to me that if she was with someone else, I might need Budgie.

"She's alone," he said. "Hanging up now. She's going in to pay for the rental. If I can overhear her plans, I'll let you know."

He really was the best.

26

I waited for Budgie to give me the "all clear" that Brigette was in her boat and headed downriver before I pulled into the parking lot. Budgie stood at the boat ramp holding the small outboard by the painter.

"I checked the gas, and you're good. Mr. Fox said if you make it down to Greenwood, you can leave the boat there and he'll pick it up this evening along with several others he's rented. It's a long trip, Sarah Booth."

"Thank you, Budgie." He'd handled everything. Except for one problem: my vehicle. How would I get it home?

Again, Budgie was way ahead of me. "DeWayne said he'd drive me here to get your car and drop it off in Greenwood for you."

"Again, thank you."

While Budgie held the boat at the small dock, I got in and steadied it for Sweetie Pie and Avalon to jump in. Pluto sat on the dock and gave me a hairy eyeball. He was not happy with this turn of events. He didn't much like water in a puddle, and the river was big and filled with currents. He looked at Budgie as if pleading for the deputy to take him home.

"Coleman told me to bring the cat."

Budgie turned away to hide his smile. When he turned back, he said, "I think the sheriff was messing with you, Sarah Booth. It's going to be a long, hot day with an angry black cat in a boat brimming with dogs."

He wasn't lying. Pluto looked mutinous. He might try to make me walk the plank. But that reminded me of the talk of treasure. "Hey, Budgie, do you know anything about buried treasure on this river?"

"Lots of stories, but no one has actually turned anything up, as far as I know. Then again, if you found treasure would you really tell anyone?"

He had a point. Loose lips would only lead to tax penalties. But what did I know? "No, I'd keep my lips zipped and bury it in the backyard for a rainy day. Or a renovation project at Dahlia House."

"I'd spread it out among the farmers."

"You are a good man," I said. Budgie would do it, too.

"You'll lose cell phone service at different points. Be careful, Sarah Booth. I don't see Ms. McEachern as a crazed killer, but you don't know who else is on the river or what they're doing. I'd feel better if I sent a water patrol."

"No, please don't. I can't spook them. If Brigette leads me to Danny, I don't want them to panic and do anything crazy."

Budgie gave me a look that clearly said my presence might cause them to panic if they were up to anything illegal. Danny Anderson was a wanted man. I didn't ignore Budgie's concerns, but I had given this plan a lot of thought, and I believed I was safe. I wasn't going to threaten Danny. I had no authority to "bring him in." I was merely going to try to talk some sense into him if I saw him.

I started the small motor and Budgie threw me the line. I was off.

The terrain of the Mississippi Delta is mostly flat and the rivers meander through walls of trees along the banks. In some areas, the Tallahatchie is very secluded. A perfect place for a fertile imagination to take root and grow. And scare me to death if I let it run too wild! The thought of the woman in white on the bridge came back to me and I pushed it out of my brain. I couldn't afford to be a sissy now. And I had the dogs and cat to protect me. Maybe.

The twenty-five-horsepower motor hummed along as I basically floated with the current. The river was empty, and I worried that Brigette had gotten too far ahead of me. I didn't hear any sounds of another person, but sound carried differently on the water.

Sweetie Pie was loving the ride, her long hound ears flapping gently as she sniffed the air. Avalon, who was less trusting, sat in the bottom of the small boat and watched the shoreline. Pluto was at the bow, like a maritime figurehead. I had a bit of trepidation thinking of his reaction once we got home. Pluto was a master of revenge.

At last, the beauty of the scenery began to calm my nerves. I found myself enjoying the day, the smell of blossoms along the banks. It was hot, but not unbearable, and I dipped my hand in the water, trailing my fingers as we moved along. Were I not on a case, I'd pull over to one of the sandbars and take a quick dip. But I had a job to do.

I rounded a bend in the river and turned my little craft in a circle. About two hundred yards away, just in a curve, a fishing boat had been pulled onto a sandbar. Was it Brigette's boat? I had no way to know. It could be her or anyone. This is what I had hoped for—and also dreaded. Was I about to confront Danny Anderson face-to-face?

I angled toward the sandbar, intending to park beside the beached craft. When I was thirty yards away, a shot rang out and a bullet zinged into the water not three feet from my boat. Sweetie Pie and Avalon began to bark at full alert. Pluto ducked down behind the seat, showing uncommon good sense.

I angled hard away from the sandbar, using the motor to get back into the main current. I didn't know who was on the sandbar, but I couldn't risk finding out.

"Brigette! Danny!" I called out to them. "I'm here to help!"

Though I searched the wooded area behind the sandbar, I didn't see anyone. They were well hidden. There was only the one boat. If Danny was there, he'd either hidden his craft or had come in another way. I took a moment to photograph the sandbar and the boat.

"Danny! Brigette!" I called out again.

Another gunshot and the bullet hit the water closer to the boat. If the shooter wanted to hurt me, they could.

"This isn't helping anything! Please! Danny, give yourself up!"

The answer was another shot, this one even closer. I had two options. To get out of Dodge before I had a hole in my boat—or me—or to boldly continue to the sandbar and confront whoever was shooting. I chose the former option. I turned downriver and left. I had the dogs and cat to consider. If I was injured or killed, what would happen to them? When the sandbar was behind me, I checked my phone. No service here.

My grand plan to talk to Danny had evaporated in the reality that whatever I had to offer, the person with the gun wasn't interested. I couldn't prove it was Danny or Brigette, but I believed it was. Who else would have cause to try to scare me off? They could have killed me if that was their intent. They didn't seem to want to hurt me—but they were not going to make it easy.

I nosed my boat into the current and opened the gas. I'd make it to the very next area where a boat could be put into the water and then call for help. Assuming I had cell phone coverage. And that was a big assumption.

I'd studied a map of the river and the public and private boat ramps. Fox's was the full-service public ramp that most people used. There was safe parking for vehicles and boat trailers. A full-time employee kept Fox's open seven days a week, offering boat rentals by the day or week. They sold bait, tackle, ice, and sandwiches made fresh daily by Bertha Fox. Her sausage biscuits were famous across the Delta.

But I intended to check each ramp along the way, even knowing that such a time-consuming maneuver would put me in a position of being tailed by the people I had meant to tail. Brigette—I wasn't worried about her proving violent. But Danny, if he was robbing places and committing acts alien to his nature, how big of a push would it take for him to reach violence as a solution to his woes? I was struck again by the fact I learned with each new case: no one ever really knows what another person is capable of. Often, we didn't even know our own capabilities until pushed into a corner.

27

It seemed like half a lifetime passed before I came upon another sandbar, which would give easy access to a boat. I was utterly tired of the sun, the river, and the insects that had begun to devil me. The yellow flies could smell my blood from miles away. A swarm of them circled the boat, looking for my exposed flesh. Even the dogs were snapping at them. Pluto was under a few towels I'd thrown in.

This sandbar looked promising. I could see that the trees weren't as dense. Perhaps there was a trail through the woods to an access road that led to a main thoroughfare. I couldn't tell by looking, so I had a decision to make. To thoroughly check the area, or to slip on downriver until I had a phone signal. Because I'd been shot at upriver, I was now downstream from Danny and Brigette—or whoever had shot at me. This meant checking this sandbar for them would be a waste of time. But since I was here . . . I ran up on the sandbar, got out of the boat, and pulled it up enough so it wouldn't float away. The dogs and cat jumped out, apparently ready to be landlubbers again.

Sweetie Pie and Avalon instantly went into search pattern, combing the small sandbar before heading into the woods. I let them go while I checked on Pluto, who looked a little seasick. It had been a bad idea to bring the cat.

He came over when I called him and rubbed against my shins. I could hear his purr loud and clear. "Oh, Pluto, I'm so sorry."

He gave a sweet meow and then hurled on my shoe. Before I could react, he scampered away, his thin black tail forming a question mark.

I danced a jig, finally kicking my shoe into the river. I'd rather wear it wet than pukey. When I had it washed off and back on my foot, I decided to wade into the river a little to cool off. The dogs thought this was a fine idea. They gave up sniffing for tracks and romped in the cool water. I couldn't help but smile at their antics. Pluto had taken a position in the shade of a sweet gum tree.

The dogs hadn't found anything in the woods, and I'd wasted enough time. I didn't want someone with a loaded gun coming down the river on top of me. Of course they could go upriver, against the current, but it would be slow going. And I doubted Danny would put in an appearance at Fox's place since he could easily be recognized. No, it was time to move on.

We loaded up and pushed off the sandbar. An hour later, my shoulders and arms were baking in the sun. I didn't want to stop, though. We'd checked four more sandbars without success.

I found a signal at the last sandbar and called Tinkie.

"Where in the dickens have you been? We've been worried sick."

I checked my watch, surprised to find it was late afternoon.

I'd been on the river for hours. "Sorry, Tinkie, I'm fine. I didn't have a signal."

"Not a signal in all this time?"

She had a point. I hadn't been checking my phone like I should. I decided to ignore the question. "I've examined all the sandbars for an exit to a main road, but nothing." I didn't want to tell her about being shot at until we were face-to-face. She'd only worry.

"Where are you?" Tinkie asked.

I gave her my location on the river and hung up. It was time to get on to Greenwood. The sun had sucked all the energy from me.

I came up on a big sandbar with signs of camping. This looked like a place people could get to from a road. It was well worth investigating. I pulled the boat up on the sandbar and the dogs, cat, and I set out on foot to see if we could find a vehicle. I grew excited when I kicked at the remains of a burned campfire and found a gardening trowel. Had someone been digging for treasure? There'd been no signs of such on the other sandbars I'd checked. I had a sense that I was closing in on Danny Anderson. I still believed he and Brigette were upriver of me, so it was safe to explore.

If that was the case, I could call Coleman to get in touch with the Leflore County authorities. I didn't want to see Danny arrested, but I was out of other options. He needed to come in and explain his actions—and let his family know he was alive.

The dogs coursed over the sandbar, sniffing and exploring. It was a lovely sandbar, shaped like a comma, with white sand beaches. Pluto had found a shady spot and was licking a back foot. Whenever he looked at me, he gave me a death stare. I'd have to order some expensive cat food for him to forgive me.

When Sweetie Pie gave a loud yodeling howl and struck out on foot for the woods that fringed the white sand, I followed.

The day had turned really hot, and the yellow flies were a torment as we stepped into the woods. Sweetie Pie and Avalon hit a trail, and they were off. Pluto, who'd decided to go with, and I were slower.

Once we walked inland and left the sandbar and the river breeze, it was stifling. We'd gone maybe half a mile when Sweetie and Avalon came running back to me. Instead of going forward, they rushed back to the sandbar where I'd left the boat. Were they playing around? I was about to turn back myself when I saw tire tracks coming out of a mud puddle. The tracks told me it was a big pickup. As I moved along to the south, I had a sinking feeling. The truck tracks went down to the water. As I had feared, it appeared someone had loaded a boat into a truck and left the river by driving out. If this was Danny and Brigette, they'd outsmarted me.

"Dang it." I said the words aloud and then whistled for Sweetie Pie and Avalon. The dogs began to bark excitedly. I was turning around to go back to them when I heard the roar of a loud motor and the sound of a vehicle crashing through the narrow trail. Whoever it was, they were getting away. I ran after them, only to realize it was too late. They'd escaped.

Sweetie's frantic barking, blended with Avalon's softer barks, let me know something was happening on the sandbar. My boat—and my only means to get downriver to Greenwood—was on that sandbar. I rushed back to the river and stopped. I was in big trouble. My boat was gone. Someone had pulled it off the tip of the comma on the sandbar where I'd beached it. Had they taken it or simply let it free to make its own way downriver? I didn't know. I only knew that I'd been played by someone smarter than I was.

To add insult to injury, Pluto sauntered up to my feet. He looked up at me and then flipped over and sprawled out, like he'd fainted. Yeah, that was my life. A wiseacre cat and a case that got the better of me at every turn.

I pulled out my phone and for a minute, my heart stopped. I had zero bars. I turned in a circle, holding the phone up until two appeared. And then I called Tinkie to come and find me. There was nothing to do but wait for rescue.

"Don't look so chagrined, Sarah Booth," Harold said when he and Tinkie joined me on the sandbar. "It could have happened to anyone."

"I lost my boat." My pride was smarting.

"Like I said, it could have happened to anyone. Do you think someone pushed it off and left you stranded?"

"Yes. I know that's what happened."

"Any idea who?"

"Brigette McEachern and Danny Anderson, but before you ask, I don't have any proof." I felt my eyes fill with angry tears, but I blinked them away. If I bawled like a crybaby, I would only look more foolish. Still, I felt like crying big-time. My face, shoulders, and thighs were sunburned. About a billion yellow flies had feasted on me, leaving behind saliva in my skin that made me want to tear a hole in every part of my body. And I'd accomplished nothing but losing one of Mr. Fox's rental boats.

"Let's get you home," Harold said, taking pity on me.

Tinkie offered me a hand and pulled me to my feet. Sweetie Pie and Avalon rushed into the river for one last dip. Pluto only looked at them with contempt and started toward the trail that would take us to Harold's truck. "I've lost that rental boat," I said. "It's probably on the way to Vicksburg."

Tinkie's delightful laugh echoed off the trees. That's when I noticed the yellow flies weren't biting her or Harold. How was that possible?

"You didn't put on any poisonous fly spray, did you?" I asked.

Tinkie and Harold both laughed. "It's some perfume my mother loved. Insects hate it. I guess that was one good thing she gave me."

"I want the name."

"I'll get you a bottle when we get home," Tinkie promised. "Now let's get downriver to Greenwood and see if anyone found your boat and turned it in."

The truth of the matter was I'd rather be flayed alive than get back on the river; I was delighted to ride to Greenwood in a vehicle.

28

Harold called the water search and rescue as we drove, and I basked in the truck's powerful air-conditioning. We weren't far from town when Harold's phone rang. The water rescue had recovered the boat and was towing it to the landing in Greenwood. They'd found it in time to get it on the transport Mr. Fox ran for fishermen who floated downriver. I sighed in relief. But the bottom line was that Brigette and Danny had outsmarted me.

Coleman met me at the boat ramp. If he was amused, he was good at hiding it. His suggestion of stopping at a local restaurant was met with approval by all, and once we'd made sure Mr. Fox's boat was on the way home, we could relax. Calamity had been averted, but I'd wasted the day. We checked with the folks at the ramp, and they said that no other boats from Mr. Fox had been brought in.

When the waitress put the tall glass of Jack and water in front of me, I took a long sip. The tension in my shoulders relaxed, and even though the sunburn was painful, I was on the mend.

"I can't believe I fell for this," I said.

"You're not certain who set your boat free," Coleman pointed out.

"Who else could it be?" I asked. "Brigette never brought her boat to Greenwood. I'll bet anything they were hiding in the woods, pulled up deep in a small creek or branch that feeds into the river. They were watching me. When I went to look for them, one of them snuck down to the river and pushed my boat off. Then they jumped in the vehicle and took their boat back to Mr. Fox, leaving me stranded."

"It's a theory, not a fact," Coleman said.

I wanted to argue, but he was right. It could have been anyone. But if that were the case, where was Brigette? She left her vehicle at Fox's and took the boat downriver. She never showed up at the ramp in Greenwood.

"I'll drive up to Fox's and see if she returned the boat," Coleman said.

"Thank you." I should do it, but I was glad he'd volunteered. He'd get more and better information anyway because of his badge.

"While you were out playing Huck Finn, I learned some interesting stuff," Tinkie said. Her blue eyes were twinkling. She'd found something good. Man, I needed to hear something good.

"What?"

"There really is supposed to be treasure buried somewhere along the Tallahatchie."

"I thought the buried treasure was just an old folktale."

"Apparently, it's true. But it wasn't rich people fleeing from the Union troops. It's much more interesting." Tinkie was paying out the details like a professional storyteller.

"So, tell me!" I was all ears, and even Coleman had leaned

in to listen. Harold obviously knew this, because he was grinning.

"Back during the Civil War, there was a group of outlaws who roamed this area. They were called the Norton Clan."

"I've heard stories," I said. "They robbed people who had very little to give."

Tinkie nodded. "They also kidnapped the enslaved and instead of freeing them, they took them down the Mississippi to New Orleans and sold them at the slave auctions."

The sugarcane fields around New Orleans were infamous for the hardships the enslaved workers endured.

"These outlaws were brutal. So many people were barely hanging on, and the Norton Clan would come in and steal everything of value. Chickens, hogs, horses, any valuables, and actual human beings." Tinkie nodded at Harold, who picked up the story.

"There was a family, the Sullivans, who had a large plantation tucked away on an oxbow lake that formed along the Tallahatchie. Their entrance to the property was hidden from the main waterway, deliberately constructed so. Because Columbine Plantation was so isolated, the Sullivan holdings missed most of the fighting and the worst of the scavenging that often comes with war," Harold said. "When the Southern troops pulled back during a Civil War battle, deciding to take a stand along the Yazoo rather than the Tallahatchie, the area's residents went into panic mode. They felt they'd been abandoned, and as the Confederate troops left, full-scale terror set in.

"And folks had every right to be afraid. The Northern troops were in hot pursuit of the retreating Southern forces. Much of the land and most of the plantations and farms had already been destroyed by the fighting. The Sullivan family did all they could to hide from the coming mayhem. They destroyed the waterway that led to the lake and did their best to cover any trace of their existence. And it worked, for a while."

"The armies went through the area, but Columbine Plantation and the people there remained virtually untouched. The Sullivans shared what they could with their neighbors, but word about the fine plantation got out. Weeks before the war was declared over, the Norton Clan came through the area. They killed the Sullivan family, raided the house, and stole everything they could carry off."

Tinkie picked up the story. "A neighbor, some think the very person who alerted the Nortons to the untouched plantation, supposedly helped the outlaws load the silver, jewelry, and money on a boat on the lake to take it down the Tallahatchie. For his pains, he was shot and left on the sandbar. Several of the outlaws took the boats with the valuables, while others forced the enslaved people onto larger boats and headed south down the river."

Harold nodded somberly. "Greed. Same old story. The outlaws in the boats with the jewels and gold could move faster than the larger boats filled with human cargo. The head of the clan, James Norton, saw that one of his outlaws was making off with the valuables. You know, the old saying 'there is no honor among thieves' held true. Norton called for the thief to stop, but the man didn't heed his boss. It was clear he meant to steal the valuables."

"James Norton would never allow that," Coleman said. "My great-grandfather knew some of the members of the Norton Clan. James ruled them with an iron fist. No one double-crossed him and lived to tell the story."

"So what happened?" I asked.

"James Norton shot at the betrayer. He fell out of the boat and the other outlaws jumped ship and swam to shore."

"And the money and stuff?" I asked.

"The boat was found the next morning along the bank. The money was gone. It was heavy stuff, so a man walking wouldn't be able to carry a lot. Most historians believe the outlaws buried the valuables on the river, intending to come back for them later. They didn't live that long. James Norton tracked them down and killed them all."

"And the money and jewels were never recovered," I guessed.

"That sums it up," Harold said. "Over the years, there have been treasure-hunting parties scouring the river, but if the valuables were ever found, no one admitted it."

"And you think Danny Anderson may have found that treasure?" I asked.

"We don't know," Tinkie said. "But what if he did? What if he's been on the river recovering the treasure all this time?"

"I think his parents are going to want to wring his neck," I said. "He should have let his folks know he's okay if this is the case. They've been worried sick something has happened to him."

Tinkie laughed. "Your point is taken. He should have."

"Do you have any evidence any of this is true?" Coleman asked.

"This is where it gets good," Tinkie said. "We do."

"Spill it." I wanted to hear this.

"When Todd Jenkins's body was recovered from the river, he had an 1861-D gold coin in his pocket." Tinkie almost whispered the words, and she did indeed have us on the edge of our seats. "Tell them about the mint, Harold," she said.

"Most folks don't know that the Confederate states actually minted a small amount of gold coins in 1861. In the 1820s, the federal government allowed the creation of three branch mints: the Dahlonega, the Charlotte, and the New Orleans mint. It was too dangerous to transport gold up to Philadelphia to be minted. When war broke out, the Confederacy had some gold and decided to mint their own coin. The one found on Todd Jenkins came from the Dahlonega mint in Lumpkin County, Georgia. An 1861-D gold dollar. It's extremely rare and very valuable."

"Gold is gold. It wouldn't have mattered the origin of it," Coleman said. "While the paper money of the Confederacy became worthless, the gold coin would have been incredibly valuable."

"Exactly," Tinkie said. "And Harold and I believe that Danny found the hidden treasure. Todd may have been a partner or he could have been a plain thief. But somehow he came to have that gold dollar."

Despite my attempts to shoot holes in Tinkie and Harold's theory, I couldn't. It was the only thing that made any sense about Danny's ongoing absence. "And you think Brigette is helping him?"

"Brigette has the money to buy whatever land this treasure has been found on. Or to pay for excavation." Harold saw the logistics clearly. "It's too bad Danny had too much pride to ask her to pay off his loan. She would have helped him."

"If true, this story will make headlines around the globe," Coleman said.

"It sure will." I was having a hard time even grasping all the implications. "Who will the money belong to?" I asked.

"Finders keepers," Harold said. "The Norton Clan killed the Sullivan family. There are no survivors."

"What about the land where the treasure is found?"

"Either they're digging it up to move it right now or Brigette will make an offer to buy the property. She has a fat bank account. And this story could only enhance her modeling work. I mean, a woman who found a real buried treasure . . . That's solid gold material. I can see it now, The Model with the Golden Touch."

Harold wasn't wrong about that. This crazy case had taken a strange, strange twist. From legendary songs to ghosts to land pirates and buried treasure.

"And we have even better news," Tinkie said.

"What?" I bit hook, line, and sinker.

"We still haven't launched the drone. We were going to track you, but we lost your cell phone signal when you were on the river. Harold and I went up to Fox's and tried to find you, but we couldn't. But we *can* use the drone to find an excavation site."

I'd been so frazzled by losing the rental boat that I'd forgotten about the drone Harold was going to use. This was, indeed, an excellent turn of events.

"Let's go!" My enthusiasm was short-circuited when I felt razor-sharp claws in my shins. "Damn!" I nearly flipped over backward getting out from under the table. Two golden-green eyes glared back at me. Pluto. He was not having another moment of a trip involving the river.

"The day is almost gone," Coleman said. "Let's start fresh in the morning. This time I'll help. I finished the reports on the burglaries in Sunflower County. I'm pretty sure it was Danny, or someone pretending to be Danny. I need to find him, bring him in, and question him. That means I need to help with the drone. I've alerted all the proper agencies to be on the lookout for Danny and/or Brigette. We'll get to the bottom of this."

It sounded like the perfect solution to me.

29

After a night of suffering from horrible sunburn, I dreaded going back to the river, but the possibility of the drone intrigued me. Could it find what I'd been unable to? I'd withheld the fact that someone shot at me from my posse because it wasn't a serious attempt. If I told Coleman or Tinkie, they'd worry far too much. Still, it would have been terrific to have footage of the incident from the drone. Someone was trying to intimidate me and I didn't like it.

Before I left my bedroom, Coleman slathered my arms, face, and neck with sunblock. He didn't say the obvious—that I was unwise not to have done so the day before. My world at Dahlia House was normally jeans and T-shirts with a hat and sunglasses. Exposure to the brutal rays of the sun was minimal. If I was working outside, I often wore long-sleeved shirts. Yesterday, I'd just failed to put on my thinking cap. I hadn't considered the long hours on the water and under the sun. Today, I was older and wiser.

Coleman put the cap back on the tube of sunblock and

handed it to me. "I'm going to the office to see what Budgie and DeWayne have turned up," he said, referring to his deputies. "They were rounding up some folks who really know the river. Folks who might be able to help Harold with the drone. The good news is that Harold feels that Brigette and Danny, if they are treasure hunting, will be looking downriver of where Harold picked you up. And that portion of the river is a bit more accessible by drone. Or at least it's an area that is known to more hunters and fishermen. Harold can pick his launch points with more accuracy."

"Thank you for helping, Coleman. And that is good news."

"If you do find Danny and Brigette, what is your plan?" Coleman asked.

"You'll arrest Danny for the burglaries. I'll talk to Brigette and see if she'll tell me the truth. She knows a lot more than she's letting on. She needs to talk. Arrest her if it will encourage her to tell the truth." Coleman wasn't in the habit of arresting people on a whim or request, but heck, it didn't hurt to make a suggestion.

He grinned at me and kissed the top of my head. "Maybe, if I have to. But I'm not going to arrest an international model because she went on a boat ride. Not a chance. But keep throwing out ideas." He turned serious. "I was thinking about that coin and Todd Jenkins. If he or Danny found the treasure and they fought over it . . ."

"As desperate as Danny is, I don't think he'd hurt anyone. I don't." I'd uncovered nothing that changed my mind about Danny.

"And Brigette?"

This was a meatier issue. Why was Brigette back in Mississippi? "She seems real and nice. And she's invested in Mississippi and folks here. She appears to be a loyal friend who will take action instead of offering platitudes. That's what I've observed, but I don't know her."

Coleman pressed harder. "Brigette came home to help Danny. Why?"

"Talk to Cece. She may have insight. And I'll be back in an hour to pick you up. When you were in the shower Tinkie called and gave me the timeline for Harold and the drone."

"I'll be ready. And calling Cece is a great idea. Thank you."

I got my boots and tied the laces. I was dressed and ready, so I poured another cup of coffee and went to the front porch. The day was just beginning, and already the heat and humidity were taxing. We desperately needed rain.

Cece answered on the second ring. In the background I could hear reporters chattering about their stories. The newsroom at the *Zinnia Dispatch* had a comforting rhythm of steady work during most hours, but then those frantic pushes to meet deadlines. Cece seemed to thrive on the pressure.

"What's up?" she asked.

"What's the scoop on Brigette McEachern?"

"She's something else, isn't she? Why are you asking?"

I filled my friend in on the happenings of the day before. The coin was of specific interest to her. "How much is that coin worth?" she asked. "Wait, I'll look it up online."

I gave her some time while I sipped my coffee and stroked Sweetie Pie's sun-warmed back. I was so lucky. My hounds were in good health. Pluto, for all of his aristocratic airs, was loving and had saved my bacon in the past. Even Poe, the raven who was sitting on the back of a wicker chair giving me a death stare, could be nice. My horses frisked and romped in the pasture. When the real heat came down, the equines would seek shade and snooze or graze. The only thing out of kilter in my world—this week—was a dead-end case. If I could find Danny and prove he wasn't a thief, I'd be set. Well, there was the ghost on the Tallahatchie Bridge. That needed a resolution, but Jitty had taught me such things were often not granted.

The call of a woodpecker—a wild sound that made me think of dense jungles—caught my ear, and I strained to listen so I could find the bird's location. I loved the redheaded little devils. I'd learned that the woodpecker's long tongue wrapped around the inside of its skull and helped protect the bird's brain from the repetitive, hard pecking that allowed them to eat insects. The birds were a marvel of nature.

I listened for the tapping of the woodpecker's beak, but instead the strum of a guitar came to me. I instantly knew the song. I'd sung it along with my mama as we'd driven the back roads of Sunflower County. "If I had a hammer . . ."

Though Pete Seeger and Lee Hays had penned the song in 1949, it was Peter, Paul and Mary who sang to me. I couldn't help myself. I sang along with the trio that I had loved since I was a tot. I loved all of their music. Their song about a magical dragon could make me cry to this day.

"I'd hammer out jus-tice . . ." That line never failed to make me think of my dad. I was thinking of him when Mary Travers stepped out from behind a front porch column. Her contralto voice—the protest sound of the 1960s—made me suddenly melancholy.

"Don't be sad, Sarah Booth. Justice is never easy to gain," Mary said.

She wore a peasant top and cut-off jeans. Her long blond hair hung straight on either side of her face, which was framed by bangs. I'd aspired to be Mary Travers when I was a kid.

"Where's Peter and Paul?" I asked her, thinking I was a pretty good smart aleck.

"Busy. They sent me to help you out."

This was welcome news. I knew it was Jitty, and she was never allowed to help me with a case. "Where is Danny Anderson, and has he committed a crime?" Even though I knew it was forbidden, I wasn't going to let this opportunity slip away from me. After all, Jitty had offered help.

"'I'm leaving, on a jet plane,'" she sang out. She began to flicker and fade.

"Wait! Don't leave," I said.

"Don't ask questions you know I can't answer," she replied.

"Sorry." I really wasn't, but Jitty or Mary or whoever apparently expected an apology. "What is it with all the folk singers?" I asked.

"Protest. The right to protest is one of the most sacred of American rights. And it is also one of the first things a dictator will take away from citizens."

She was right about that. Marching and singing were tools of demanding social justice in a world stacked against the little guy. Mary Travers, Joan Baez, both were justice warriors. They'd sung out against the Vietnam War and for civil rights for all Americans. What was Jitty getting at? That the deck was stacked against farmers?

"Are you urging me to take physical action against those who are oppressing farmers?" I asked her.

"Maybe."

Oh, my, goodness! Jitty was more frustrating than trying to pull on skinny jeans on a humid day. "You wouldn't like it if I were arrested."

"Fact," she conceded. "My suggestion is that you fight the man, but don't get caught."

"The man?" I asked. "Who is that?"

"The cops. The law. The man. Back in my day, they were all men. The oppressors."

In the 1960s and '70s there were no female law enforcement officers—or at least very few. Law enforcement, like many other professions, was male dominated. Women were outright banned in most departments.

"In this instance, who, exactly, do you see as 'the man'?" I asked. I wanted to bite my tongue after I said it. Jitty had sucked me into another debate where I'd never win, no matter what I said.

"The boss, the head guy, the ruler."

"And who is that?" I asked. Was I actually about to get something over on Jitty? A miracle!

"The person who opposes justice," Jitty/Mary said cagily. She tossed her long silky hair over her shoulder. "Time to check in at the Great Beyond." She began to morph from the blond Mary to the beautiful mocha Jitty.

"At least finish the song," I begged. "That's another of my favorites."

She cleared her throat and her lovely contralto rang out on the crisp morning air.

I caught sight of Coleman's truck coming down the driveway and Mary quickly changed to Jitty amid some musical notes and guitar picks that whirled and spun in the air around her. Before she completely disappeared, I heard her say clearly, "Your father is very proud of you, Sarah Booth. Very proud. You are also a warrior for justice."

And then she was gone.

30

Coleman stopped in front of Dahlia House. Even though he saw me sitting on the porch, he tooted the horn. My aunt Loulane would have taught him some manners. A gentleman always came to the door for a lady.

"Impatient some?" I asked as I hurried down the steps toward him.

"Don't want to keep a lady waiting," he said. "Then again, I don't know where to find a lady."

I shook a fist at him but laughed. I'd never made any claims to be ladylike. And never would. I was a tomboy through and through. "Where are Tinkie and Harold?"

"They're meeting us at Broussard's Landing. That's a good place to launch the drone. It can cover a large portion of the river from there. We'll gradually move down the river until we find where someone has been digging. Or some sign of Brigette."

I jumped into the truck and was about to slam the door when Sweetie Pie and Avalon forced their way into the front seat and then jumped into the back. "Should I put them inside?" I asked Coleman.

"No, they're good. We might need Sweetie Pie's snout," he said. "That terrain can be slow going. If she hits on a scent, it could save us hours."

Yet again, he was correct. And I was glad to take the dogs. They loved to go with us and they loved the water. The minute Pluto had heard the word "river," he'd jumped out the truck window and disappeared in Dahlia House. He wasn't about to be taken back to the Tallahatchie for any reason.

We pulled out down the drive, and I settled into the seat. I watched the scenery flash past the window. It was another blistering June day. Robin's-egg-blue sky. Not a cloud to be seen. Mississippi was heading into a real drought, and that was more depressing news for farmers.

Driving through the Delta with Coleman was one of my simple pleasures. We were connected to this soil, this land, in a way that enhanced the bond between us. We shared a love of something much bigger than we were.

"Are you going to arrest Danny if we find him?" I asked. It wasn't the resolution I wanted, but it would conclude my case in a way that was so much better than finding his body.

"I have to, Sarah Booth. He's a person of interest in burglaries and a murder. Todd Jenkins was killed. Doc's autopsy proved it. If Danny did it, then he'll have to pay."

If Danny was charged, tried, and convicted, the Anderson family would certainly lose their land. But it would be the same outcome if he was dead. I hoped we would find him alive and safe. The rest could be sorted out at a later date. I would work to help prove his innocence.

The rows of cotton and soybeans flashed by my window in a blur that was mesmerizing. My fate had been connected to this land for generations. The Delaney family was part of a multicolored fabric of tragedy and happiness, brutal practices and great kindnesses. I could not speak for the ancestors who had owned slaves. How anyone could think that was okay was beyond me. But not a single family member had fought to preserve slavery. Rather the opposite—they'd fought to end it. But that stain of slavery still touched the land. Each acre. I'd heard it said that anyone who sought to understand the nation had to first understand Mississippi. That was a stretch for many people. How could Jitty love me so much, coming from a place where she'd been viewed as livestock? I couldn't answer that. I could only be grateful she chose to stay in my life.

"What's on your mind, Sarah Booth?" Coleman asked, calling me back from my musings.

"This land. This state. How my life is built on the bones and dreams of so many."

"You're worried about Danny, aren't you? You fear he's guilty?"

Once again, Coleman understood me better than I understood myself. "Yes. I don't know him, but I've met his parents, his friends, the farmers who respect and look up to him. The women who care about him. If he has done these terrible things, it will change them profoundly."

"Most people sitting at home never think about that fact. They see a crime, a person charged, and they hope the perpetrator gets swift punishment. They never, ever comprehend that the ripple effects of a crime never stop with the perp. They don't understand that most prisons today are pay-to-survive. The prisons are for-profit, so they feed the worst possible food and not enough of it. Inmates rely on family to send money so they can survive. It's not a system devoted to rehabilitation and teaching inmates a skill or trade. It is merely intended to punish. And that attitude doesn't help society at large."

I'd visited my share of local and state prisons, and knew how terrible the conditions could be. "You're right. Why is it that people are so thirsty to see others in dire circumstances?"

"It stems from our Puritan ancestry," Coleman said without batting an eye.

I looked at him to see if he was teasing. He wasn't. "You really believe that?"

"I do. Like some religions are all about fear and punishment. Those are effective cudgels to keep people in line, but they don't really touch the heart of the penitent or the prisoner. The Puritans came to America to escape religious persecution and then busied themselves inflicting that same persecution on Native tribes, slaves, and folks with different beliefs. 'Believe as I believe, or suffer' is kind of the way folks think."

"Freedom of religion." I spoke mostly under my breath.

"Only good as long as the courts uphold it. There's a move afoot these days to tell people who and what they can worship. And believe. Rights that we've viewed as inalienable are under fire."

I nodded. I'd seen the same thing. "Unless we demand due process, the rule of law, and protections for all citizens, we each stand a chance of becoming the next victim of a would-be dictator." But we'd fallen down into the tar pit and it was a lovely summer day that held potential for finding Danny and getting answers to some of the pressing questions.

"Maybe when we get on the river we should do a rain dance," I said.

Coleman laughed. "You go right ahead. I'll watch. Maybe you can talk Harold and Tinkie into it."

We fell back into silence as we left the lovely fields behind and entered an area where the wild brakes created a habitat for wildlife. We weren't far from the river, though we'd come at it from a different direction. I saw the sign up ahead for the boat landing, and Coleman turned in. Harold and Tinkie were already waiting for us.

"Now that's a mighty fine drone," Coleman said when he examined the equipment Harold had brought. "We're getting drones in the sheriff's office, but that thing is state of the art."

"The camera is excellent. Great detail and enlargement. And we can add an infrared component if we need it."

"I can't wait to see this thing work," Coleman said.

The boys prepared the drone while Tinkie and I went into the bait shop and tiny store to buy cold drinks and snacks for us. It was going to be a long day. And hot again. I also bought some sausage biscuits for the dogs—they were all there. My two, Tinkie's two, and Harold's two.

"Do we have a plan?" Tinkie asked.

"Let's see what Coleman and Harold suggest." I could come up with a plan, but the boys might have something better. They both worked too hard to get in a lot of fishing, but they still knew the terrain far better than I did.

Sure enough, when we joined them with colas and snacks, they'd come up with a way to search the area most effectively. Harold and Tinkie would launch the drone here and begin to track it downriver along the bends and twists of the Tallahatchie. Coleman and I, with the second remote control, would drive to the next landing and pick up the drone there and fly it down to the next sandbar. We'd work our way downriver, leapfrogging each other. It was the most time-efficient way to do this. If we spotted anything, we'd call the other party and meet up to confront Danny and Brigette—or whoever we found—with a united front.

Coleman and I left Harold and Tinkie as they watched the drone buzz behind the treetops. It was an art to keep it below two hundred feet and above the treetops. Harold had apparently been practicing.

Coleman drove to the next pig trail through the woods that would also take us to the river. He'd found an extensive topo map that was a great help. I could have used it yesterday when I was floating along the river. Some sandbars were not accessible from a road. The map showed it in clear detail.

"Do you think we'll find anything?" The sun was already sparking rebellion in the burned skin on my shoulders, arms, and thighs.

"I do. Look, Danny has to be on the river if he isn't dead. I don't think Brigette would have come all this way if she believed he was dead. I suspect he contacted her and she came to assist him in whatever plot they're carrying out."

The limbs of small trees and bushes slapped the truck and tried to force their way into the windows as we drove toward the river. The dogs were quiet in the back seat, drinking in their surroundings. They were eager, but well-behaved.

At last, we came to a footpath leading to the sandbar. We parked and got out, checking for any indication that another vehicle had been down the path. To my excitement, there were tire tracks in the loamy soil. A truck had been through here. I looked at Coleman, who opened the back door of the truck and released Sweetie Pie and Avalon. The dogs were on the trail.

My hopes rose higher and higher as Sweetie Pie's loud bay echoed off the trees. We had lost the advantage of surprise, but it was possible we'd gained the advantage of terrifying whoever was down by the river.

We raced after the dogs. Coleman tried to block the

whiplike fronds from coming back and slapping me, but it was a narrow trail. At last, we burst into the clearing. A pristine sandbar stretched in front of us. It could have been a photograph for a book about the beauty of Mississippi, but the sand was empty. Not a trace of a human being. The dogs raced toward the water and dove in. The day was hot, and I didn't blame them.

Coleman and I took a more restrained approach. He was a far better tracker than I, and he motioned me over to two sets of footprints. One was clearly a man's. The other could be that of a woman, a small man, or a child. I knew in my gut it was Brigette and Danny. And they were gone.

It was then I saw the pile of sand at the north end of the sandbar. I nudged Coleman and we walked toward it together. We came upon a large, deep hole. Also empty. Shaking water and sand, Sweetie Pie and Avalon joined us. Sweetie jumped into the hole, which was at least four feet deep. It was square, rather than the rectangle of a grave. There were drag marks where something heavy had been pulled over the sand.

"Do you think they found a treasure?" I asked.

Coleman examined the area around the hole. "Something heavy was pulled out. They dragged it to here. Judging from these indentations, it rested here awhile."

"How much would a thousand gold coins weigh?" I asked.

"I don't know, but a lot."

"The value of the coins, if they are actually the 1861-D golden dollars, is in the rarity, not the actual gold," I said.

"Budgie tried to look up the value, but neither of us could really determine anything. He's been calling a numismatist in DC to try to get a value, but so much depends on what a collector is willing to pay."

"So, they got the treasure and escaped."

"That's an assumption, not a fact," Coleman said. He put a hand on my shoulder. "We'll find them, Sarah Booth. If Danny is alive, he will come to the surface eventually. He won't abandon his family. If he found this treasure and is innocent of the burglaries and the murder of Todd Jenkins, he should come forward."

"He should. But woulda, coulda, shoulda doesn't always happen."

"Brigette will have to return to her work. Time doesn't stand still for a model. Either they're hot or they're not. She can't afford to disappear on bookings."

He was right about that. Too right.

Coleman pulled out his phone and called Harold, canceling the handoff of the drone. "I think we found where they were, and they're gone. The boat Brigette rented hasn't shown up in Greenwood, but it could later." He gave Harold the details about the hole in the sandbar.

"It would make sense that they spent the night there gathering the treasure before anyone else found it," Harold said. "Then they loaded whatever was in the hole. Danny probably took the truck and sent Brigette downriver with the boat to turn it in. Maybe we can catch her in Greenwood. Of course, they could have gotten someone else to take the boat."

"We're headed that way as soon as we round up the dogs," Coleman told him.

It was the best plan we could come up with. I photographed the area as I waited for the pups to join us. Together, we pushed through the underbrush as fast as we could. The yellow flies and mosquitoes were as big as the Wicked Witch's flying monkeys, and I was eager to get in the air-conditioning of the truck.

31

By the time we drove to the Greenwood boat landing, a very fancy affair compared to the smaller places upriver, I had eaten a lot of the snacks Tinkie had bought for Coleman and me to share. I crumpled up the little snack bags and stuffed them in my pockets. Deny, deny, deny—that was the way I planned on handling any accusations.

I headed to the landing to check with some of the good old boys hanging around. If Brigette had been there, they'd dang sure remember her. Coleman stopped to take an urgent phone call. Curiosity was eating at me, but finding Brigette took precedence.

When I called out a hello, two of the men signaled me over. I took my phone and showed them Brigette's photo. "Have you seen this woman?"

"What's she done, increase the earth's body temperature by ten degrees?" They both cackled.

"She didn't do anything. I just need to talk to her."

"Isn't that Coleman Peters, the sheriff from over in Zinnia?"

the man asked. They were old, but they were also keenly observant.

"It is. He's my fella. We were planning on a picnic on the river."

"Don't get a case of those sand fleas. You'll be sorry." The men cackled again. They were in rare form.

"I'll be careful. That's how my mama raised me. Careful, but willing to take a risk." I winked at him and he blushed with delight.

"You're a mess, aren't you? You remind me of Libby Delaney."

The smile fell off my face. His words were like a stab in my heart. Not because he was being mean, but because more than anything I wanted to be like my mama. "Thank you. I'm Sarah Booth Delaney, her daughter."

"I thought so," he said. "Ms. Libby was kind to me and my wife when our first child was born. Helena had trouble with the birth. She spun down to a terrible place. Your mama took her to a doctor in Jackson and got her some help. I was afraid she'd harm herself or the baby."

"People didn't understand the hormone fluctuation back then. I'm glad she got help."

"She did. We had two more children and everything went just like clockwork. But your mama checked on us. She took the time to make sure."

To my utter horror, I felt tears sting my eyes. "Thank you." I had to turn the conversation. "Did either of you see this woman?"

"She was here." He stretched his head up and nodded toward a small café serving breakfast all day long. "She was over there a few minutes ago."

I couldn't believe it. My heart began to thud. She might

still be here. I swung around to see what Coleman was doing, and I felt the air leave my lungs. His face was red, and he was speaking tersely into the phone. When he was furious, Coleman didn't yell or romp and stomp. His enunciation became clipped and his jaw hardened until it looked chiseled. Whoever he was talking to had majorly pissed him off.

Instead of calling out to him, I ran over. He saw me coming and abruptly got off the call.

"Brigette may be in the little diner over there. Those men down by the dock said they saw her just a few minutes ago."

"Let's go." Coleman put his phone away and strode toward the café. He was still angry, but it was wearing off. Coleman never stayed angry. He had the ability to get over something and when it was called for, to truly forgive.

I wanted to ask him who he'd been talking to, but I didn't. We were focused on finding Brigette. We could talk later, when he could get aggravated if he needed to. Now, he had to be calm, steady, and bring Brigette in peacefully.

The delicious smell of bacon wafted on a lovely breeze, teasing me. Despite my newfound vegetarianism, the bacon smelled delicious. The screen door creaked with a sound that brought back childhood. Coleman walked into the tiny dining area. A woman sat at the last table, her back to us. Her hair was pulled up in a tractor cap. Her posture was impeccable, and her shoulders were square. It was Brigette. I knew it. Coleman did, too.

"Ms. McEachern," he said as he approached. "I need to talk with you. Would you mind coming with me to the courthouse in Zinnia?"

"You don't have any authority in Leflore County," she responded. She didn't turn to look at Coleman. If she had, she might have reconsidered her words.

"Fine," he said. He pulled out his phone and called the Leflore County sheriff. "I have a suspect in several burglaries and a murder sitting at Londie's Diner down by the bridge. Yeah, yeah. Thanks."

He turned to Brigette. "You can go with the sheriff here. He's got a nice cell waiting for you. I only wanted to talk to you, but you chose to do it your way."

"Call him back. I'll go with you." She took off her hat and shook out her beautiful dark hair. She removed her sunglasses. "I'm sorry. I was being a bitch. I'm hot, tired, and itching from a billion bug bites. It's all I can do not to claw the skin off my legs."

Oh, I felt her pain. I did. Coleman considered for a moment and then called to tell the sheriff he had it handled. "Let's go," he said to Brigette.

"Good thing I've finished eating," she said.

I, on the other hand, was eyeing a catfish plate. But Coleman was ready to go and he was in official mode. I got up, smiled, and headed for the door. But not before I nabbed a basket of hush puppies for the dogs. They shouldn't have to suffer starvation because Coleman was suddenly in a hurry.

The interview room at the sheriff's office in Zinnia didn't have all the latest technology, but I could sit behind the two-way mirror, watch, and listen. Coleman sat across from Brigette. Budgie brought her a cup of coffee and then joined me.

"She sure is pretty," he said. "Why would she risk her modeling career to help Danny break the law?"

"Maybe she didn't. We don't really know what she did or didn't do."

The door creaked open and Tinkie joined me. "We need to talk," she whispered.

Torn between watching the interview or hearing Tinkie's news, I said, "Will it hold for a minute?"

"Sure, but Harold has to get back to the bank soon, and he's waiting."

I didn't have to wait long. Coleman got right to the point. "Brigette, were you with Danny Anderson?"

"I want to speak to a lawyer," she said.

Oh, this wasn't how I wanted it to go. She'd come willingly, and now she was going to stonewall? Coleman didn't really have any evidence to hold her, so this was a dang waste. I gathered my things and started to exit the room with Tinkie when Brigette spoke.

"I will tell you that Danny hasn't done anything wrong. Not really. He's a very good man who is only trying to save his family farm."

"Were you digging on the river?" Coleman asked.

"That's not illegal even if we were." She folded her arms across her chest. Even Tinkie was now focused on the interview.

"Danny needs to come in and clear all of this up. It's the only way," Coleman said.

"I don't disagree. My only issue is the timing. He'll come in when he can." She leaned forward and put a hand on Coleman's arm. "I promise. I promise he'll turn himself in just as soon as he can."

My first reaction was relief, followed by annoyance. Danny had no right to worry so many people. When I found him, I might have to hurt him. I realized Tinkie was looking at me in a strange way. "What?"

"Brigette is flirting with Coleman."

She was, and I didn't like it. But I didn't want to act like a fool. "Fie on her. She's flirting, but Coleman won't bite."

"You're probably right," Tinkie said. She nodded to the interview room, where Brigette's hand had moved up to Coleman's bicep. She gave it a squeeze.

"How do you stay so fit, Sheriff Peters?" she asked.

Oh, it was a ploy as old as the ages. Delilah after Samson's hair. "Coleman is too smart to fall for that," I said stoutly.

"Sarah Booth, Coleman loves you with his whole heart. I don't question that. But never, ever underestimate Brigette McEachern. Or any other self-confident woman who's used to getting her way."

I forced a smile. "I'll heed your words. Thanks, partner. Now, show me what Harold is so excited about."

Brigette's flirtations amused me—because I knew my man. Just the same, I needed a distraction. Tinkie didn't intend for her words to affect me, and I simply had to ignore them. I did trust Coleman. Implicitly. But Brigette was beautiful, wealthy, and smart. I'd be stupid not to see it—and keep it in mind.

32

Harold was hanging out with our pack of dogs on the courthouse lawn when we walked outside. He was trying to teach the dogs to fetch. I knew for a fact that Roscoe and Sweetie Pie would fetch. Chablis was far too prissy to perform a trick, and Zelda and Avalon were just learning to be part of the pack. But it was amusing to watch the dogs teach Harold to fetch. He'd throw the ball. They'd run after it, colliding in Keystone Kops fashion, and then run back to him without the ball. Harold would then go pick up the ball. He was perfectly trained.

When he saw us coming down the courthouse steps, he whistled up the dogs and came over.

"Did Tinkie tell you?" he asked.

"No." I looked at my partner. "Tell me what?"

"Show her," Tinkie said.

Harold obliged, bringing his cell phone from his pocket. "There are some photos and video from the drone flight over the river."

I took his phone and studied the snapshots he'd transferred from the drone to his cell phone. The images were detailed; I could clearly see two other sandbars where a deep hole had been dug. So, Brigette and Danny had merely moved down the river searching for the buried treasure. But had they found it?

"We don't have any images of the sandbar where you and Coleman found the deep hole," Tinkie said. "We didn't get that far downriver with the drone. But at least it shows consistent effort to dig something up."

"Can I borrow the drone?" I asked Harold. "I want to check the rest of the sandbars. There should be three or four from where we tracked Brigette. It shouldn't take long, but I just want to be sure we've covered everything we can."

"Is the drone complicated to work?" Tinkie asked him.

"Piece of cake. Let me show you."

We went to his pickup and he got the drone from the back. He gave me the controls and showed me how to fly it, hover, and take photos or videos. It wasn't all that complicated, but it was a lot to manage.

"I can help," Tinkie said. "Tomorrow. Let's go early before it gets so hot."

That was reasonable. It was well after lunch—actually closer to five than noon. I was hot, tired, and ready for a shower. "Tomorrow is a plan. Just let me take the drone up right now to see if I can manage it."

"Sure." Harold put it down in a clear place on the lawn of the courthouse.

At first I was tentative, but I got the hang of it and sent it soaring into the sky.

"Remember, you can't get above a certain level. It could interfere with planes."

"Right." I nodded. "I think I can do this. Let me bring it down."

Before I could touch the controls there was a loud bang and the drone exploded in midair. Someone had shot it out of the sky!

Coleman and the deputies heard the shot and came boiling out of the courthouse and onto the lawn. Harold, who looked stricken, was picking up the pieces of his drone that had fallen to the ground. It was destroyed.

"What happened?" Coleman took in the basics—the blasted drone—but he needed details. Harold supplied them. I was still a little speechless. Somehow I felt this was my fault.

"You didn't do anything," Harold reassured me.

"But I—" Sweetie Pie, leading the pack of dogs, took off toward the local hardware store. Somehow, tiny little Chablis was keeping up.

"Let's go!" Coleman said. "DeWayne, Budgie, jump in a patrol car and follow us. The dogs know who did it."

Coleman and I set off on foot while the deputies jumped into patrol cars and Harold and Tinkie took his truck. The chase was on.

Coleman was two blocks ahead of me, hot on Sweetie Pie's trail, when he turned down an alley. A blind alley, as I knew from past bicycle adventures as a kid. Whoever had shot the drone was about to get arrested.

By the time I got there, Coleman had the culprit in handcuffs. When he escorted him out of the alley, with the help of the dogs, I stopped. It was Wylie Moulton. He glared at me as Coleman pushed him along.

"You can't charge me with anything," he said. "You can't prove I did anything."

Maybe, maybe not. I motioned Coleman away from the suspect. "When I was on the river, someone took a potshot at me. They didn't try to hit me. It could have been Wylie."

"And you're telling me this now?" Coleman was a little exasperated.

"It was more intimidation than trying to hit me. But I knew I needed to tell you."

He gave me a long look. "Sarah Booth, he dumped his rifle in the trash can. Can you grab it for me? Remember not to touch any part of it."

"I can do that." I dropped back and went over to the big can painted like a cotton bale that the city council had installed. The cans were all over the town. A clever way to encourage folks not to litter. When I lifted the lid, I saw the barrel of the rifle. I stepped into the hardware store and got a pair of cleaning gloves. Those would work perfectly. I picked up the gun and headed back to the courthouse.

The deputies had turned around and gone back, and so had Harold and Tinkie. I needed to walk because I had a passel of hounds on red alert. The pooches, whom I was praising lavishly, pranced along the sidewalk, obviously proud of themselves. To my surprise, a large black raven circled overhead. Poe had joined us. He didn't often leave Dahlia House unless he was following me. But somehow, he'd known to come to town.

I held out my hand and he settled on it. Boy, I was glad he wasn't flying around when Wylie Moulton went on a shooting spree. "Go home," I told him. "Fly low and fast! I'll be there shortly."

Folks would say the bird couldn't understand what I said, but Poe flapped his wings and took off. He circled me once and then disappeared into the tree line, in the direction of Dahlia House. Now it was time to get back inside the courthouse and see if Coleman could get Wylie Moulton to confess to digging up buried treasure or, more seriously, to murdering Todd Jenkins. Todd was the odd man out in the whole case. Had Wylie killed his friend Todd? Was he in cahoots with Danny? Did he have the goods on Danny and Pearl? Or Danny and Brigitte? Why had he shot Harold's drone? Had he shot at me on the river? Oh, I had questions for him.

33

By the time I got the critters rounded up and settled in the sheriff's office, Coleman was well into his interview of Wylie Moulton. He'd allowed Brigette, who'd pleaded a headache, to go to her hotel. She'd promised to make herself available when he needed her.

I slipped into the room where DeWayne and Budgie were listening in. Tinkie and Harold had driven to an electronics specialist to see if any footage from the blasted drone could be salvaged. It only made sense that Wylie shot the drone because he feared it had captured something incriminating. Well, that was the logical way to look at it. Logic didn't always walk hand in hand with Wylie.

"I told you a million times, I haven't done anything wrong," Wylie said with a huff. He never looked into the two-way mirror, so I didn't know if he was aware he had a bigger audience than Coleman.

I took a seat between the deputies, who were watching the interview with amusement.

"He's drunk as Cooter Brown," Budgie said. "He said he shot the drone because a big black raven had been following him around and he thought the drone was an alien raven sent to harvest his organs."

"Good grief. And he's allowed to carry a loaded gun," De-Wayne said. "We need some better gun laws."

We quieted and our focus turned to Coleman when he started talking. "Were you on the Tallahatchie yesterday or today?" Coleman asked Wylie.

"No business of yours if I was or wasn't." Wylie folded his arms and pursed his lips. "I ain't talkin' no more."

"Good, because he's about as useful as a screen door on a submarine," Budgie said. "I think he's brain damaged."

I sat quietly. I was lucky Coleman allowed me to sit in at all, so I kept my yap shut. I'd told him that someone shot close to me yesterday—a warning. I was pretty sure it was Wylie.

"Did you kill Todd Jenkins?" Coleman asked.

Wylie shook his head. Then said, "We were best friends. Why would I hurt him?"

"Money," Coleman said. "You know that buried treasure rumored to be on the river? Well, someone dug it up."

That got Wylie's attention. "That Todd. We had a pact. We were gonna split whatever was found. If he found it, and now he's dead, then it should all belong to me."

"What were you searching for?" Coleman asked.

"Silver and jewels from Columbine Plantation. Those plantation people were killed by that outlaw gang. My granny told me all about it. She knew people who lived at Columbine and knew the real story. They were shot dead by the Norton Clan, who buried the treasure on the river. All those riches have been on one of those sandbars for over a hundred years. Heck, Todd and I searched with metal detectors. We even got one of those gizmos that x-ray the ground. We never found anything. But that Danny, I think he stumbled on something and wouldn't tell us. Todd must have followed him or something."

This was getting closer to motive than I'd been all day. Maybe Todd's death was self-defense. If Danny had found the treasure, and Todd felt he had a claim on it—Todd certainly had one of the valuable gold coins in his pocket when he died—the men may have fought and blood was shed. Whoever found the treasure, the three men might have had a set-to. Once Todd was dead, Danny may have panicked and called Brigette to help him hide the treasure.

But why not Pearl? How did the preacher's wife fit into the story? Was she Danny's lady love, or was it Brigette? I hoped Coleman would pursue this line of questioning.

Almost as if he could read my mind, he cleared his throat. "You're in a lot of trouble, Wylie. You can help yourself out by giving me some information. Has Danny been hiding out on the river?"

"I don't know what Danny does or doesn't do."

"Was he hunting the treasure with you?"

"Not with me. Danny thinks he's smarter than me and Todd. He's always felt he was smarter."

"What's Danny's relationship with Pearl Wingard?"

Wylie shrugged. "The preacher's wife! She and Danny were always together, whispering and plotting. The women love Danny. All of them. Even that rich broad, the model from New York."

"Did Pearl help Danny hide out on the river?"

"You ask her. She's not hard to find. She's up on that bridge almost every day, pining for Danny or—" His expression turned mean. "—maybe something else entirely."

Coleman chose to ignore the implication. "Wylie, did you

kill Todd? Before you answer, know that he had a very valuable 1861-D gold coin in his pocket. It seems he may have found the treasure."

Wylie started out of his chair, but Coleman rose quickly and pressed him back into the seat. "Stay calm. Do yourself a favor."

"Todd had a gold coin?"

Watching the interview, I believed Wylie had not been aware.

Coleman pulled up his phone and showed Wylie a photo of the coin.

"He found the treasure. He really found the treasure." Wylie was more bemused than angry. "Where was it? How many more coins are there? What about the jewels and silver?"

"Was Todd trying to cheat you out of your share?"

Wylie frowned and his brow furrowed. "Todd wouldn't do that. It was Danny Anderson. He found Todd with the treasure and he killed him. Todd would have called me. He would have shared. We were in it together. Danny never shared good stuff with anyone."

"Did anyone else know you were looking for the treasure?"

Wylie nodded. "Folks on the river. They'd see us sometimes. A few asked questions, but most of them laughed at us. Said we were fools for believing in a fairy tale. But look! We were right! All along, we were right! What did you do with the rest of it?"

"First, you tell me where Danny is hiding out." Coleman played him like a fiddle.

"He might be at the oxbow lake that the Columbine Plantation was situated on," Wylie said. "'Course you got to know how to look for that. The river changed course a few decades ago and water stopped feeding into the lake. Over time, it just dried up. Only the old-timers knew where it once was or how to go about looking for it. Todd and I figured the treasure would be buried not too far from that lake."

"Okay, so where would that be?" Coleman plunked a map of the river down on the table. "Show me."

Wylie studied the map. He traced the river with a finger, checking the area around the water's path. "Can't tell on the map. The river shifts all the time. The lake once fed off the river and went deep into the interior. It was smart because Columbine had access by road and water. And the lake was hidden. You had to know where to look to find the opening. Or that's what my grandpa said. He helped us figure out where it might be." His voice wavered. "That was better than ten years ago when we were all in school. Then, the treasure hunt was about adventure, not desperate need like it is now. It ain't no game now. Especially not for us farmers."

He wasn't exaggerating. Finding the treasure—if it was as plentiful as everyone anticipated—would settle the debt they all carried. A fairy-tale ending.

"Wylie, your friend is dead. Murdered. Now I'm going to ask you a question and I want an honest answer. When did you last see Danny Anderson? And where?"

Wylie looked around the room as if someone might have written the correct answer on the wall. At last, he spoke. "The day before Todd died we all met up on a sandbar. Todd took some supplies to Danny, who was hiding out from the creditors. He figured if he wasn't around, they couldn't foreclose on his property. That Levi Butler had been hunting for him, trying to pressure him into a bad deal. Danny thought if he could just stay out of the way and hunt for the treasure, he might turn things around. We all hoped that."

Grown men hoping to find a buried treasure to save their heritage—it was heartbreaking.

"You and Todd were helping Danny?"

Wylie nodded. "Danny hadn't done anything wrong. He was just laying low for a few weeks, hoping to see some rain, to even have a flicker of hope that he'd have a banner crop this summer. Pfft! Not even a drop of rain has fallen in the last two weeks. Each day, the hope dies a little more."

"And Pearl, was she helping him?"

"When she could. Pearl . . ." He didn't go any further, and I knew he wouldn't. Whatever the relationship between Pearl and Danny, Wylie was not going to spill the beans. He may have been drinking, but the alcohol hadn't loosened his lips enough to reveal those secrets. I had to wonder, too, why Wylie still had such loyalty to Danny. Wylie had indicated that he believed Danny had killed Todd. He'd even talked of revenge. So why protect Danny now? The dynamics of these men—and women—were hard to figure out. What looked like betrayal ultimately came across as loyalty. I wanted Coleman to press him hard on Danny's location. I started to tap on the window, but DeWayne shushed me away.

"We're going to find Danny," Coleman told him. "And if he's broken any laws, you'll be a conspirator, and you'll be prosecuted. I know times are hard and the crops are drying up in the fields right now, but think how much worse for your farm and family it will be if you're in prison."

Coleman's words hit Wylie hard. He literally paled. "I haven't done anything wrong. I haven't broken any laws."

"Someone killed Todd Jenkins. You've admitted you were treasure hunting with him and Danny. That's a mighty big motive staring me right in the face, especially since Todd had that gold coin in his pocket."

"I didn't hurt Todd, and if Danny has found that treasure and isn't planning to share, maybe Todd couldn't take it. We're all in a sinking ship. That money could save us all." Maybe

Wylie was still a little tipsy. Or maybe he believed what he was saying. Either way, Coleman wasn't buying it.

"Wylie, you need some time to think. Go home and sleep it off. I can find you if I need you. And, by the way, if you ever fire a weapon at Sarah Booth again, you'll regret it. Warning or not."

There was a light tap on the door and Tinkie was peering in the little square window. She signaled me to come out. A wave of remorse for Harold's drone came over me. His expensive drone was destroyed because he was helping me. Somehow, I'd have to make this right. I just feared the cost of such a high-tech little flying machine would break me.

I stepped out of the room and closed the door. Tinkie looked at me with consternation. "Coleman is just going to let Wylie go home? He blew up a drone and shot at you."

"Coleman has a plan. If Wylie is free, he can maybe lead the law to where Danny is hiding. If he isn't lying about the whole thing. Did you find anything?" I asked her. She was excited, so I felt a surge of hope.

"We did. Harold was able to salvage most of the photos and some of the video footage. When Wylie shot the drone, he didn't hit the camera, just the flying mechanism."

"Okay. I just wish he hadn't shot it at all."

"Harold isn't mad," Tinkie said. "He had the dang thing insured. He'd tell you himself but he had to get back to the bank. Coleman acquired a court order, so Harold's digging into Wylie's and Todd's financials for him. To see if they came into any money unexpectedly."

"Harold is a good friend."

"Uh, he left Roscoe and Pumpkin for you to babysit. He didn't have time to take them home. You know they always manage a jailbreak from his place. Those two dogs can open doors, scale fences, climb vines—and who knows what other mischief."

"Where are they?" I loved them, but I knew them too well. Roscoe was always up to no good. In fact, he was probably already out there peeing on the shoes of some pompous person. Pumpkin, on the other hand, was known to tear into people's garbage and drag empty prescription bottles for little blue pills and empty liquor bottles to the steps of the Baptist church.

A lot of private and personal details of a person's life could be found in their trash. Irate didn't begin to describe most people's reactions.

Harold had gotten death threats because of his dogs' actions. Animal control had been called numerous times, but Roscoe and Pumpkin were the Bonnie and Clyde of the canine world. Someone had even started a Facebook fan page for the dogs. They were notorious with a capital N.

"See if Budgie can download those photos," I said. "Let's take them to Dahlia House—with the dogs." I had to find Roscoe and Pumpkin. My dogs were quietly snoozing under the desks in the sheriff's office. "Once Coleman has a chance, he can look at the pictures. Then we'll talk when he gets to Dahlia House."

"Good idea," Tinkie said. "An excellent plan!"

34

On the way to Dahlia House, we stopped by a local camera shop. The owner, a friend of Tinkie's, let us use her magnifying light table to check out the photos from the drone. When we'd selected a dozen photos, she was able to print the digital images for me. It was much easier to see the details in a print rather than a digital image.

And what we found was well worth pursuing.

Tinkie and I spread the photos on the counter and waited for Coleman. We'd only finished one martini each by the time he got there.

"Did Wylie tell you anything useful?" I asked.

"Let me see those photos first. Then I'll tell you everything."

Coleman pored over the images. Finally, he pointed to the one I'd also pinpointed as the most significant. But I wanted to know if he saw what Tinkie and I had seen.

"That's Brigette, isn't it?" He pointed to a person.

The figure in question was partially obscured by a canopy of tree leaves, but I was certain it was the model. So was Tinkie.

But there were two other people in the photo. A male, likely Danny Anderson. And Pearl Wingard. She was in a clearing and easily identifiable.

"How did Pearl end up with them?" Coleman asked.

Neither Tinkie nor I had an answer. Just a guess. "She had to have driven in and met them. Maybe that's how they got the treasure off the sandbar."

"Folks at Fox's Landing would have mentioned seeing Pearl if she'd been there. She's too well-known," Tinkie pointed out. "The gossip would have been flying. It would have beat us down the river."

She wasn't wrong about that. "But why is Pearl involved?" I asked. "This is only going to hurt her husband. He's a tolerant man, but Danny is wanted for questioning in a murder and several burglaries. Not a good look for a preacher's wife to be with a suspect in some crimes."

"Reverend Wingard may be a little too understanding for his wife's own good," Coleman said. "It would behoove Pearl to steer clear of Danny, at least right now."

"Knowing the right thing to do and doing it are two different things," Tinkie mused. "We all know that."

"Look at this," Coleman said, tapping one of the photos. "It looks like they are each carrying something heavy."

The leaves blocked so much of what we needed to see, but the stooped posture of the three people did make it seem they were each carrying a heavy load.

"If they got the gold to a vehicle, where would Pearl take it?" I asked. "Did Danny go with Pearl?" We already knew that Brigette had brought the rented boat in at the Greenwood landing. It made sense that Danny and Pearl had taken the treasure—if there was one—with them. But to where?

"I'm going to see if Budgie can enhance these photos,"

Coleman said. "Can I have the memory card from the drone? Just in case he needs it."

"Sure." Tinkie pulled it from her pocket and handed it to him. "That's a good idea. Budgie is smart with technology."

"Yes. Thanks. I'll—" His phone rang before he could finish his sentence. When he looked at the caller ID he frowned. "I need to take this call." He stood up and answered.

A loud male voice came over the phone. The man was near hysterical, bellowing and cussing. Coleman was not an excitable man, but the blood flushed up his neck.

"Could you please quiet down?" he asked in a super-calm voice, which told me how angry he was.

The yelling on the other end continued.

"Your Honor, please stop yelling." Coleman was icy.

"You don't tell me what to do." The man was so loud I could even distinguish his words.

"Judge, I'm going to hang up if you don't get yourself under control."

Coleman was not a stickler for decorum, but he wouldn't tolerate abuse from anyone. Not even a judge. I was dying to know which judge. Tinkie was also drinking in every syllable.

"I don't know what you're talking about," Coleman said. "No one has been harassing Levi Butler or any other land agent. But if these farmers catch Butler out on their property without permission, they're going to kick his ass, and I won't be arresting them for it. Butler is a parasite."

"You'd better watch your step, Peters. You aren't impervious to an election challenge. Butler and his friends may just fund your opponent."

Coleman also didn't respond well to pressure. "Give it your best shot, Truett."

I gripped the countertop. Mark Truett, the circuit court

judge who'd taken my father's place on the bench. He'd been the attorney for the school board when Daddy was alive. Now he was the top judge in the district, and in my investigation, I'd learned his name had been linked with the young woman, Charlaine Smith, who was said to haunt the Tallahatchie Bridge.

Judge Truett was undisguised ambition. He'd steadily worked his way up the food chain of the local justice system. My father hadn't cared for him—thought him overly ambitious and basically uneducated about how the law should be applied. But Truett had raised the money to campaign for the circuit court judgeship, and once he was in office, he was popular with the money men who funded so many candidates that did their bidding. One election year, when Truett had run unsuccessfully for district attorney, my dad had put a FOR SALE sign in his yard—as a prank, but a prank with meaning. Ever since then he'd despised my parents.

"Tell him to piss off," I said.

Coleman nodded. "I have to go, Your Honor. Have a good evening." He hung up before the judge could reply.

"What was that?" Tinkie asked.

"Judge Truett is upset that you've been questioning local residents about their farms."

"Me?" I was a little shocked. "I haven't offended anyone."

"Oh, but you have." He was amused.

"Who?" Tinkie and I asked together.

"It would seem Vera Volt has taken real offense at the cruel and unrelenting grilling you gave her."

Tinkie and I burst into laughter. It was the only suitable response.

"Just as I thought," Coleman said. "Vera is stirring the pot. Again."

"Coleman, I think Vera stole that christening gown from Pearl and buried it on the river trying to start trouble for the Wingards. Or at least for Pearl. She has a crush on Micah. She'd be really happy if Pearl evaporated."

"What would she hope to gain?" Coleman asked.

"As you said, just stirring the pot. It made me think maybe Pearl had done something." I held up a hand. "It was a jump to conclusion, I know. But if it occurred to me, wouldn't it also occur to others?"

"Sarah Booth is right," Tinkie said. "It isn't a far jump to think that maybe Pearl and Danny had an affair."

"And they got rid of the evidence?" Coleman didn't fall victim to assumptions and gossip as easily as Tinkie and I did. "That's a little far-fetched."

"You're forgetting that gossip can do as much damage as the truth," Tinkie said. "There are some people only too willing to believe the worst of someone they're jealous of. Micah loves Pearl completely. He would do whatever is necessary to protect her and shield her from any threat. You wouldn't believe she and Danny threw a baby off the bridge or harmed an infant—or anyone else. But there are people like Vera who want to believe the worst of others. And once the gossip starts and the rumors are passed around, it would make it hard for Pearl and Micah to stay in Leflore County. He might be voted out of the church. Life isn't fair."

Her words hit me hard. Gossip was treacherous. It could have far-reaching consequences. And if the congregation of Micah's church began to view his wife as a criminal, it wouldn't be pretty for him. Or for Pearl.

"But why would Vera, or anyone, do that? If she's fond of Micah, surely she would see that such damaging gossip would ruin him as well as Pearl."

"Some people will try to destroy what they can't have. You know that." Tinkie pushed her martini glass toward me and I got up to refresh our drinks and fix a bourbon for Coleman. It had been a long, hot day. We'd made some progress on finding Danny, but he was still out of pocket.

"I'm going back to the office for a little bit," Coleman said, waving the drink away.

"What's up?" I asked.

"I want to bring Brigette in. Now that I know she was on the river with Danny, she needs to tell me where he's hiding. I'm thinking he has a river house or someplace safe where he's staying. You know those houses are scattered all down the river, and most folks only use them for fishing weekends. We have to find him and bring him in."

"Do you think she'll tell you?" I asked. I hated myself for the little twinge of jealousy I felt. Coleman was true blue. I believed that. Brigette was the wild card. I remembered her hand on his arm. And the look Tinkie threw at me told me she had her own concerns.

"For Danny's sake, I hope she will."

"Why not ask Pearl?" Tinkie asked. I could have kissed her.

"Pearl is in the most precarious position if she knows Danny is up to something. I think Brigette would be more likely to talk. She has her whole big life in New York. She has money to burn. She'll be more comfortable."

Coleman's logic wasn't wrong, but I could also make a case that Brigette had little to lose by obfuscating the facts.

"Want us to go with you?" Tinkie asked.

I wanted to kiss her, but didn't.

"No, you girls stay here and finish your drinks. I want to take these prints to Budgie, and I'll be home in time to put something on the grill, if you'd like."

"Sounds perfect." I grinned, following it up with a big kiss.

"I'll hurry home," Coleman said, smiling. "I have plans for you tonight, Sarah Booth."

He was out the door when I looked at Tinkie.

"I'll have the fire department stand by in case you two get so hot you burn the house down."

It felt good to laugh. I'd been far too tense. "Now let's see about figuring out where Danny might be. Wouldn't it be fabulous if we beat Coleman to the punch?" I asked.

"Indeed. Hey, have you talked to the Leflore County sheriff? Shouldn't he be up to his ears in this case?"

She had a very good point. "Maybe I should speak to the water rescue, too."

"Let's make some calls."

35

I called the water rescue while Tinkie called Pearl Wingard. Both sessions ended up being brief. The water rescue said Fox's Landing reported that all of their boats were accounted for. They did give a list of rentals—Brigette McEachern and fifteen other people, all male fishermen and none with connections to Danny Anderson that I could pinpoint.

Tinkie's call to Pearl was short-lived when Micah answered and said that Pearl had gone to West Point, Mississippi, to visit her aunt. He agreeably supplied the aunt's name and address. If he suspected an underlying motive for Tinkie's call to his wife, he didn't let on. But of course we knew Pearl wasn't on the other side of the state in West Point, because she'd been on the Tallahatchie River with Brigette and the man we believed to be Danny.

"She's lying to him," Tinkie said. Her disappointment in Pearl was clear. Tinkie might not condemn people for bumping uglies, but she couldn't abide a liar. "Tell the truth and shame the devil" was her motto.

I didn't much cotton to liars, either, but I was sometimes in the habit of fudging the truth. Sometimes to spare another's feelings. Sometimes to get myself out of a jam. My attitude was a bit more lax than Tinkie's when it came to holding to the absolute letter of the truth. Lying was not a good thing; it was a moral quagmire. But life sometimes depended on the white lie or the lie of omission.

"Sarah Booth!" Tinkie's voice whipcracked me back to the present. "What are you lying about? Or what do you intend to lie about?"

"Nothing!" I gave her my wounded-puppy-dog eyes.

Instead of being remorseful for accusing me, she laughed. "Stop acting the fool. I know you lie when it's convenient."

"I do not!" I lied.

"Can the false outrage. You do it all the time, mostly with good intentions. But good intentions aren't a substitute for good choices."

This time I rolled my eyes—aggressively.

"Oh, stop it." She laughed long and hard. "I am upset that Pearl has lied to Micah. I'm tempted to tell him."

"No, you aren't." That was a bridge too far. "She has her reasons."

"Because she's boinking Danny?"

Now I laughed. Tinkie and the word "boinking" did not go together. "Because that isn't your job or your place. Let them manage their own relationship. Think about it. No good will come of telling Micah. He either already knows, or he doesn't want to know."

"Are you aware that 'boinking' comes from the sound that mattress springs generate when a couple makes love?" Tinkie asked.

I was definitely in awe of my partner. "Where did you hear that?"

She shrugged. "I have my sources, and I won't lie about them."

"I'm going to get even with you, Tinkie. Sooner or later."

"You can try."

"Sassy wench" was a term that suited Tinkie. But I was done with wordplay. We had a missing farmer and a missing preacher's wife to account for. "Since you already called Micah and he said Pearl was visiting her aunt, why don't you call him back to see if you can weasel any more info from him?"

"Weaseling a preacher may get me sent to hell."

"And?" I asked.

"What are you going to do?" she countered.

"Give Vera Volt a call."

Tinkie's perfect mouth formed a big red O. I knew it wasn't a job she wanted. "Why would you do that?" Tinkie asked.

"Because I'm going to trick her into going on the river with me tomorrow. And once I get her out in the wilderness, I'm going to find out exactly what her role in all of this really is."

"I don't want to go, but I sure want a recording of this," Tinkie said. "How do you purport to make her tell the truth?"

"I found out a juicy little tidbit from Cece the last time I talked to her."

"That would be what?"

"Vera never learned to swim." My smile went from ear to ear. I felt as if maybe I had grown a few crocodile teeth to go along with it.

"You can't dump her in the deep water." Tinkie's eyes widened. "Can you?"

"Only if she won't talk."

Tinkie knew I'd never endanger a person's life, but as she had commented before, I was a very strong swimmer. And frightening a person didn't equal endangering. Again, Tinkie was a more black-and-white kind of gal. I leaned more gray with the ability to blur the sharp edges.

"Now let's mix some drinks for Coleman and Oscar. They'll be here soon. Coleman is grilling and you're making a salad."

"I am?" Tinkie was always shocked when anyone let her near food preparation.

"You are. And I'll help you chop. Tomorrow, I'm taking Vera to the river."

"And I'm taking Brigette to lunch. If she plans to stay in the area much longer, I'll find out for sure."

She was the best, best friend ever.

36

A heavy fog hung over the land as I set off the next morning. Vera had tried to worm out of the river trip, but the thought of catching Pearl in a compromising position—which I had dangled as bait—was too much temptation. She couldn't walk away. But it sure didn't keep her from whining and moaning.

"Can't we take your vehicle into the woods?" she asked. "They aren't going to be on the water this early. No civilized person is up and about at this time."

I'd rented a boat from a small tackle shop closer to Greenwood. There was no need to go all the way upriver to Fox's Landing. I didn't want to be on the water all day again either. I knew where we'd found Brigette, Pearl, and the man I presumed to be Danny—though that was still unconfirmed. Brigette had pretended to work with Coleman, but she hadn't revealed anything. Budgie and DeWayne had been tasked with running her down. Soon the deputies would have her back in the sheriff's office.

"You look like you're contemplating suicide," Vera said to me as I pushed the boat off the dock and into the river.

"Thanks for those cheerful words."

"What's wrong with you?"

I sighed and looked at her. "The company I keep gives me stomach cramps."

She shot the bird at me and laughed. "You're clever, Sarah Booth. Way too clever. And yet here you are, ferrying me around like precious cargo. What are you getting out of all this?"

"I know my actions don't make sense to you." I decided to change tactics and go for humble and stupid. "It's kind of you to help me with my investigation. I guess I'm going to be obligated to you for the rest of my life."

She brightened up. "Yes. Yes, you are. I like that."

"Vera, do you know Danny Anderson at all? I mean, I'm sure he found you attractive, like all the rest of the men. Why didn't you ever date him? Or did you?"

Vera's lips thinned. All around us were the sounds of early morning on a fine June day. She was too busy listening to her thoughts to hear any of the birdcalls or whir of insects.

"Danny didn't date. Not anyone. Plenty of women tried, but he was married to that land. Or so it seemed. He had a few flings in high school, but as an adult he always had his focus on Pearl."

"What's Danny like? I mean, is he kind? Is he controlling?" As I questioned her, the boat gently drifted along with the current. I wasn't in a hurry. I had a lot of questions. If I played to Vera's vanity, she might answer them.

"He's smart. Everyone says that. And he's focused on bringing Mississippi into the future of clean farming."

"That's a good thing, right?"

"As long as it doesn't impact the bottom line. And I think you have your answer to that. He's losing the farm. All this green insanity and whining about climate change. Just grow some plants or quit farming."

"The weather's been hard on everyone."

"Oh, yes, I forget you have acreage that you pay someone to farm for you."

Oh, brother. "Yeah, Billy Watson does a great job managing the land. He knows more about farming than I could possibly learn. You know, he's an advocate for halting herbicides and other cancer-causing agents that farmers have been using."

"Good for him. And good for you."

We'd gone off on a tangent and I needed to correct course, with Vera and with the boat. We were about to coast up onto a sandbar.

"How much longer do we have to drift like this? Turn the motor on. It's getting too hot."

The sun had burned off the layer of fog that had kept the temperatures tolerable. Now it was just bright and hot, with an expected high of near a hundred degrees. I'd grown up playing outside in the Mississippi summers, riding bikes, and playing kickball or softball, but this heat was unrelenting. It was one more element in the battle the farmers were fighting.

Per Vera's request, I started the small outboard. We picked up a little speed and I had to admit the breeze felt good. I let Vera enjoy it for a few moments before I cut the motor, tossed the anchor over, and leaned back in my seat.

"What are you doing?" Vera asked. "Start it up again. Get us moving."

"Can you swim, Vera?"

The question shocked her. I had both life preservers under

my feet at the stern of the boat, and I knew Vera wouldn't attempt to get them. If I rocked the boat just a little, she'd have a conniption.

"What's wrong with you? Point the boat to the sandbar and let me out."

She was gripping the sides of the boat. I gave it a gentle little rock. She squawked like a chicken.

"You're crazy," she said. Her voice was quieter. "What are you trying to do?"

"I'm intent on getting the truth out of you. One way or the other. See, if I rock the boat a little harder, and if you fall out, and if you can't make it to shore, then I'll just tell everyone you confessed to . . . whatever I decide. No one will dispute it because you'll be, well, dead."

"You better take me to shore. Right now."

"Folks say the Tallahatchie is haunted, Vera. I believe it, too. This particular part of the river has the deepest hole in the whole length of the Tallahatchie." I was making it up as I went along. "Folks around here say that a whole family drowned right here. They were picnicking on the sandbar and a teenager swam out to right about here, where we're sitting. Somehow he got caught in a current that pulled him under. When he didn't pop up, his brother went after him. The same thing happened. Then the sister rushed out to try to save them. She disappeared, too. The last to try to swim to their rescue were both parents. They went under and never came up."

"You are lying through your teeth," Vera said. "You're just trying to upset me."

"No, I'm just giving you a little history lesson. You know they found all five of those bodies right here. A tree had washed down the river and sank in this deep hole. The currents going around that big tree caused a suction that pulled that whole family to their deaths."

"No such thing ever happened." Vera wasn't quite as sure as she'd been before.

"Call Cece and ask her. Here." I pulled out my phone and dialed my reporter friend. "Cece, I'm on the river with Vera Volt. I was telling her about the family who all drowned about three miles from the Big Switch Landing. She doesn't believe me."

I put the phone on speaker. "Vera, it was awful. My folks talked about it when I was little. That family . . . What a tragedy."

"I was telling Vera they pulled them out with grappling hooks. They died with horror on their faces. Folks speculated that some evil monster caught them one by one and held them under." I gave a dramatic pause. "But I don't believe in monsters. It was just the river."

"Ms. Falcon, please call the law and tell them Sarah Booth is holding me hostage on the river." Vera was screaming.

"I'm sorry. You're breaking up, and I have a deadline." Cece disconnected. Thank goodness she'd played along.

"Vera, did you steal the christening gown from Pearl's attic?"

"Why do you care?" Vera asked, searching for her normal bravado that had abandoned her.

"That's an easy question. You're so delighted to ruin Pearl's life because you're jealous of her. I thought a little payback was called for."

"Buzz off, Sarah Booth. Get a life. You're poking around into everyone's business. Micah Wingard deserves a loyal, loving wife, and Pearl is not that. She's a hussy. A two-timing hussy."

"And you know this how?" I pressed.

"I know plenty. And one thing I know is that once I get back to town—and I will get off this stupid river and get home—

you are going to jail. I'm going to press charges of kidnapping and endangerment. You'll see. Not even Coleman Peters is going to be able to save you from the fate you've earned. Speaking of Coleman, Brigette has been asking around about him. About how serious you two are. I told her you refused to commit so Coleman is pretty much a free agent."

I felt the strong urge to throttle her. I couldn't let her see she was getting to me. "Always plotting to ruin someone's relationship, right, Vera? Do your worst. Coleman isn't that kind of man."

"Every man is that kind of man. You don't know a thing about men, do you?"

"Maybe not. But what I do know is that there's a long stretch of potential accidents and a sunburn between sitting here with me and getting back to Zinnia. If you don't want to answer my questions about Danny and Todd Jenkins, I can wait."

After thirty minutes of sitting in the very hot sun in the middle of the river without seeing or hearing another living soul, I realized that I didn't have to throw Vera in the river to make her talk. The sun was going to cook the answers out of her. I was suffering, too, but I was okay with that. Whatever it took. Because I was in control of when we ended this test of wills, I had the upper hand.

"You're going to pay for this." Vera had slumped into the bottom of the boat. She was dipping her hand in the river and bringing water up to splash on her hot face. At least I'd brought an old straw gardening hat. "You're sitting out here in the middle of nowhere with me while your beau is making time with a supermodel. You're not very bright."

"Give it up, Vera. I trust Coleman. But you can answer some questions and I'll take you to shore. Did you bury the christening gown you stole from Pearl's attic?" I just kept on with the same questions over and over.

"Yes! Okay? Yes! I did that."

She was cracking! "Why?" I kept my voice without inflection.

"Because I wanted to upset Micah, to make him see what she was up to with Danny. I wanted him to divorce her so he would see me."

That was more honesty than I'd expected. "To what end, Vera? Micah loves Pearl. If he gave up on her he'd probably give up on romance forever. Did you ever think of that?"

"As I said earlier, you don't know a damn thing about men, Sarah Booth. As soon as Pearl was gone, I would have been the most compassionate person he ever met. He would cry on my shoulder, and I would mourn with him. Men are easy to manipulate. Make them feel strong. Make them feel like the heroes of the story and you can get whatever you want."

I didn't doubt some men were like that. But not Micah. He sought deeper, more complex relationships. I told her so.

"You think Micah is so different. Well, he isn't. I would have been in his bed within three weeks of him kicking her out. Men aren't built to be alone. They need a woman. I'd be willing to bet Coleman is lining up your replacement."

I rolled my eyes. "Do you know where Danny is?"

"I do not. You can broil my brain in this sun, but I can't tell you what I don't know."

"Who killed Todd Jenkins?" I asked.

"I don't have any proof."

Vera had a grapevine of gossip. I was curious who she blamed. That was the first time Vera had let the lack of proof slow her roll. "Who do you think did it?"

"One of two people—Danny or Wylie Moulton."

"Why would Danny or Wylie kill their friend?"

"You really don't understand dynamics, do you? Danny is viewed as the smartest farmer in the region. He's a national figure. Other farmers look to him for advice and help. Todd and Wylie have worked just as hard as Danny, but none of the accolades fell in their laps. That's hard on a man's ego. Here again, your lack of knowledge about the male of the species is your downfall."

Vera was a parasite, sucking my energy with her ugly view of men. "Not all men are such simpletons. Some have values and heart and depth."

"I'll put money on it that my view is accurate. In fact, let's run a test case with your beau."

"I'm not involving Coleman in any of your conniving scenarios."

"Chicken." She grinned. It was the first time she'd had a spark in the last hour.

"I'm not a chicken. I don't play with my friends in an effort to win an argument."

"I'll bet you that I know more about men than you do. If I'm wrong, I'll answer any ten questions you want to ask."

This was a pointless and dumb conversation. "Just tell me where you were the day Todd was killed."

"The old 'turning the tables' trick. That doesn't work on me either. I was at the church sewing circle. I go every week. I was there with Micah and six of the women from the congregation. But you know who wasn't there? Pearl Wingard. That's who."

"Are you implying that Pearl killed Todd?" Of all the people I'd suspect of a murder, it wasn't Pearl Wingard. But then again, I'd thought it possible she'd gotten rid of an unwanted baby—which to many would be far worse than killing a grown man.

"I didn't imply anything. You did." Vera smiled, and I'd never seen a more dangerous creature. Vera was capable of murder. I should have seen it before I found myself isolated on a river with her. Maybe my hostage situation wasn't the best plan I'd ever hatched.

"Now you're thinking you made a mistake bringing me out here. Alone." Her grin widened. "Not very smart, Sarah Booth. What if I told you—" A shot rang out, echoing loud along the water. It was impossible to tell the direction it came from, but the bullet zinged into the water only inches from the boat.

I struggled to get the anchor up and start the motor. When it caught, I opened the throttle wide and aimed downriver. We'd make better time going with the current, and I didn't want to remain stalled in the middle of a river like sitting ducks.

"A friend of yours?" I asked Vera.

"No. No it isn't. I think whoever it was, they were aiming for me."

I couldn't tell. And I didn't want to discuss it. I only wanted to beat a trail down to the Greenwood landing and get off the river. The Tallahatchie had suddenly become a very dangerous waterway for me.

37

I had the small outboard motor wide open, and we were about to make it to a bend in the river. If we could get around the curve, I would feel like we had some cover, at least. Vera was nobody's fool. She was hunkered down in the bottom of the boat and had ceased all moaning and whining.

I eased the boat into the turn without reducing speed. I was about to relax when a bullet tore into the side of the boat and through to the bottom. Water started gushing in. We were sinking.

"Do something!" Vera ordered.

"You either steer or bail." I tossed my hat to her. It wasn't a great bucket, but it was better than nothing.

She set to work dumping out as much water as she could, but the boat was filling faster than she could bail. We were going down.

"Vera, if we have to abandon the boat, I'll get you to shore. Remember, don't struggle and don't try to drown me or I *will* leave you to figure it out on your own."

"I'm terrified of the water. Please, just get us to shore. We're close."

I tossed her both life jackets. "Put them on. You'll float, I promise. I'll drag you to shore. I swear it."

"I'm going to sue you into next winter," she said in the most ungracious fashion. "You think you're so special because of your parents. Well, not everyone feels that way. Your folks were troublemakers, just like you. The sheriff may protect you, but if you ever go to court, you'll have a harder road to travel, and I intend to take you before Judge Truett and make you pay."

"Dream on." Truett didn't like me and he'd disliked my parents. Simple facts. But our paths seldom crossed.

"You think you can get away with anything. Coleman Peters can't keep me off your back."

I ignored her. It wasn't worth a fight when I was struggling to navigate the boat as close to the sandbar as I could. If the shooter was north of us on the sandbar, he would still be able to get to us on foot. The sandbar wasn't a safe option, by any means, but it was better than drowning in the river. And at least the ground sloped at the sandbar, giving a gentle incline. I could get purchase with my feet and drag Vera, if I had to. The danger was that the sandbar was wide open, without any hiding places. The opposite bank had dense vegetation where we could hide from the shooter, but I couldn't count on the ground not being a sheer drop-off.

Water lapped just inches from the top of the boat. "Get ready, Vera." Who the heck was shooting at us? I hadn't advertised my trip. None of my friends would ever discuss my plans. It had to be Vera's big mouth. As soon as I got Vera on shore, I'd choke an answer out of her. She'd probably been flapping her gums all over town. God knew how many people wanted her dead—she was that annoying.

The water in the boat rose to my seat, and I checked Vera to be sure she had her life jacket snapped properly. I wouldn't weep if she floated downriver, never to be seen again, but I couldn't be responsible for her drowning.

"Just ease over the side," I told her as I cut the motor.

"So you can take off without me? I'm not that big a fool."

"Vera, the boat is sinking. Really, ease over the side and try dog-paddling toward the shore."

"You go first."

I grabbed my nose and fell backward out of the sinking boat. I came up near her and offered my hand.

"Get away from me!" She slipped into the river just as another shot zipped into the water. I dragged her to the offside of the boat. We could use it to block us for a few minutes, before it disappeared beneath the choppy waves. Grabbing the back of her life jacket, I struck out for shore.

"Kick! Kick!" I gasped.

Another bullet smacked the river not five inches from my head. Did that mean the shooter was in a boat? Or had they walked down the sandbar enough to still have a clear shot at us? I couldn't answer and I didn't have time to ponder the question.

"They're going to kill us," Vera screamed.

"Shut up and kick!" I put everything I had in stroking for the shore. When my feet finally touched bottom, I hauled Vera to her feet and marched her up the bank. When she wanted to fall in the sand, I made her keep running to the safety of the trees.

"How are we going to get home?" she wailed.

"Let's try to live long enough to worry about that."

That was the wrong thing to say. "We're going to die! We're going to die!" she wailed.

Oh, I was ready to kill her, but I couldn't. I managed to get her up into the tree line and push her down into a depression made by a big tree trunk. "Stay here. Shut up and don't move."

"What are you going to do?"

I didn't have a lot of options since the rucksack I'd put in the boat with my gun in it was at the bottom of the river. Along with my cell phone.

"Did you bring a phone?" I asked her.

"Maybe."

My fingers literally itched to circle her throat and squeeze. Oh, the satisfaction I would derive. I shook my head and snapped out of the fantasy. "Vera, get out your phone and see if it works."

She reached into her shirt and pulled a heavy-duty freezer bag with her phone in it from her bra. Damn. She was smarter than I was!

"I have a signal!" she announced.

"Give it to me."

She reluctantly turned it over. I quickly called Coleman.

"Where are you?" he asked. "We've been at the landing for half an hour."

"We ran into a sniper. He sank our boat. We're on a sandbar and I don't think we're safe."

"Who is the sniper shooting at? You or Vera?"

"I can't tell. I don't think he's a very good shot, or he wasn't trying hard. Just find us. Please. Before I choke the life out of Vera."

He started laughing. "You can't do that now, because I'd have to arrest you."

Vera, who had been listening to the conversation, said, "Thank goodness that man has some sense, Sarah Booth, because you don't. Does Coleman work out? He is built!"

"Bring some stakes and rope. I may leave her on the sandbar as a sacrifice to the river gods." That took the grin off her face.

"Did you find out anything?" Coleman asked.

"Plenty. And I'm about to find out a lot more." When Vera started to protest, I shushed her and pointed upriver. A boat with two figures in it quietly floated toward us. The figure at the bow was likely a man, but I couldn't tell because he had a life jacket on and a hat shaded his features. There was also a rifle in his hand, and it was pointed in our direction.

"Get deeper in the trees," I whispered to Vera. "Now!"

She scrabbled deeper into the woods. In a moment I heard her hand connect with flesh. "Damn yellow flies."

Maybe if they got a taste for her they'd leave me alone.

If I'd thought the heat on the river was bad, the humidity in the woods was suffocating. Huffing and puffing, I trudged forward. When Vera pleaded for me to stop and rest, I ignored her. Someone was trying to kill us.

"Sarah Booth, I'm not taking another step. I can't. I'm dying."

"Maybe the people shooting at us were actually trying to hit you. If they find you sitting here on your ass, maybe they won't chase me."

"Stop, and I'll tell you who killed Todd."

I almost got whiplash from my instant reversal. I wasn't certain Vera had any useful information, but it was always possible. "Tell me. And make it fast."

Vera sighed and sank down to sit on the root of an old tupelo gum tree that had fallen over. "Give me a minute to catch my breath."

Her face was red and sweat coursed down her cheeks and neck, darkening her shirt. She did look like she was about to have a stroke. Apparently, fitness was not a high priority for her.

"Spill it, Vera. No procrastinating, or I'll just leave you here. I don't mind doing that at all."

"Okay, okay. But what are you going to give me in return?"

"What? What do you want?" I wanted to bite my tongue the moment the question jumped out of my mouth. "This isn't a negotiation." But I was a day late and a dollar short. I'd already opened that door.

"I want full immunity."

"What?"

"I don't want to be charged with any crime."

"Vera, I'm not a law officer. I can't grant you immunity, full or otherwise."

"But you can make Coleman do it."

"I can't *make* Coleman do anything. And neither can you. So, who killed Todd?"

"What's the point of sleeping with the sheriff if you don't get any benefits?"

Every action with Vera was transactional. Where had I seen that before? "Tell me or not. Up to you." I took two steps backward. "I'm walking to the road. Maybe I can flag down a car to catch a ride to Greenwood."

Vera held up her phone, which I'd foolishly given back to her because she had the ziplock bag to keep it dry. "You do that. I'll call an Uber."

Rage swept over me. A pulse pounded in my temples, but I took a deep breath and laughed. "A great plan, Vera, if you can find your way to the road." I set off at a brisk pace.

"Wait! Wait. I'll tell you." I wiped the grin off my face before I walked back to her.

"Spill it. Now."

"Wylie Moulton killed Todd. They had an argument about the treasure, got into it, and Todd hit his head."

I thought about it before I responded. Todd, Wylie, and Danny had all been friends. They'd all grown up with the legend of the outlaw gang and the buried treasure from Columbine Plantation. It made sense.

"Do you have any proof?" I asked.

The sound of someone moving through the underbrush halted her answer. I put a finger to my lips to warn her to hush. Dammit! I'd let a potential killer slip up on us because I'd been trying so hard to take Vera down a notch.

"Vera, come on out. It's the other one I want. I won't hurt you."

I didn't recognize the voice, but I was willing to bet it was Wylie Moulton. And he meant to do me harm. Where in the heck was Coleman or some deputies who were supposed to be tracking him?

38

Vera started to answer, and I pulled her down behind the tree root she'd been sitting on. My hand cupped her mouth to emphasize I meant for her to shut up.

"Vera, come out, come out, wherever you are."

The man's taunting, singsong voice scared me. He sounded like a psychopath. Someone who could, and would, kill with impunity. Even Vera seemed to sense the danger. She grew very still. I removed my hand.

Fallen tree limbs crackled only thirty yards from where we hid. We hadn't taken precautions not to leave a trail behind us. We'd been moving too fast, and I'd underestimated my foe. Plus, there had been two people in the boat, so another man was somewhere in the woods, probably also trying to find us.

"Give me the phone," I hiss-whispered, sealing my seriousness with a pinch to the tendon in her shoulder.

"Ouch!" She jerked away.

The man had shifted to our west. "Oh, little Vera and her

friend, the pain-in-the-butt private investigator. I'm gonna find you."

I snatched the phone from Vera's hand and shot a text to Coleman. "Please get here fast. A killer is following us. Track Vera's phone." Coleman would have already figured out to do that, but just typing it made me feel I was being proactive.

"Vera!"

The voice was closer. Holy cow, Wylie Moulton was going to step on us in another five minutes. I looked around and found a sizable limb. I wasn't going down without a fight.

"Vera, what are you doing hunkered down in the dirt?" Wylie had crept up on us. He was standing not twenty feet away. He looked at me. "Ms. Delaney, you just can't keep your nose out of other people's business, can you?"

"I can learn," I said.

Instead of getting angry, he laughed. "Too late to learn now."

"Wylie, she is the sheriff of Sunflower County's girlfriend."

"I know. So what?"

"You can't run fast enough to get away from Coleman Peters if you hurt her."

"Once I get that money from Danny, I'll fly somewhere they won't extradite me."

Wylie Moulton was not only dumb, he was delusional. But this was the time to let Vera's motormouth do the work.

"Think, Wylie. Think. You're already on the line for a murder rap."

Oh, that was the wrong thing to say. The slight smile dropped off Wylie's face. He looked at Vera. "You know, you're right. And they can't kill me but once. So, I might as well get rid of both of you."

Too late, Vera realized what she had unleashed.

I looked around to find cover if I made a break for it. Wylie had a gun, but I wasn't certain he was a good shot. He'd missed us on the river, but maybe he'd only meant to drive us to shore.

"Wylie, I can help you." Vera held out her hand to him. Wylie was having none of it. He aimed the rifle at Vera's heart. I held my breath.

The sound of a baying hound dog came to me and my knees almost buckled. I'd recognize the voice of my Sweetie Pie anywhere. Her cries mingled with Avalon's sharp bark, Roscoe's snorting little bark, and Pumpkin's excited cacophony. The rescue was under way.

Wylie heard it, too. He aimed at Vera. "You bitch."

Before he could pull the trigger, Sweetie Pie flew out of the woods at about four hundred miles per hour, or at least faster than a speeding bullet. She caught his arm in her teeth and dragged him off his feet. The gun discharged, and I saw Vera fall to the ground. And then all hell broke loose.

Coleman and Harold crashed through the trees. Coleman jumped on top of Wylie and Harold rushed to Vera.

"She's hit," he said. "Shoulder. Looks like just a graze. Not serious."

"What do you mean 'not serious'!" Vera was in full battle mode. "I've been shot. I may die. I'm going to sue everybody. Just you wait and see."

I sank down in the dirt and leaned back against a small sapling. Sweetie Pie rushed to me and licked my face. Avalon sat down beside me and leaned against me, giving comfort.

"Wylie killed Todd Jenkins," I said to Coleman.

"Get off me," Wylie said. "You can't prove that."

"I think we can," Coleman answered. "Just as soon as we bring Danny Anderson in to testify."

"Do you know where Danny is?" I asked.

"He's on his way to Zinnia. He called the sheriff's office and said he was coming in to talk to me. Brigette convinced him to turn himself in."

"They're both okay?" I asked.

"They are." Coleman cuffed Wylie and forced him to sit on the ground. He came over to me and lifted me to my feet. "Are you okay?"

"I'm good. Did you interview Brigette this morning?"

"She came in early, then went to talk to Danny. She's the one who talked him into turning himself in. She can be mighty persuasive."

"Yes. Yes, she can."

Something in his tone gave me pause. At the moment, though, I let it go. Once Danny was returned to his family and the case fully resolved, I'd talk with Coleman. It was stupid to let Vera or anyone else get to me. He'd assuage my concerns and that would be that.

I glanced at Vera as Harold pulled her to her feet. She grinned. "I told you so," she mouthed at me.

Before we could make it to the road where Coleman and Harold had parked, we were met by the deputies. They'd come to help Coleman track Wylie.

Coleman put his arm around my shoulders and kissed my cheek. "Get Vera to the hospital. Tell Doc to keep her there until I get back."

"Okay." The prospect of more time with Vera depressed me. I had bigger fish to fry—the kiss from Coleman had been perfunctory. "Are you okay?"

"Sure, sure!" But he didn't meet my gaze. "See you back in Zinnia."

Coleman called the deputies over for a powwow, leaving me and Harold to see that Vera got medical attention. When they disappeared into the trees, I put Vera in the passenger seat. "Harold, are you coming with us?"

"Coleman asked me to go upriver and rent a boat and meet them. He wants to talk to the other guy in the boat with Wylie."

I'd already filled Coleman in on the fact that Wylie had a boat and a partner. There was nothing left for me to do but head to Zinnia and Doc Sawyer.

Vera was in the passenger seat and started slapping the dash. "Hurry up, Sarah Booth. Turn on the car! I'm suffocating."

Oh, if only that were true. But there was no point in putting off what had to be done. I waved goodbye to Harold, aware that he, too, didn't seem to want to make eye contact. I opened the back door of the cruiser and whistled the dogs up. Sweetie Pie and Avalon were the first to jump in the vehicle, and Rosco and Pumpkin were also glad to go with me. They'd had enough of the heat and sun, too.

"What kind of kiss was that Coleman gave you?" Vera was determined to provoke me into doing something stupid.

"Shut up, Vera."

"Y'all act like you've been married fifty years. All the dew is off the rose, eh?"

I ignored her.

"I've seen this same scenario play out dozens of times. You think it's forever, but it's just forever until the new girl comes along."

There was a pothole in the road and I hit it going too fast. I was in no danger of losing control of the car, but the jolt made Vera scream in pain.

"Maybe you should be quiet so I can focus on driving," I said sweetly. She got the point and shut up.

39

While Doc examined Vera, I walked around the hospital, too antsy to stay in one place. I finally went out to my car to listen to the radio. There was a local farm report show on NPR I enjoyed, and I was about to jump out of my skin just sitting around.

Something was on my car windshield. The paper tucked beneath my wiper blade fluttered in a gentle summer breeze. I grabbed it and got in the car to read it, turning the AC on full blast.

> *Mind your own business before you meet the same fate as your parents.*

The note was like a kick in the gut. I opened the car door and looked around, hoping to catch a glimpse of whoever had left it. The parking lot was empty of people, just cars baking in the sun. No movement. Nothing. Around the back side of the hospital, a red convertible disappeared. I ran after it, too late to identify the make of the car or driver. Had I seen red hair? Was I hallucinating?

I still clutched the note, and when I looked at it, nausea surged. The low-grade headache I'd attributed to too much sun expanded into a booming pain. I held tight to the note and leaned against my car.

Doc came out to talk to me while Vera got her blouse on. His white hair was disorderly, as always. His face reflected his personal kindness, his trademark. "I wouldn't ever think that you'd be helping Vera to the hospital," he said, gently teasing me.

"I hope she gets the psychiatric help she needs," I said, trying hard to pull myself together. I had no emotional space left for Vera.

Doc laughed and patted my shoulder. "Flesh wound. She'll be fine. She said Wylie Moulton shot her?"

"That's likely the first true thing she's said all day."

"What were you two doing on the Tallahatchie?"

Doc was a vault. Whatever I told him would go to the grave with him, and I wanted to talk about anything other than the note I still held. "We were hoping to find Danny Anderson."

"When I talked to Coleman this morning, he said Brigette was working to help him convince Danny to turn himself in."

"Yes."

"I saw the photo Cece ran of Brigette in the newspaper today. She just gets prettier and prettier."

"Yes." This wasn't the conversation I wanted to have with Doc. Brigette had become something of a sore tooth to me. "Did Vera say anything informative about Danny, Todd, or Wylie?"

"She said Wylie probably shot Todd Jenkins. A dispute over

the Columbine Plantation treasure that James Norton and his clan were supposed to have stolen." He sighed. "I always thought all that talk of treasure was hooey, but then they found that gold coin in Todd's pocket. Did they find any trace of the treasure?"

"I think they may have. Or at least some of it." I remembered the image of the three people trekking through the woods all hunched over like they were carrying something heavy.

"Who has it now?"

"I don't know."

Doc lifted my chin gently with his hand. "What's going on, Sarah Booth? You're acting like a kicked dog."

I felt tears building and I looked away. "I'm just tired. Vera has sucked my soul out through my nostrils."

He laughed. "She can do that. That woman is like Lyme disease. You can't get rid of her. She's set her cap for every man in the area, and none of them have fallen for her."

"Because she's mean."

"Some men like a mean woman."

I looked at Doc. "Are you kidding?"

"Halfway. But some men enjoy a woman who will fight with them and for them."

"Vera only wants a man if he belongs to someone else."

"There is that, too. But you have no worries. Coleman is still smitten with you, isn't he?"

I forced a smile. "Of course."

"Good. That's good. Now I'm sending Vera home. She said you'd drive her. She shouldn't be alone—"

"Coleman said to keep her at the hospital. I am not nurse-maiding that viper!"

"Okay." He held up his hands. "But I can't keep her here against her will. Just get her home and get her to take another pain pill. She said she'd drive back tomorrow for me to check the dressing."

The truth of the matter was that I didn't want to spend another minute in Vera's company. She'd gotten to me with her digs about Coleman. And she knew it, which made it even worse. She was relentless and I was an idiot. Coleman was the most true-blue and honorable man I'd ever known. Why was I letting her get to me? I couldn't answer that, and I didn't want to bring it up to Tinkie. She would think the same thing I thought—that I was acting like a fool. Besides, I had bigger fish to fry. Who had left the note on my car?

"Sarah Booth, you do look a little peaked, despite that sunburn," Doc said, drilling me with his gaze. "What's up?"

"This case is driving me to drink." I laughed. "As if I needed a reason. But seriously, it should have been a simple case of finding Danny. He never even left the region. But we've gone from possible Billie Joe McAllister scenarios to now land pirates and treasure. It's just been a lot. I've got a headache and my emotions are all over the place." I was shaken by the note. "I thought I saw Gertrude Stromm. Maybe I'm hallucinating."

"Why don't you come in tomorrow and let me run some tests? Just to check everything out."

"Tests? For a headache? That's a little over the top."

"Just some basic tests to rule out anything serious. How about you take a pregnancy test? Couldn't hurt."

His words stunned me. "No! Unnecessary. Every time a woman goes to a doctor they want to run a pregnancy test. Ridiculous." I couldn't tell him about the note on my car, the real source of my mood fluctuations. At least not until I had more information.

"Sounds to me like your hormones are all over the place. This isn't like you. Pregnancy could be one simple reason."

Oh, it was not simple. Not at all. "I'm fine. Really." I stood up. "Would you tell Vera to call an Uber? I just remembered something I have to do right away."

"Will do." He started to say something else, but walked away. I fled the hospital and went straight home to Dahlia House. When I arrived, there was no sign of Coleman. He was likely still searching for Danny—or explaining his interference to the Leflore County sheriff, who might not be so happy to have another lawman poking into his business.

I was glad to be alone. I intended to take a ride on Miss Scrapiron. I needed to think. To try to determine what I'd really seen and what I may have imagined. I uncrumpled the note and spread it out on the kitchen table. It was real. And the implication was clear. My folks had been murdered. The car wreck wasn't an accident.

I pulled on some long pants and boots and went down to the barn. The horses came running as soon as they saw me, and I threw out several flakes of hay for them. Miss Scrapiron was ready and willing for a ride. She nudged the English saddle with her nose. She seemed to understand that I needed to ride—to get away from my thoughts and worries.

The sound of a harmonica stopped me short. I finished cinching the girth on the saddle when I heard a lovely voice singing about sunshine and the high cost of love. I looked over Scrapiron's back and saw a beautiful brunette woman with bangs and a headband wearing jeans and a boho blouse.

"'My daddy, he once told me . . .'"

"Who are you?" I asked. I didn't recognize her, though from her voice I knew she was a singer.

She stopped her song and came forward. "Gale Garnett. I had some hits, but I was more popular in Canada than here."

My brain was doing a fast shuffle to try to put it together.

Then it hit me. "'We'll Sing in the Sunshine.' Right?" My mother had a strong contralto voice and she'd loved to sing this song when we were flying over the back roads in her Roadster.

"That's me."

Of course I knew it was Jitty pretending to be Gale, but why?

"Sing with me," she said, and launched into the second stanza of the song. I had no time for a sing-along. I'd just been handed some evidence that indicated my parents may have been murdered.

"What did Doc have to say?" Gale asked as she slowly transformed from boho folk singer to my favorite haint wearing my favorite jean shorts and red pullover. Jitty took whatever she wanted. She never asked permission or begged forgiveness.

"He said Vera would be fine."

"And that's all?"

I got the bridle from the tack room and took the halter off my horse. "What are you driving at, Jitty?"

"Something is eating at you. What? Maybe I can help."

If only it were that simple. "Everything is fine. I want to go for a ride and clear my head."

"You look pretty wrung out, Sarah Booth."

"Thanks. What a lovely compliment." She eyed me. "I'm okay. All that time on the river and I'm simply tired." I had to derail this or she'd get to the nut of my discontent. I couldn't ask her about my parents. I couldn't. If she'd known this all along . . . the betrayal would be unforgivable. "Jitty, is the Tallahatchie River haunted?"

"Every place is haunted, Sarah Booth. Most people just can't see it."

"Why can I?"

She thought for a minute. "Because you are open to it. Because you've lost too much, too soon. Because you can hold yourself still long enough to see things others rush by."

Those were all good reasons, but why the woman in a white dress on the bridge? It had to relate back to my case. Because if it didn't relate to my case, did it relate to me, personally? Was I destined to be a ghost haunting a landscape of betrayal? Even the whisper of that idea made me break out in a sweat. It couldn't be. And on top of that, Doc had put a real scare into me. I was not pregnant.

Jitty/Gale picked up her song again.

All the singers and songwriters Jitty'd appeared as sang about loss. Gale Garnett said it in her song—the cost of love was too high. Was this the bitter lesson I was about to learn?

"Earth to Sarah Booth!" Jitty watched me intensely.

"What?"

"What's going on with you?"

"Leave me be. I've got a lot on my mind."

"Clearly. You're troubled. Change is coming, Sarah Booth, and change is part of life. Bend with the wind and survive."

I wanted to tell her everything. I needed to talk to someone. Tinkie, preferably. I owed my partner a phone call, but as soon as she heard my voice she'd know something was off with me. "I'm tired of bending, Jitty."

"Tell me what's wrong. I can't help you if you don't confide in me."

Would Jitty help me? If she could, maybe. I was never certain if Jitty used the "rules of the Great Beyond" because she didn't want to help, or if she really couldn't.

In truth, I needed to talk to Coleman. He was the person who needed to hear my fears. The thought of that conversation filled me with dread. I'd lived assuming one thing. That thing, if it was a lie, had allowed me to go on with my life never understanding the true consequences.

I couldn't think about this. I couldn't even look at Jitty. "I need to be alone."

Miss Scrapiron took the bit, and I finished tacking her up before whistling for the dogs. Pluto had come out to the barn, but in typical cat fashion, he showed no interest in what I was doing. Poe was waiting for me out on the fence rail.

"I have to go," I told Jitty.

"I'm concerned, Sarah Booth." Jitty wasn't pulling any punches.

"Yeah, me too. See you when I get back." For the first time since I'd been home, I walked away and left Jitty standing alone.

I mounted and set off at a trot. Miss Scrapiron strained at the bit—it was a very gentle snaffle—and as soon as we crossed the road, I let her go. She was a Thoroughbred, and when she stretched out into her long stride, she could cover ground. Sweetie Pie and Avalon raced beside us. Hound dog joy! Poe circled over us, keeping watch.

Slowly the tension began to leave my shoulders. The note had been left to upset me. To throw me off my stride. There was no truth to it. The red car had been a hallucination brought on by the gut-punch of the note. My reality was unchanged. I had to hang on to that.

My body moved with my horse, and I focused on the joy of riding on a perfect summer day in a world where land and growing things were valued.

When Scrapiron began to slow of her own accord, I took a path that would lead us home. The ride had worked its magic. My head was clear, my emotions under control. I would call Coleman as soon as I got home and tell him that we needed to talk. Later, when we were having a drink together, I would show him the note.

I'd just turned down the drive to Dahlia House when my phone dinged. It was a number I didn't know, but I checked the text.

"I'm going to the courthouse to turn myself in. Please meet me there. Danny Anderson."

So Danny was doing the right thing. I hurriedly untacked my horse, brushed her out, hosed her off, and set her free in the pasture. I dashed inside, took a five-minute shower, threw on some clothes, and headed to the courthouse. Danny Anderson was coming home. Voluntarily. My case was concluded, with a positive outcome.

So why wasn't I more thrilled?

I called Tinkie on the way to the courthouse. She was already en route. "All I can do is thank the people and forces who brought this about," she said. "Oscar is so relieved. He's talking about throwing a party for all the searchers."

"That would be fun."

"What's wrong with you, Sarah Booth?"

Tinkie was too perceptive for her own good. "Heatstroke, I think. I was out on that river too long. I'm just tired."

"Ri-i-ight." She wasn't fooled at all. "We'll talk once Danny is reunited with his parents. Should I call Pearl Wingard?"

That was a question for sure. "Yes." It might not be the smartest thing, but Pearl deserved to know Danny was okay.

"Where is Vera?"

I felt like a bad person, but I had to own it. "I left her at the hospital. Told her to call an Uber to get home."

Tinkie started laughing, and she was still laughing when I pulled in to the courthouse. She pulled up beside me seconds later. She hurried out of her Cadillac and came over. "You just left her at the hospital with a bullet wound?"

"I did. She'd gotten on my last nerve. I might have killed her if I'd had to spend another minute with her."

"Yeah, I can see that." Tinkie's eyes widened. "Uh-oh, look!" She nodded behind me. I knew without looking it was Vera.

"She has a lot of nerve being here."

"Nerve is one thing Vera does have a lot of . . . Not sense. Not heart. Not kindness. But she has a lot of nerve." Tinkie stepped in front of me. "Get inside the sheriff's office. I'll run interference."

"Thank you!" I turned tail and hurried away. Once the mess with Danny was cleared up, I could go home and wait for Coleman.

In the sheriff's office, Budgie and DeWayne were relieved that Danny had turned himself in. He'd flatly refused to go to Leflore County and insisted he'd come here. He was in the interrogation room waiting for Coleman. "Danny didn't do anything wrong, as far as we can tell," DeWayne said. "Disappearing for a few days isn't a crime."

"We think it was Wylie who burglarized the stores, trying to throw the blame on Danny," Budgie added.

"And the treasure?" I asked.

"Danny said they found it. No one knows the value yet, but it is going to be a lot of money. Those coins are valuable."

"Enough to resolve his debt?"

DeWayne nodded. "His debt, and he said he's going to help some of the other farmers. He said the treasure was a gift that was meant to be shared."

Danny was a remarkable man. "Is Brigette here?" I hated myself for even asking.

"She went to get coffee and donuts for everyone. She is a sweetheart."

Good grief. Even the deputies were singing her praises. "Great. Can I speak with Danny?"

DeWayne nodded. “Coleman told me to call you, so go ahead.”

“Where is Coleman?”

“He just said he had an errand to run. He’ll be back.”

“Thanks. Would you send Tinkie back with me?”

“I’m right here,” Tinkie said, walking up to us. “I wouldn’t miss this for the world.”

40

We walked into the interrogation room together. Tinkie nudged me with her shoulder. “This is the best outcome we could hope for. Danny has been cleared of killing Todd. Budgie said that Wylie admitted to killing him.”

“And the evidence supports the theory that Wylie robbed the local businesses,” Budgie said. “But best of all, the treasure will save Danny’s family land. And help others. It’s a great outcome.”

“What about the second man in the boat with Wylie?” “No loose ends” was my motto.

“He was just a local guy Wylie duped into going fishing with him. He had no idea what Wylie was really up to. I don’t think he’s going to be charged with anything.”

“I agree.” My mood was still tainted by my earlier concerns, but I was better able to disguise it. And Danny was alive—unharmed. When I saw Danny Anderson sitting at the table in the empty room, I felt a swell of emotion. He was sunburned, disheveled, but grinning.

Danny stepped forward. "Thank you, ladies. Thank you. I heard that you were looking for me and giving my family hope. Mrs. Richmond, I owe your husband an apology. I never meant to get people so worked up."

"You had a lot of folks worried sick," Tinkie said. "Oscar included. He felt this was his fault."

"Oscar should know that a banker can't control the weather or the market. He's a good man and he bent over backward to try to help me. Now Levi Butler, on the other hand, he's a skunk."

"Sarah Booth's horse dumped him in the middle of the road." Tinkie was gleeful.

"Oh, that is the best." Danny's smile was a hundred watts. He was a man of the outdoors, but I could clearly see why he was also a leader for the farmers. "Sheriff Peters says he's investigating Butler for possible charges. Seems he has a habit of lying to people and bilking farmers out of their land."

Happy news! I didn't like Butler and I didn't like his business. If Coleman could charge him, it would make my day.

"Danny, why didn't you contact your family?" I asked. It was the question that he needed to answer most, in my opinion. "You let them worry and suffer, thinking you were dead."

"It's a long story. The bottom line is that I did it to protect them."

"How so?" Tinkie followed up.

"You know I grew up with Wylie and Todd. We share a lifestyle and a value system, or so I thought. When I hatched the idea of looking for the Columbine Plantation gold, it was more of a lark. We were all so depressed about the huge loans we owed and how time was running out. We started looking for the treasure as a way of getting back to the three young boys who'd played imaginary games on the river."

I understood that completely. Sometimes the past was the only safe place to go.

"We didn't expect to find anything, but then Todd was digging near where the mouth to the dead lake was and he found two gold coins. Wylie showed up and said that Levi Butler was talking to my folks about buying the land. The thing was, they needed my signature to close the deal. That's when I decided to disappear. As long as I was gone, everything was on hold with selling the land."

I had done far worse than that to save Dahlia House. In fact, if Tinkie ever knew I'd stolen Chablis and ransomed her back, she would never forgive me. It was an action that made me squirm with shame whenever I thought of it. I wanted to confess to Tinkie. I did. But I couldn't risk losing her friendship forever, so I had to live with the guilt. That was my cross to bear.

"But you could have contacted your family," Tinkie said.

"My folks are good people. Too good. They're honest and would have felt compelled to tell the truth. I needed time. And I didn't want to ask them to lie. It would have hurt them too much."

"It makes sense," Tinkie admitted.

Danny continued talking. "Todd was with Wylie when they found the two gold coins. Wylie had one and Todd had the other. I don't know what really happened. A few days later, they got into a fight and Wylie demanded that Todd hand over the second coin. They both knew they were very valuable. Todd refused. They got into a shoving match and Wylie flipped out. He pushed Todd down in the sand and struck him in the head, then dragged his body to the river. I guess he was too scared to steal the other coin from Todd's dead body. Or maybe remorseful. We were all very close."

"Did you witness this?" I asked.

Danny shook his head. "Wylie told me, and then he decided he was going to have to kill me. That's when I went deep into the woods and couldn't let anyone know where I was. If I'd called my folks and Wylie found out about it, he might have killed them. It's like he lost his mind. Thank god for Brigette. She came through."

"And what about Pearl?"

Danny inhaled and blew out his breath. "Pearl. That woman is something special."

"Are you in love with her?" Tinkie asked.

"I fell for Pearl in tenth grade. I've always loved her. Always. She is loyal and kind."

"Were you having an affair?" Tinkie went for it.

"No. Never. I missed the opportunity when I had it. Then she met Micah, and he's been her whole life."

Hearing this was a big relief.

"The thing is, Pearl always put our friendship high up on her list. She never failed to help me if she could. When folks started gossiping, she refused to back away from me. Micah never questioned me—he knew who Pearl was."

"And she was never pregnant?" Tinkie asked.

The word gave me a start.

"Never. We didn't have an affair. We were friends who shared a lot of troubles and childhood joys. That's it. But I do know this. Pearl wants a baby. Desperately."

"Does Micah want children?" I asked.

Danny frowned. "You should talk to Pearl. Or Micah. That's their business."

"Were you going to be a surrogate father?" Tinkie asked. Her question reflected brilliance. "Is Micah sterile?"

He only shook his head. "Talk to them. This is not my business to share."

"I would want a trusted friend to father my child if Oscar couldn't," Tinkie continued, unfazed. "I had my own serious issues with pregnancy, but I can tell you I wouldn't trade anything in the world for my daughter, Maylin. She is the best of every moment of life."

Danny's smile was sad. "Maybe one day I'll know that for myself. If I can save the land, then I can plan a future."

"Will Brigette be part of that future?" I asked.

"I wouldn't do that to her. I clearly see that her life is in New York. She's the toast of the town. You know I loaned her the money to make that first trip to New York. I supported her for six months until she got her first modeling job. She paid me back and more. And she came here to look for me. She's a real friend. Her work as a model is important, too. She helps people. When she finishes a shoot coming up in Italy at the end of this month, she's coming back here with a bunch of her model friends to host a fundraiser for the farmers of the Delta. She's trying to help them save as much of their land as possible."

"She's also doing that photo shoot with children on Friday to help some local charities," Tinkie said. "She's a very good egg."

"That she is."

But Danny looked almost as sad as I felt. "Is there anything else you want to tell us?" I asked.

"Like what?" He seemed to be at a loss.

"Like where the treasure is?" Tinkie asked.

"Sheriff Peters is sending some men to bring it here. I don't know who it really belongs to. If I have a say, I want to sell the coins and split the money with the local farmers. Those coins could mean saving family farms. They could be salvation for my family and others. Do you know who the coins belong to?"

"I don't. Are there any living relatives of the family that owned Columbine Plantation?"

"Cece and Millie are checking into that," Tinkie said. "So far, none have been found. Folks who grew up in that area said all the heirs are dead. The plantation went to ruin when the oxbow lake dried up. It looks like the money may belong to Danny."

"What about Wylie?" I asked.

"Where he's going, he won't be able to spend any money. Once Coleman takes him to the Leflore County sheriff, he'll be charged with the murder of Todd Jenkins." Wylie had earned his own date with destiny.

Danny blinked several times, as if something was in his eye. "Wylie and Todd were my friends. I don't know what happened. I just don't know."

"Danny, this is a far better outcome than I anticipated," I said.

"So why aren't you happy?" Tinkie pressed. "You look like someone stole your dog."

"Sun poisoning." I looked the part. I was badly sunburned. "I'm fine. Just drained."

It was all coming to a close. Soon. But I had a few more questions. "Danny, have you ever seen a woman in a white dress on the bridge?"

Danny's gaze flicked up at me, then away, then back. "I've seen her. So has Pearl."

"But Pearl . . ."

"We agreed not to talk about it. People tend to think you're nuts if you admit to seeing ghosts."

He wasn't wrong about that. "Who do you think the woman is?" I asked.

Danny thought about it for a minute. "I always thought it was Charlaine Smith, the woman who supposedly fell or jumped or was pushed from the bridge. But I don't know. I never got a clear look at her face. Her curly dark hair was always blowing around and obscuring her features." He chuckled. "Classic ghost story, right?"

Tinkie followed up on my question. "Did Pearl see the same thing?"

"Pearl has been drawn to the bridge for as long as I've known her. I think the story of Charlaine Smith got under her skin and stuck. Pearl was always a person who had sensitivities. She felt other people's emotions, their grief. In some ways, I think she identified with Charlaine Smith."

"I can see why she would," I said. "Do you know anyone else who has seen the ghost?"

"I did." Tinkie spoke up. "I didn't tell you, Sarah Booth, because I didn't want you to think I was losing it."

"Have you ever seen another ghost?" I asked.

"Maybe." She looked down and a smile touched the corners of her lips. "Have you?" Her blue gaze rose, found mine, and held steady.

"Maybe," I said.

Her grin widened into a smile. "We should compare notes when this case is over."

"I'd really like that." If only I could share Jitty with Tinkie—that would be wonderful. I needed to ask Jitty first, though. I didn't want to break any rules of the Great Beyond and lose my ancestral ghost. "I'm going to check with the deputies to see when they expect Coleman back." I was bone weary and ready to go home, soak in a cool bath, and slather my tight skin with Noxzema or some sunburn agent.

I stepped away from the interrogation room and walked back to the main office. The desks were empty. I walked out into the hallway of the courthouse, my footsteps echoing. As a child, I'd loved the sound when I raced through these halls to meet my father. Those times were beyond my reach now.

I looked around. The place was also empty. It was only four o'clock in the afternoon. Where was everyone?

The courthouse had doors that opened in all four directions, and I went to the north entrance near where the law officers parked. I stepped into the sunshine, aware immediately that a hot, hot summer was on the way. Again. The sun hit my skin, igniting the deep sunburn with pain.

Movement by the patrol cars caught my eye. I started to walk that way and stopped. It was Coleman. And Brigette. The tension between them was electric. She stared up into his eyes and swayed toward him. Behind her, on the road, a red Roadster passed. The woman behind the wheel had red hair—just like Gertrude Stromm. I followed the car with my gaze, unable to move or say anything. I couldn't deny it or wish it away, Gertrude was back in Zinnia. This wasn't a hallucination.

The series of shocks was so profound I didn't hear the door open behind me. I felt someone step up close, and I heard DeWayne say, "Damn, what is Coleman up to?" He didn't wait for an answer. He put a hand on my shoulder, turning me away from the scene as he called out. "Peters, you'd better get your ass in the sheriff's office. Judge Truett is on the line and he is pissed at you."

DeWayne's arm circled my shoulders, effectively blocking me from the scene on the courthouse lawn. Did Coleman kiss Brigette? Is that what DeWayne was trying to protect me from seeing?

I tried to twist out of his grip, but he propelled me through the door and inside the cool courthouse. "Let me check on the sheriff," he said. He turned and moved toward the door.

"Tell Coleman that Gertrude is in town. I just saw her."

DeWayne stopped in his tracks. "Just now? She's here?"

"She just rode by."

"I'll take care of this. We'll get her this time." DeWayne raced to the sheriff's office to sound the alarm and prepare for the chase.

There was nothing for me to do but go back to the sheriff's office, grab my dogs, my purse, and my keys, and go home.

41

I managed to get my things and escape down the hallway to the first-floor restroom without seeing Tinkie or anyone else. My thought of going back to Dahlia House was nixed by DeWayne. He insisted I was safer at the courthouse. Dahlia House was my haven, but I couldn't disagree with DeWayne's assessment. I stepped into the ladies' room to compose myself.

By the time I'd reined in my tears and emotions, I'd come to a conclusion. DeWayne's behavior supported my fears about Coleman. True. But if Coleman was deceiving me, I couldn't change that. If he was lying to me about my parents, I could—and would—confront him, not run away like a coward. I was raised better than that.

My cell phone rang. Tinkie. "Sarah Booth, what in the world? You disappeared before Oscar could thank you. He has the gold coins from the treasure, and he believes they're valuable enough to settle Danny's debts and a number of other farmers'. It's going to be a new day in the Delta for those who work the land."

"That's great news."

"Have you been crying?"

Damn. Tinkie was an emotional bloodhound. "I'm fine. I'm washing my hands and getting some water for the dogs."

"You're in the ladies' room? I'm on the way."

"No, please don't."

Her response was a dial tone. Neither hell nor high water would keep her away, now that she thought I'd been crying.

I took water to the dogs in the sheriff's office and decided to head Tinkie off at the pass. When I opened the main courthouse door, Tinkie was coming up the steps. She took one look at me and stopped.

"What in the hell, Sarah Booth? What happened?"

"Nothing."

"Did you hear that Judge Truett is holding Coleman in contempt? And there's some issue with him working in Leflore County. Exceeding his authority or some such nonsense. The Leflore County sheriff is pissed. This is all bull crap, but it is annoying. Sarah Booth, what's wrong with you? You look like death warmed over."

The pounding pressure of tears built behind my eyelids again. "I have to go."

"Go where?" Tinkie put a hand on my arm. "What's going on?"

"I have to ask Coleman something." I couldn't explain. I had to take action. Right away. I couldn't wait.

I ran down the steps and toward the parking lot. I caught Coleman just as he was leaving the courthouse. One look at my face told him a story he didn't want to hear.

"What on earth is wrong?" he asked.

"Were my parents murdered?" I blurted it out. "Were they?"

"What are you talking about?" he asked, and I feared it was a delay tactic.

"Just tell me the truth. Did someone kill my parents? Did you know about it?"

He blew out a breath. "Let's go to Dahlia House and talk."

I shook my head. "No. Tell me now. I can't wait." I'd expected Coleman to deny it. To put my fears to rest. To reassure me that my parents' deaths had been an accident. Tragic, yes, but not an act of evil. If someone had harmed them . . . I could not accept that. It put every single thing I'd believed in doubt. My whole past would be a lie.

Coleman must have read the distress on my face because he tried to embrace me. "Sarah Booth, let's go home. We can talk."

"No!" I pushed him away. "No more talk. Were my parents murdered? Someone left a note on my car at the hospital."

"What note? Who?"

I waved his questions away. "Tell me the truth."

Before he could answer, the courthouse door opened and Vera Volt blasted out to stand beside us. Tinkie, who followed Vera out, also joined us.

Vera grinned like a shark. "Congratulations, Coleman, you found Danny alive and well. Good for you." She tapped Coleman's arm twice, then faced me. "Good detective work, Sarah Booth, but at a price. I think Coleman is falling for Brigette."

Tinkie simply stared at her. "That's a stupid thing to say, Vera. Coleman loves Sarah Booth."

"That's not what I saw—"

"Vera, you'd be wise to mind your own business here instead of trying to create trouble." Coleman was pissed and didn't bother to hide it. He reached for me, but I stepped back. "We do need to talk. Come back to the office with me. Please."

I felt myself softening. I owed him a chance to explain.

"I would never deliberately hurt you, Sarah Booth." Coleman held out his hand. "I love—"

"Oh, really. That's rich, Coleman. Then why were you about to kiss Brigette McEachern in the courthouse parking lot? I would have photographic evidence but Budgie dragged me inside so I couldn't see."

Vera's words sliced as effectively as a knife. I couldn't listen anymore. I backed away from them.

"Stop it, Vera. You've done enough harm." Tinkie was in her face. She turned to me. "I'm driving you home. Now."

Coleman reached out a hand, but I avoided it. He opened his mouth as if to say something, but no noise came out. He turned abruptly and went to his patrol car.

"Come on, Sarah Booth." Tinkie aimed me toward her car and propelled me forward. She called back over her shoulder, "Vera, why don't you go back to your crypt and wait for nightfall?"

I didn't have it in me to fight Tinkie. I got in the passenger seat. I didn't look back, but I knew Coleman was watching us drive away.

Tinkie was silent as she drove, and I was lost in the whirl of my thoughts. The image of a Chinese-red Mercedes Roadster, circa 1979, flashed in the back of my brain. Sunlight hit the red hair of the older woman driving. Gertrude Stromm was in town! I hadn't imagined it. I wasn't delusional. I hadn't imagined any of it.

When we got to Dahlia House, I paced the front porch.

Tinkie watched me with alarm. "I don't know what happened, but I'm making you a fresh martini."

"Okay." I didn't care. My world was upside down. The person I trusted the most, Coleman, had kept information from me. Why?

Tinkie returned with a martini and I obediently took it. My hand was shaking so badly the vodka sloshed all over me.

"Sarah Booth!" Tinkie took the drink before I dropped my glass. "Damn! Sit down. You're about to faint."

"I never faint," I said through gritted teeth. "I saw Gertrude in town."

Tinkie pushed me into a rocking chair and she knelt down at my feet. "You might not faint, but you're going to make me. Are you sure it was Gertrude? Did you really see her?"

"I'm sure. She was driving a Roadster exactly like my mother's." I might not be able to prove that Gertrude was near, but I had seen her driving around the courthouse square. I wasn't delusional; I'd seen her.

"We have to call Coleman." Tinkie pulled her phone out of a pocket on the calf of her pants.

"No! Call DeWayne or Budgie."

"I've already told DeWayne."

"Did he say anything?"

"Only that he would put out an APB immediately. She won't get away this time, Sarah Booth."

"Why is she even here?" But I knew. In my heart I knew the truth. Somehow Gertrude was linked to the accident that killed my parents. It was so clear now that I finally had the truth.

"She hates you. She hates me, too, just not as much." Tinkie sipped her drink and stood up. "Let's get the critters and go to Millie's. I'm starving."

"You go on. I want to talk to Coleman."

"Leave it until tomorrow, after you've had a chance to think it all through."

"No. I have to do it now." I sipped my martini and my stomach suddenly recoiled. The desperate need to hurl came over me. I barely made it to the edge of the porch before I heaved up everything I'd eaten that day.

"Let me take you to the hospital. That sunburn looks bad, and now you're throwing up," Tinkie said.

There wasn't anything Doc could do for me. I knew that. "No point. I'm okay now. Let me brush my teeth." I didn't wait for a response. I hurried in the front door and up the stairs. My stomach was better, but it wasn't settled yet. I had to brush my teeth or I'd upchuck again.

The urge hit again, and I knelt down by the toilet, resting my forehead on my arm after a round of dry heaves.

The sound of someone playing a guitar echoed around the bathroom. Whoever was playing was damn good. Then a harmonica kicked in and a nasally voice. ". . . when your rooster crows at the break of dawn . . ."

I sat up and leaned against the cold side of the tub. I could see him in the bathroom mirror: the curly hair, dark sunglasses, black leather jacket with his harmonica and guitar. Bob Dylan. Oh, I knew this song. "Don't Think Twice." And I knew exactly why Bob was there. Jitty had all the answers and this time she was giving me one. Was this what she'd been trying to tell me since I first took this case?

"Stop singing, Jitty." I meant it, too. I'd had more than I could take.

I got to my feet. I was upstairs in the home I'd loved since I was born. Instead of the love and laughter of my family, I was surrounded by the dead. Surrounded by memories and loss.

A fiery rage began to spread through my body. It was incendiary. Everything I'd ever believed was a lie. Everything. All the people I could trust were dead. Even Jitty had betrayed me. She'd hinted and teased about betrayal, but she'd never come out and told me. She should have. My parents had been murdered. She should have told me so I could protect my heart. Instead, in her selfish quest for an heir, she'd left me wide open to bone-crushing grief.

Still looking like Bob Dylan, Jitty stepped through the bathroom door. "Are you okay?"

For the first time ever, she sounded scared. And well she should be. I would not be betrayed again. "You knew it was never an accident. Get out of my house. You get out and Coleman will be right on your heels."

"What?" she slowly transformed into Jitty, my ancestral ghost, a woman of beauty and style.

"I said, get out of my house. I don't want you here. You've played me. You've betrayed me. Get out!" I roared the last two words.

I could hear Tinkie downstairs, scrambling up the steps as fast as she could. "Sarah Booth, are you okay?" She stopped on the landing.

"Get up here, Tinkie. Now!" The pure hot fire of my anger had burned away all other emotions, even reason. "Get up here! I have something to tell you. Something you really want to hear."

"What?" Wide-eyed and trembling, she asked, "What is wrong? I can help."

"No one can help, but there are things you need to know about me. Things I haven't told anyone else. I won't be betrayed again. Not by Coleman or anyone else. Coleman knew my parents were murdered and he never said a word."

"Sarah Booth!" Tinkie was pale. "He didn't want you to be hurt. That Judge Truett. He has a long reach and Coleman wanted to protect you. I'm sure he was looking for evidence—"

"Everyone has to go. Right now. You, too! This is my home and I want everyone else out."

Tinkie looked at me like I'd lost my mind, which maybe I had. "Who is everyone else?" she asked. "Only Coleman lives here with you."

"Not anymore, he doesn't. Now, get out!" I'd carried my secrets for too long. I would be done with them, with the past, with the future I'd once cherished and believed in—trusted even. Coleman, Jitty, and my friends, everyone had lied to me.

I was ready to burn it all down.

Acknowledgments

Sarah Booth and her sidekicks have starred in a long-running series and it takes a lot of work from many people to keep it all on track. First of all, thanks to my agent, Marian Young, and to my editors at St. Martin's, Hannah O'Grady and Madeline Alsup. Getting a book in shape to print is a long process. From the acquiring editor down to the copy editor and all the folks in publicity, it is a massive effort to bring a book to print. Many thanks to the copy editor on this book, Lisa Davis.

I also want to thank the art department and artists who create such wonderful covers. The book designer also deserves thanks. It's the little details that make a book polished and professional.

I've developed a lot of friendships via the Zinnia characters, and I want to thank all the readers, booksellers, and librarians who have faithfully recommended and read my Sarah Booth books throughout nearly three decades. The terrific publicity team at St. Martin's, Sarah LaCotti and Kat White, have been fabulous. We've had help from many mystery lovers on social media and WriterSpace, which handles my newsletter and online promotions.

These characters have shared my life and my friendships. I've spent more time with them than most other people in my "real" world. And the books have allowed me to share my love for—and disappointment at times with—my home state of Mississippi. Mississippi, like all of us, is a work in progress.

I want to also thank Priya Bhakta, a talented writer who heads up KaliOka Press and helps me with social media, newsletters, and everything in between. Jennifer Haines Welch, my niece, is smarter than I am and reads my manuscripts first to be sure I haven't made factual errors or left threads unresolved. And this book wouldn't exist if it weren't for Bobbie Gentry and her haunting ballad, "Ode to Billie Joe."

I've been blessed with a terrific team. I couldn't do any of it without all of them—and the readers.

About the Author

Hope Harrington Oakes

Carolyn Haines is the author of the Sarah Booth Delaney Mysteries. She is the recipient of both the Harper Lee Award for Alabama's Distinguished Writer and the Richard Wright Award for Literary Excellence. Born and raised in Mississippi, she now lives in Semmes, Alabama, on a farm with more dogs, cats, and horses than she can possibly keep track of.